Tickets

THE GOLDEN BOWL BOOK THREE

MAEVE CHRISTOPHER

Tickets
The Golden Bowl Book Three

Maeve Christopher

Published by HNI Books
Copyright © 2018 Paula M. Scully

Editor: Janet Hitchcock
Cover: Dar Albert of Wicked Smart Designs
Formatting: Nina Pierce of Seaside Publications

ISBN: 978-0-9993905-2-8

Dedication

For Mum, who taught me about "tickets"

Acknowledgments

My thanks to Janet Hitchcock, Chris Senechal, and
Tracey Quintin for helping me make this book
the best it can be.

ONE

~ *Lena* ~

"Lena Goodwin to the ticket office, please. Lena Goodwin."

Ugh. I knew getting two balcony seats at the last minute was too good to be true. I sure wasn't going to trudge back to the ticket office to hear that there was some big mistake, and we'd have to give up our seats. Besides, I had a perfectly good excuse for not leaving this spot.

Mom was settled in her seat, riffling through The Golden Bowl Tour program. I think she was a little frustrated. Reading was difficult or impossible for her now, depending on the day, and all the noise and activity was distracting for anyone, never mind an Alzheimer's patient.

"Lena Goodwin to the ticket office, please. Lena Goodwin."

Mom looked up. "Lena Goodwin!"

"I know, Mom. It's okay." I sank back into my seat, like someone might recognize me, and laughed at myself. I didn't know a soul in Philadelphia, and I was pretty sure no one but the ticket lady cared if I sat there.

But I guess she really cared. The voice became insistent over the din of the sold-out crowd. *"Lena Goodwin to the ticket office, please. Lena Goodwin!"*

"Lena Goodwin, please," Mom repeated.

I smoothed some of the wiry silver hair that had overtaken Mom's formerly brunette curls then patted her back to try and calm her and me. A momentary flash forward put that same gray hair on me. I stroked my frizzed curls, making sure they were still dark, if not well behaved.

I was exhausted already, and I hadn't even started to execute my plan. It was no easy task getting Mom out of bed and dressed in the morning, never mind getting her *to* the train and *on* the train. I'd bundled her in layers to assure she'd be comfortable in iffy October weather. I'd put her in her red woolen coat, so I'd be able to find her easier if she slipped away from me.

The trip from New York was eventful. When I couldn't wait another second to use the bathroom, I walked the two rows back and did my business in record time. When I came through the door, I could see Mom had already disappeared. The conductor wasn't happy with me.

Fortunately, she didn't get too far, and she was okay—just a little too insistent on petting some woman's faux fur collar.

"Lena Goodwin to the ticket office, please. Lena Goodwin!" I buried my face in my hands, frustration at the boiling point.

"Lena Goodwin, please. Lena Goodwin." Mom tapped my arm.

I didn't raise my head. "It's okay, Mom." How would I ever get my mother and me in front of Cat Clemente? It was a herculean task just to get the two of us here in the concert hall. Security was intense, and I hadn't considered how much time and effort it would take to wait in line and finally get through to our seats. There'd be no way we could sneak backstage or even throw ourselves on their mercy. The guards weren't taking any nonsense from anyone.

I couldn't believe I missed meeting Cat in person at my office. I knew she was a friend of my boss, but Cat was a mega rock star with a talent for healing people. Never in a million years did I think she'd come to our office in New York. Stupid me was off in Philadelphia trying to get tickets for their concert here, thinking there was no way to see them in New York. *Dumb.*

Superstar Aubrey Rose was opening for the Clementes' band. I knew she wouldn't be on long because she often joined them during their performance, too. They were all best friends. I knew a lot about them. They were like one big happy family—and over-the-top protective of each other. They had to be. So many crazies would have done most anything to take them down.

Mom started singing her favorite song of Cat's. At least she was settling in. I took a minute to glance at my program. The Golden Bowl Tour was inspired by the restaurant owned by my boss's fiancée, Annie, who was kind of a relative of Cat. Both Annie and Cat were philanthropists and proponents of the power of prayer. So it was not surprising the Clementes' band started The Golden Bowl Tour to raise money for their charities.

As the hall lit up in soft gold light, I remembered the prayer I put in the golden bowl at the restaurant up in Maine. *God help me.* I should have insisted on seeing Cat there and then. She and her family were vacationing on the coast of Maine, staying with Annie in Marberry.

But then I couldn't let on I needed to see Cat. My ex-husband was in charge of security for The Golden Bowl restaurant, all their businesses, and their family. I wasn't about to tell him my little secret at this late date.

A sudden uproar exploded behind us in the hallway leading to our balcony. People were shouting and screaming. Mom started to panic. I grabbed hold of her. "It's okay, Mom." I couldn't see a thing except the backs of everyone in our balcony jumping up and down. It dawned on me there was no way for us to get out of here in an emergency. Mom wouldn't make it. I started to panic. Did I smell smoke? I yelled, "It's okay, Mom!"

I began to hyperventilate. I was in an aisle seat. We could make it out. Was that a flicker of fire near the stage? *God help me.* We could make it out. Somehow. I grabbed Mom and held her. It could be fire. But there was no alarm sounding.

I noticed the balcony had quieted. There was no alarm. It was too quiet.

A hand landed on my shoulder blade. "Lena." The voice was soft and comforting. I turned to see Cat.

I almost fell out of my chair. "It's *you!*"

"Will you join me for a cup of tea?"

"Uh … yeah." I popped out of my seat and grabbed Mom and all our stuff.

I felt like a rock star myself as we made our way backstage covered by armed guards and swarmed by fans who only wanted a minute of Cat's time, just like me. I think I was in shock. Mom sure was, but the guards were super-careful with her. She called one of them Ricky and then got upset when he put her in a chair in Cat's dressing room and started to leave.

Cat took her hand and knelt in front of her. "Ricky is helping us all stay safe today, Kay. He'll be back to see you after he's done with his work."

"Okay." Mom gave him a big smile and waved him on his way.

Somehow I wasn't surprised at that strange scene, but I was surprised that Cat had an actual pot of tea in her dressing room. She poured three cups and offered a plate of scones from The Golden Bowl's Bakery & Sweet Shop. Mom took a blueberry scone and savored every tiny bite as her finger traced the outline of a rose decorating the china teapot. I wondered why I wasn't surprised that Cat knew Mom's name.

I choked up, and my voice turned to a croak. "Thank you, Cat … for seeing us today … I can't tell you how much it means."

She took a seat, pushing her blond hair out of her face. "I'm so happy I found you in the crowd. When you didn't come to the ticket office, our security force was not happy about my idea to go and find you."

Her giggle and her strange accent comforted me somehow. Cat was from Austria and married to a Spanish billionaire businessman. According to rumor, they lived in a castle in the Austrian Alps. They were one of the most powerful couples in the world and also one of the most generous. They gave away many millions in charity every year.

But what I needed from her wasn't money.

I wasn't sure how much time I'd have with her before the guards would throw me out, so I came right to the point. Still croaking. "Mom's Alzheimer's is getting worse. She's only in her early sixties. I need you to heal her."

Cat carefully refilled Mom's cup and put the pot down. This little tea party thing was nice, but my palms were getting sweatier by the second. "Cat?"

"I'm sorry, Lena, I cannot heal your mother. Only God can heal her. Scripture tells us, 'I am the Lord, your God, who heals you.'"

I wiped my hands on my jeans, mad at myself for missing that little point. Cat was one of the humblest people on earth. Now I'd have to waste time trying to straighten out my blunder. "Okay, that's fine, but God listens to you. I know you heal people all the time. People leave your concerts, and they're healed. You even healed a little kid with cancer up in Maine. I know it's true, and I want Mom to be healed. I've already asked God a hundred times. But he'll listen to you."

I wondered if Cat was even paying attention to me. She was now engaged in a smiling game with Mom. I thought I'd lose it. "Cat?"

She kept her hand on Mom's hand and said a prayer … then another. When Cat said amen Mom repeated it, then started singing, "Amen … amen … amen . . ."

I felt a surge of happiness at Mom's joyful outburst, but I turned to Cat with my serious voice. "We might not get her to stop singing. Once she gets started on something, it can go on and on."

Cat smiled at me. "As it should." She turned back to Mom and began a chorus of halleluiahs. It wasn't long before Mom was singing that, too.

I could hear the sound of the crowd welcoming Aubrey Rose to the stage. Time was running out for Mom and me. I wiped my eyes and cleared my throat of emotion. "Is Mom healed now, Cat?"

"The Lord is in her heart."

Mom was practically dancing in her seat doing halleluiahs to the beat of Aubrey's music. My happiness at her happiness was dashed with doubt. "Are you sure she's healed, Cat, cuz she's still stuck on that one word. When is she going to speak normally again?"

Cat's magnetic blue eyes locked on mine. "Know that God loves Kay with a love that's beyond all understanding, and nothing can change that. That's the important thing, Lena. Love is what is important. God's ways are not our ways, and Kay might not be healed in the way that suits you. But believe that God is good, and God has what is best for her, no matter what it looks like in the natural."

A shudder went through me. "Uh … okay."

Mom was still singing the same refrain.

Cat reached for my hand. "You made a big effort to get here today, Lena. You weren't looking for me. You were looking for God."

I nodded, and my eyes filled. I wanted to take back my hand to wipe them, but I couldn't move. I let tears drip. "I don't think God likes me very much."

"You're believing lies. God loves you as much as he loves Kay. As much as he loves me. You've faced horrific tragedy in your life, Lena, and you've suffered terrible consequences through *no* fault of your own. You've pushed as far as you can, all under your own power. It's left you empty and stressed. Now you know there's something better. So much better. You've been seeking God, and when you do, you find him. Ask God into your heart. Pray with me now, Lena."

I did. When I finally said, "Amen," Mom switched her song back to amen. I laughed as I wiped the tears.

By the time I got myself under control again, Mom was interspersing her amens with bites of another berry scone. I had to chuckle. "Well, I guess Mom isn't healed the way I hoped for. But she sure is happy. I guess I need to order her some scones from The Golden Bowl."

Cat put her teacup down. "They do bring a smile. I can also recommend their lemon bars."

"Oh, yeah. I read that in a magazine. Good marketing." We both laughed.

There was a rap on the door and the guard walked in. Mom sat straight up. "Ricky!"

I burst into tears, and Cat jumped out of her seat to hug me.

Two

~ *Annie* ~

January could be fierce on the coast of Maine. Buck had almost convinced me to extend our Hawaiian honeymoon by a week or two. It would be the slowest time of year for my restaurant, The Golden Bowl, and The Bakery & Sweet Shop. But the food prep facility was another story. With the launch of our new "Super Club" line of packaged meals for the diet and health conscious, January looked to be setting an all-time record for sales.

Since my new husband was also my consultant—a partner at Brooke, Lewis & Wynn, the experts in the restaurant and food service industry—Buck had an interest in getting us back to the continental U.S. in order to take advantage of all the media attention around the new product line. Although he had expected a successful launch, sales were soaring straight to the stratosphere. We both agreed we'd need to keep a close eye on things. We arrived in New York to spitting snow and headed to his office in Manhattan.

We were barely through the impressive mahogany doors when Buck's partner, William Brooke, sprang from the conference room and motioned us over. "Great to see you! Amanda James is here with her camera crew. She's doing a story on your new diet products, Anne. It'll be aired this weekend." He almost jumped out of his skin, whispering loudly, "The number one news magazine show in the world!"

I couldn't help but chuckle. Will was normally all business, at least when I was around.

Amanda peered around the doorframe. "Welcome home, newlyweds. Put a brush through your hair, Annie, and we'll get started."

It was fun to see Amanda again. We'd developed a friendship of sorts, so my nerves remained in check for the interview. No hard questions.

After the camera crew packed up, I sat with Amanda chatting over coffee. Not surprisingly, Buck had a hundred things to deal with in the office. We'd been gone a solid month. I was still in relaxed mode, which was a new feeling for me. But Amanda was gone after one cup.

I wandered toward Buck's office and chitchatted with Janice, his administrative assistant, but Buck was nowhere in sight. Janice gestured with her thumb. "He's in Lena's office with Will and Carter."

"Okay, I'll wait in Buck's office."

Janice raised her brows. "Well, I know we've got the joy o' the Lord since the last time you were here, but you're a better woman than I, Annie Wynn. That girl singlehandedly almost destroyed your whole business. Not to mention how she was trying to seduce your husband. I wasn't a bit surprised she was the only employee of Brooke, Lewis & Wynn who didn't attend your wedding."

It was more Janice's attitude than worry over Buck and Lena that propelled me down the hall to Lena's office. Carter Lewis stood in the doorway punching one hand against the other, a straw hanging out of his mouth. He removed the straw to say, "Hi, Annie." Then he turned back into the room. "Lena needs to stay here in New York." He replaced the straw.

Buck rose from his chair. "Have a seat."

I plopped into the comfortable upholstery and said hello to Lena.

"Hi, Annie. Sorry it's so crowded in here." Lena looked to be at wit's end. Her wavy, dark hair was unkempt, her chocolate brown eyes stormy. Her gray wool business suit was disheveled.

Will pushed his chair closer to the wall to make room for Buck to stand by me.

Lena handed Buck a folder and resumed her seat. "Look, I know it's a good idea to take on this job at The Golden Bowl. From a career point of view. From a personal point of view ... not so much. But I need to think of my career." She cast a quick stony glance at Carter. It looked like his heart would break. I didn't think Carter was her favorite person.

She made a face. "Okay, Buck, I'm taking the job at The Golden Bowl. I'll need a couple weeks to get packed and make arrangements. Meanwhile I can work on some of the issues here."

Buck nodded. "Very well."

Will clapped his hands. "Good. All set."

Carter left without a word, the straw sticking straight out from tight lips.

Buck escorted me back to his office to face a mound of paper on his desk. I took a seat across from him. "Um ... Buck?"

He looked up. "Yes, my dear?"

I could never keep a straight face when he called me "my dear." It threw me enough that I didn't prioritize my questions. But I did keep my voice low. Janice was ever-present, opinionated, and loved gossip. "Why does Carter have a straw hanging out of his mouth?"

He smirked. "It's his way of quitting cigarettes. I suppose it helps with the scotch, too."

"Oh. He's tackling all the vices at once, huh?"

"Indeed." He winked at me. "Now he needs to quit harassing Lena, his latest vice."

Hmm. "Is that why Lena's coming to The Golden Bowl to work? To keep Carter out of trouble? Or is this one of those keep-your-enemies-closer things?"

His steel gray eyes bulged a bit, signaling his irritation. "I need the best person I can find for a new position at The Golden Bowl. We're ready for a full time IT expert. Hopefully, Lena will keep things professional. I think she's learned her lesson. Frankly, she's done some wonderful work for us in our absence."

He came around the desk and pulled me from my seat. We were almost nose to nose. "Why don't we go have lunch? I could use a cheeseburger."

I giggled. "Okay. We'll see how New York cheeseburgers measure up to The Golden Bowl." I put my hand to his handsome face and smoothed back his dark hair. I could see the stress in those steely eyes, and I didn't want to push him. Keeping Buck sober was a top priority. We'd both been concerned that staying on at his firm could jeopardize that.

Buck was the cornerstone of Brooke, Lewis & Wynn. He'd been the driving force since founding the firm nearly thirty years ago. He was the one who was largely responsible for their global success. Since he was half British and half American, he had a perspective, as well as the smarts and perseverance, that put the firm at the forefront of the restaurant and food service industry.

But he'd also learned his lesson about smelling the roses. Our month-long Hawaiian honeymoon during a major product launch was proof of that.

He tipped me over his desk and kissed me until I gasped, "We're getting too old for this."

Our laughter sent his papers flying and crashing to the floor. Janice's voice came from the doorway. "I thought decorum was the new watchword at Brooke, Lewis & Wynn."

Buck made the face he usually had for Janice, a mix of displeasure and surprise at her nervy intrusion. But underneath it all, he knew he needed to keep her on as a key employee. He deftly tugged me up and to his side as he addressed her with his usual, "Indeed."

He turned to me. "Shall we adjourn to lunch, my dear?"

In short order we were checked into our hotel, one of the best in the world and a client of Buck's firm. Our cheeseburgers from room service were "top class," as he would say.

"Um ... Buck?" I snuggled into his side, nestled in the bed munching on a French fry. "Did you tell Nathan about Lena?"

He drew me closer. "No. Why would I tell Rhodes?"

"Okay." *To be continued.* I would have thought Nathan, our director of security at The Golden Bowl, would want to know his ex-wife would soon be working on our premises. But Buck was the business mind here.

He brushed the top of my head with a kiss. "Frankly, I should have discussed it with you first. But you were in with Amanda, and I needed a competent IT person in Maine yesterday. I knew the Super Club would succeed, but this is beyond my wildest imaginings."

I smiled at the ceiling. *Praise God.* "Think of all that money for charity, Buck."

"Indeed."

~ *Lena* ~

I needed my head examined for moving to Marberry, Maine in mid-January. My only consolation was leaving Carter Lewis in New York—at least for now. Like a sad puppy dog, he stuck his head in my office doorway and promised me he'd come visit "when the weather is nice." I believed that would be maybe a week at the end of July. Hopefully, by then I could afford a vacation somewhere else.

I rented the biggest, most luxurious SUV I could find and packed it like a pro. I was only a little surprised to find that our stuff fit. I'd sold most of our old furniture and knick-knacks. At least I got something for it. I donated or left on the curb what I couldn't sell.

The apartment looked sad and bare when I returned one last time to take Mom out of her chair. Cracks in the walls and peeling wallpaper were more noticeable. Scuffed floors and nicked woodwork reminded me the landlord had done little to this old place in the thirty years we'd lived there.

Mom's aide, who'd been with her a few years, put on her coat and bent down to kiss her on the cheek, then encouraged her to stand and bundled her up for the cold trip outdoors. "Goodbye, Kay. I'll miss you."

Mom smiled at her.

I paid our aide in cash and gave her the recliner—the only half decent piece of furniture we'd had in the apartment.

I was pretty shocked that Mom never complained or got testy over all our belongings leaving the apartment. She'd had more periods of lucidity and spent a lot more time singing since we'd met Cat, and probably God, in Philadelphia. As I escorted her out of our Brooklyn apartment, she started in on her halleluiahs again.

It was weird to leave the place where I grew up for good.

We took our time heading north. Despite some periods of freezing rain and snow, the highways were clear. Mom was full of talk about getting her tickets. I promised I would, but I had no idea what shows we could see in the wilds of Down East Maine. Lately, I'd taken to making my own tickets out of colored construction paper with made-up show titles. She was just as happy if I waved them in her face and put them in a special envelope as she was when I gave them to her.

She never remembered what shows I took her to, or promised to take her to. I finally realized I might as well save the money and the aggravation. Of course, by that time I'd already spent a fortune on Broadway shows, even though I always bought tickets at a discount.

I stopped frequently for breaks, snacks, and finally for the night in southern Maine. I clipped a little alarm to Mom's pajamas, but there was no need tonight. She was out as soon as she hit the pillow, and so was I. We woke up to a couple of inches of new snow, but the roads were fine. They knew how to handle the stuff up here. After breakfast, I found the Maine Turnpike and put the pedal to the metal, heading to Marberry.

Mom's halleluiahs weren't helping the butterflies in my stomach. Of all the stupid jobs I'd taken, this had to be the dumbest mistake. At best, I was driving into my unresolved past and a very uncertain future. I didn't want to think of the worst.

I relived the painful burn I'd had in the pit of my stomach when I'd put a prayer in the bowl before driving away from The Golden

Bowl the first time I'd visited. *God help me.*

⌒ ◡

Late afternoon midweek in January meant you could walk in and get a table at The Golden Bowl Restaurant. Mom and I sat by the large stone hearth, a few embers smoldering there. Service was quick and friendly. We sipped the best coffee I'd ever tasted while we waited for our early bird dinners. Every so often Mom would break into her halleluiah refrain, but the people around us didn't seem to mind. We weren't in New York anymore.

Billy, a sociable security guard I'd met the last time I was here, arrived with an armload of wood and quickly revived a crackling fire to warm us. After a few friendly comments, he left us to our coffee and began to refill the woodpile by the hearth.

I looked up to see a familiar security guard come through the door, and he smiled at us. He walked over and reached for Mom's hand as he took a seat beside her.

"Ricky!" She threw herself into his side.

I choked up.

"Hi Kay, nice to see you again. Remember me? Roger."

"Ricky!" She hugged him tighter.

I couldn't speak and the tears started to drip. I found a tissue in my pocket. He seemed to go along with Ricky. *Thank God.* Mom could get pretty agitated if you didn't go along with her.

I reached over and pulled at his sleeve. I could only whisper. "Thank you. She thinks you're my dad."

He smiled. "Oh."

"You look kind of like him in his younger days. She thinks I'm her sister. It's a good thing I'm named after my aunt." I blew my nose. "Now she thinks my aunt is her mother."

He chuckled and stroked her hair a bit. It was so sweet I just couldn't stop crying. I had to because the waitress showed up with our fish and chips.

Roger helped Mom take her face out of his armpit and settled her in her seat. That wouldn't do. She needed to have her chair closer to him. He was awful nice about turning her chair to be closer to him.

"Ricky! Where are the kids?"

The alarm in her voice took me back thirty years when I saw Mom facing the fire. I jumped up with shock. Then I passed out.

~ *Nathan* ~

I buried the hatchet with Buck Wynn last December third when he married Annie Auclair Brewster Wynn. I'd had plenty of time to think it over, and I realized, despite his many shortcomings, he was probably the best husband for her at this time of her life.

They were both immersed in the restaurant and food business. Loved everything to do with cooking. They spoke the same language. She found him attractive enough, I guess. Who knows what goes on in a woman's head? Not me.

Not that I fought for her. Not really. I'm not sure what I would have done with her if I'd won her. I couldn't do *anything* to hurt her. That I knew. About the only other thing I knew in regard to Annie and Buck—I'd kill him cold if he ever did anything to hurt her.

Annie was the sweetest, gentlest, kindest woman I'd ever met.

I'd taken to a daily patrol of Miller's Way, the dirt path that led from Annie's oversized old farmhouse about three miles along the rocky beach south to The Golden Bowl. Daylight was starting to lengthen. It was a good time to think.

January was dead quiet when it came to people, but Mother Nature was a different story. I trudged across the windswept lawn and up the stairs to the back porch of the restaurant. Kicking the snow off my boots, I came through the kitchen door and found Doc, Annie's birth father. He nodded at me and poured a second cup of coffee.

I had half a sip when Ashleigh, the manager, pushed through the door yelling, "Doc! We need you." She came around the counter. "Mr. Rhodes! It's your ex-wife. Lena."

Doc was approaching seventy but still sharp and spry. He pushed Ashleigh back through the door before she could say another thing. I was right on his heels.

Billy was with Lena on the floor, and Doc landed on his knees beside them. She was half sitting, in a daze. A woman carried on nearby, trying to break Roger's grasp, screaming, "Ricky, help!"

"Get her out of here." I pointed Roger to Annie's private office under the staircase. He carried her there and Ashleigh followed, closing the door behind them. I could still hear the woman yelling.

"You're okay," Doc said. "Have you fainted before?"

She motioned him away. "I'm okay. Just a scare." She tried to get up, but Billy held firm.

I knelt over my ex-wife. "Lena?"

She focused on my face and her eyes widened. Her jaw dropped in surprise. "They said today's your day off. I wouldn't have come here ... oh, no!"

I shook my head. "Nice to see you, too."

~ *Lena* ~

I scrambled to get off the floor. "I've got to get going." I leaned a little too much on Billy until I could get a grip on the table. I turned to him. "Thanks, I'm fine. Just haven't eaten in a while."

He knocked me off my feet, and I was seated in front of my fish and chips. "Your dinner's still hot," he said.

Mom was screaming in the distance, and I thought I'd vomit. I looked up at inquisitive patrons around me. "Thanks, I'll take it to go."

I watched as Doc walked off to deal with Mom. "I gotta go." I pulled myself up in spite of wobbly legs and grabbed my coat from the back of my chair. I went for Mom's, but Nate blocked me.

His voice was hushed, but firm. "Somehow, we need to reach an understanding. I know you're on the payroll as of the day after tomorrow. You can't run every time you see me."

I looked for some glimmer of something in Nate's gorgeous brown eyes. But there wasn't anything there. Just a SEAL who'd never reveal a thing. That would never change. "Okay, Nate. Gotta run."

I used all my strength to push past him and ran to the door under the stairs. Mom was still screaming. I stifled tears and rammed through the door. "We're fine, Kay. Let's get your coat on and go home. Ricky's gonna help us to the car."

The waitress handed me a neatly packed to-go bag. As I thanked her and made my way through the front door, I saw Mom had grabbed a fistful of papers from the prayer bowl. "Tickets!" She handed them to Roger, who handed them to me. I stuffed them into my handbag.

By the time I drove through the gate at Washington Gardens, Mom had settled down and began eating the fish and chips with her hands. She was kind of a greasy mess, but I hustled her through the lobby right to the bathroom.

We looked reasonably normal when we sat at the conference table in the administrator's office. Fortunately, she understood our exhaustion after our long trip, and she wasted no time in escorting us to our newly decorated apartment. Mom was in heaven. It had been a long time since I lived in such a nice place. Everything neat, clean, and freshly painted in soothing pastels and white.

I attached Mom's little alarm and collapsed in her bed with her. I didn't come to until the next morning.

After breakfast, I unloaded the car, organized our new apartment, and returned to the community room to find Mom engrossed in arts and crafts with the other residents. Despite all the snow and cold, I knew deep down that Mom would be happy here.

The place had a perfect set-up for us. Mom and I would have our own apartment, and when I was at work, she'd have round-the-clock aides to take care of her. If she needed more attention, there was a facility on site. And there was a hospital down the street in case of an emergency.

Washington Gardens was in a scenic location near the ocean with plenty of activities and outdoor trails for walking. Mom would have whatever level of supervision and care she needed on a daily basis. If I had to leave on business, it wouldn't be a catastrophe.

It'd save me money to live in the apartment with her. It was a simple commute to work. I was midway between The Golden Bowl in Marberry and the food prep facility in Washington County. The only thing that wasn't perfect was the prospect of dealing with The Golden Bowl's Director of Security, my ex-husband, Nate Rhodes.

I took advantage of my newfound freedom and went for a walk along the trails. There were a few icy spots, but not too bad. My new down jacket sure came in handy, though. I sat in between some rocks, sheltered from the wind, and looked out over a rugged landscape that stretched down to the Atlantic.

I'd been so hoping Maine would be a good place to hide. New York was getting a little scary. But it looked like I made a wrong move.

How stupid was I bringing Mom to The Golden Bowl? Yeah, it was supposed to be Nate's day off, but what is there to do in Marberry in the dead of winter? Where else would you go? There wasn't even another restaurant in town.

Deep down, I guess I wanted him to know about Mom. I wanted him to know I wasn't a cheater. I wasn't such a bad person. Not really.

What was done was done.

I had to face the fact that Nate saw my mother. Maybe in that moment he wouldn't have concluded she was my mother, but by now he had to know. Roger probably told him. That'd mean Nate would tell Buck and Annie. Then everyone would know I was a liar, which they already knew, but they were giving me a second chance. I didn't think they'd be stupid enough to give me a third chance.

Then I wondered if somehow Cat would have told anyone about Mom. That'd be a stretch. We were just another prayer request to her. Something deep inside told me that wasn't true. She knew Mom's name. She remembered me. *She came looking for me.*

But so what if Cat did? Nate knew. I was so screwed, and I'd barely unpacked.

THREE

~ *Annie* ~

With the wild success of Super Club, Buck was already encouraging me to put together more products for the line. I sat in my office in the converted barn, drawing ideas from menus we'd tested at the restaurant last summer. After a knock at the door, Nathan walked in and took a seat in front of my desk.

"Annie, I'm trying to be respectful of your decision to hire my ex-wife, and I'm happy she finally has a decent-paying job, but you know as well as I do, you can't trust her."

Nathan's pronouncement rattled me. "I understand your point, but Buck felt she'd be the one for the job, and she seems to have turned her life around." I could feel my face going red hot. "Well, you know Buck turned *his* life around. I guess he's giving someone else a chance. Paying it forward."

Nathan's dark eyes were expressionless. I felt a need to ramble on in the silence, but what was there to say? Lena was probably not a good choice for us, considering her willingness to completely destroy The Golden Bowl a few short months ago.

But I couldn't help remembering the look on Cat's face when she handed me the old ticket stub Lena had put in the prayer bowl. She'd written, "God help me." I believed that was a turning point for Lena. I prayed for her still, and I'm sure Cat did, too.

I hoped with all my heart that Buck had made the right decision hiring her. I recalled a conversation with Cat about having faith in God's supernatural ability despite how things appeared in the natural. God most certainly was at work in Lena's life. And God would protect The Golden Bowl from harm.

A sudden loud sigh came out of Nathan. "Annie, the woman lies just to lie. Why would she tell me a big story about her parents being killed in a bus accident when they went on vacation after she'd left home for college?"

I was at a loss. "Um ... because they were?"

"She was at the restaurant yesterday with her mother. Roger met her at the concert in Philadelphia. He said Cat was praying for Lena's mother to be healed of Alzheimer's. The woman's name is Kay Goodwin. Roger said she thought he was her husband, Ricky. I finally took the time yesterday to investigate the bus accident. It made the news when it happened, but there was no Kay or Rick Goodwin on that bus. Lena's a compulsive liar."

~ *Lena* ~

I woke up Thursday morning with the thought in my head that ditching the mob would be easier than dealing with my ex-husband. I laughed out loud thinking that sounded like a "comedy-drama" movie I'd take Mom to. Then Cat's parting advice stopped me dead. "Resist the devil, and he will flee from you. Come near to God, and he will come near to you."

She said it was James 4:7-8, but I'd never bothered to look it up and read it like she suggested. I rolled over and found a Gideon version in the drawer of my nightstand. When I read those verses it hit me that Mom was coming near to God every time she sang amen and halleluiah.

I had some resisting to do, but I didn't know how. I needed the money. That thought prompted me out of bed to get ready for the new job I hopefully still had at The Golden Bowl. If by some miracle I could hold down this job with a good New York salary and living modestly in Maine, well maybe I'd consider resisting the devil. *God help me.*

Where is Mom anyway? Did I sleep through her alarm? She could be somewhere on the moors for all I knew. I hurried across the hall to her room. She was sound asleep, her alarm still attached. I turned my eyes heavenward. *Thank you.*

That was a first for me. *Thanking God?* I started a soft chorus of Mom's halleluiahs and ran for a quick shower, then jumped into my gray business suit, checked on Mom, and hurried out the door. I'd tame my thick hair into submission while waiting for the car to heat up.

I'd exchanged my luxury SUV for a compact car with snow tires, at least until I could find a good deal on my own new car. It wasn't the greatest idea with icy back roads and my tendency to drive too fast, but I was determined to save enough money to get myself out of hot water. One way or another.

My stomach started doing backflips as I pulled into the parking lot at The Golden Bowl's Bakery & Sweet Shop. Bad memories flared, not to mention fright at the thought of confronting Nate and Buck. At least I'd save money on meals today.

The wonderful smells filling the building almost changed my mind, but I gripped my briefcase and climbed the stairs to Annie's office. It was like a walk of shame, remembering how I'd intended to destroy Annie's business over stupid jealousy and revenge. The last time I made this trip to Annie's office, I was well prepared to turn her computers to paperweights, her business to nothing. I'd sunk pretty low.

I would have done it, too, if not for Annie's brother-in-law, the assassin. I turned on my heel with the eerie feeling he was behind me, ready to grab me again. But there was no one in the hall. Just me and my fear. He wasn't such a bad guy, I guess. And he was talented at his job. He'd worked for General Pearson, too. Not that I'd breathe a word to anyone. That could mean my demise.

I passed a wall of glass on my right, showcasing a state of the art customer service call center. I locked eyes with Tracey, the customer service manager, and offered a friendly wave to try and alleviate that look of fear on her face. She forced a grin and raised her hand stiffly.

On my left, Annie's door opened, and she faced me with a sweet smile. "Hi Lena. Welcome to The Golden Bowl." She held out her hand.

I shook her hand, wondering how this sweet lady ended up with an assassin for a brother-in-law. Life was strange. "Thanks for this opportunity, Annie. I won't let you down. You can count on it."

"We know you're very capable of helping us here. Buck has all the numbers figured out. The success of this new project means we can donate even more to worthy charities. With your help, we'll be able to make a huge difference in the world." Annie stepped inside her office and headed for a coffee pot. "Can I get you some breakfast?"

I followed and shut the door. "Uh … thanks, but I already ate. I'm all set on coffee, too. Thanks." I spun around and faced a framed document on the wall and stared dumbly at The Golden Bowl's mission statement, surprised by her kindness, still unnerved with thoughts of the day her brother-in-law quickly overpowered me as I began to disable Annie's entire computer system.

A flood of bad memories clobbered my brain. From the fiasco with David, the assassin, to working for General Pearson and his covert organization, to losing Nate, to my conclusion that I'd made a very bad move to Down East Maine. How could I ever close those ugly chapters of my life living here?

Annie faced me. "As you know, our mission is to feed people—body, soul, and spirit—and let them know about the power of prayer."

"Uh ... yeah ... great poster. You'll never forget your mission statement with this." How much more awkward could I be? *Shape up.* "I'm ready to get to work."

"Okay, great. Buck's meeting us in your new office downstairs." Annie led me back down the hall past the Customer Service Center and down the stairs past the bakery.

"We've done some renovations since you were here. We've expanded The Bakery & Sweet Shop and taken most all of Gerald's equipment over to the new space. He's over at the food prep facility pretty much full time now. So you'll be over there from time to time. We have an office for you in that building, too. It's unbelievable, but Buck says we'll be needing to add on to that space soon."

Buck's voice was unmistakable with that British accent, so I stopped by the office door where I heard it. When Annie and I peered in, I realized it belonged to the woman in charge of The Bakery & Sweet Shop. Buck introduced me to Karen, the confections manager. She seemed like a pleasant lady, probably in her mid-fifties, with a round face and glasses.

Then we went one door down to my new office.

I almost dropped my briefcase. It was three times the space I had in New York and equipped with the latest technology and ergonomic furniture. A giant welcome basket on my desk was stuffed with goodies and a card from the staff at The Golden Bowl. I welled up and croaked, "It's beautiful. Thank you."

Annie and Buck gave me a half hour to settle in before they'd be back to get down to business. After hanging my coat on a rack and setting my laptop on my desk, I discovered Karen and I shared a bathroom. This place had it all over New York. And I thought that was incredible.

I peeked through the open bathroom door into Karen's office. "This place is awesome, huh?"

She pushed her glasses up on her head, looked up from her desk, and smiled. "It is. I can't believe I have a modern office. All these years Annie and I shared a rickety old table in a storage room. We're both so grateful to have such a comfortable place to work now. Space to actually be organized for once."

I nodded.

Karen went on. "I'm happy we finally have you here to keep us heading in the right direction. Annie and I … well, we're not exactly tech savvy. But we're learning."

"Great." I didn't know what else to say, so I hoped I wasn't being hasty to ask the only question on my mind since I arrived. "Where's Nate's office?"

Karen hesitated. "Oh … Mr. Rhodes … he has an office upstairs, but he's not there very often. He's usually out and about or over at Annie's house. They have their headquarters there … I'm not sure if you call it headquarters … you get what I mean."

"Sure."

By the time I learned Karen's entire history and figured out the bathroom door situation, Buck and Annie were back in my office.

Buck did most of the talking, but he never referred to the fiasco I'd caused for The Golden Bowl this past summer. I didn't dare think all was forgotten. As he went on about the systems implemented by Brooke, Lewis & Wynn, I thought how weird it was that I was meeting people I'd be working with here when only a few months ago I was happily messing them all up remotely from the comfort of my home and office in New York.

I'd confessed to all of it, even bragging, after I was caught in a showdown. Why were they embracing me now? Did they really forgive me? They weren't stupid people. Maybe they were setting me up. My stomach started flipping again.

I couldn't help but stare at Annie. Nate had told me he'd found a woman who was way better than me. Well, I guess it was true that she was better than me. That rubbed me the wrong way. Enough for me to plot revenge to bring down her entire business.

But she ended up marrying Buck. I felt bad that I'd told Nate Annie looked old—right in front of Annie. I wanted to hurt him so bad.

I hurt her instead. She was really a beautiful woman—inside and out. She was forty-eight years old, only fourteen years older than me. A couple years older than Nate. I wasn't so sure I'd look that good at her age.

I guess I said that because her hair was so blond it was white. And it was natural. Annie's sister had the same color hair, and she was twenty years younger than her. They both had beautiful baby blue eyes and very fair complexions.

I was startled out of my daydreaming when Buck asked me for input on the food prep facility. I told him what he wanted to hear.

I guess it was guilt that kept me working until 7:00 p.m. I decided I'd better get home before the roads got slick. I gathered my stuff, put on my coat, and opened the door to my ex-husband. "Oh!" I jumped a mile.

He grabbed and steadied me. "Sorry. Didn't mean to startle you."

It took an uneasy minute to catch my breath.

He took my bag and put it on my small conference table, then pulled my coat off, and threw it on the chair. "I need to talk to you, Lena." He guided me to the seat and spun my chair so I faced his.

I groaned. "It's late, and I'm hungry." This wasn't good. I needed time and a clear head to figure out what to say. Instead, I noticed Nate's dark hair had gone more salt and peppery. It suited him.

"Your parents weren't killed in a bus accident. That was just another one of your stories. Why lie to me about your parents?"

"I'm not feeling well."

He took hold of the arms of my chair and reeled me closer. "Me either. But we're not leaving until I have an explanation. Why was it so important that I think your parents were dead?"

I was a trapped rat. "It's classified."

He started in on one of his famous mile-long curses. At least it'd give me time to think.

"I need this job, Nate. That's the only reason I'm here. I'm the only one my mom can count on. I've gone into debt to get her medical care, to keep her from harming herself, to keep a roof over her head, to try and get her healed." My voice was a croak again. I went for my coat pocket to find a tissue and an old ticket stub flew out onto my lap. I picked it up and held it in front of his face. "I'm just trying to give her some kind of a life."

He took it from me. "As your husband, why wouldn't I have the same goal?"

I broke into a sob. "Because we weren't married five minutes when you started calling me a liar and a cheat."

He glared into my eyes. "You were a liar and a cheat—long before I met you. You were too good at it."

My stomach flips were in full swing, but he wouldn't let me out of the chair. "I never cheated on you, Nate. I loved you. I loved you so much I lied to you. But I never cheated on you."

He reeled the chair closer. "How can you say you never cheated on me? Pearson—"

Anger pushed my words into his face. "Pearson ruined my life— along with a whole lot of other people. I worked in the same group with his son-in-law, and we were friends. Just friends. I was married. He was married. But Pearson never cared for the guy. He thought he was weak. So he didn't mind when the rumor got started that we were involved. He was happy as a clam when his daughter believed the lie and filed for divorce." I was out of breath, and Nate was stone faced.

By the time I could speak again, my voice was firm and certain. "I lost my job, I lost my reputation, I lost my ability to earn a living. Mostly, I lost you, Nate. And somewhere along the line, I lost myself." There was no change in his expression, not that I expected there would be. "Now I'm tired and hungry and sick and done for the day. I'm going home."

Without a word, he let me go.

~ *Nathan* ~

Sunrise was hardly underway when Annie took her thermos of coffee and headed outside to her Adirondack chair. The path had been shoveled and sanded, so I was not concerned about escorting her. Annie was adamant about witnessing every sunrise she could in that spot overlooking the ocean. She said she used the time to think and pray.

I sipped my coffee in the comfort of the farmhouse's warm kitchen, seated at the table in front of a large bay window, staring at the back of Annie's down hood. I was trying not to think. Or pray.

When I heard the swinging door, I turned and couldn't help a muffled laugh. "Morning, Buck."

"Rhodes." He headed straight for the coffeepot and filled the thermos Annie had left out for him.

I stifled my laughter. "Whatcha got on there?"

He flipped a hood up over his hat. "Practically everything I own. It's six below out there. Summer can't get here fast enough."

"I don't think Annie expects you out there every morning."

"I do." He fortified himself with a gulp of coffee, then swished out the back door.

I watched him land in the chair beside her and take her gloved hand in his. He was a devoted husband.

Mostly, I lost you, Nate. I wasn't devoted. I'd bailed out of all three of my marriages pretty quick. I couldn't stomach the thought of Lena with Pearson's son-in-law. Since I was overseas, I was one of the last to hear the news. It came from the top—from General John Pearson himself.

It didn't take me long to pack up and leave Lena once I got back to New York. It did take me years to finalize the divorce. I guess I didn't want to admit another failure. Third strike and you're out.

I loved you so much I lied to you. Coffee spilled down the front of my shirt. Lies and Pearson were words that easily fit in a sentence. I knew that. I was part of a SEAL team that often did his bidding, but my only communication was with a member of his organization who was a former SEAL—until Pearson himself called me about Lena.

Lena certainly knew Pearson better than I did. Was she trying to tell me the truth this time? It didn't seem like it. She'd cleverly emoted her way out of discussing her parents.

I decided to find out everything about them.

~ *Lena* ~

Of all days to oversleep, day two of a new job with security breathing down your neck wasn't a good choice. If the aide didn't show up, Mom and I would probably have slept in till noon. As I ran through the shower and jumped into the first suit I pulled out of the closet, I remembered to be grateful that Mom felt so comfortable here. There were more than a few cold mornings I'd chased her down the streets of Brooklyn.

By the time I coaxed my car to The Golden Bowl, my stomach was in full revolt. I'd eaten so much sugary stuff last night, I knew I needed a decent meal. I tiptoed down the hall past Karen's door, and she didn't look up from her computer. Once I set up my work for the day, I went to her office via the bathroom. "Morning, Karen."

She popped her head up. "Hi, Lena."

"Uh … any idea what's up with Buck and Annie today?"

She grabbed a notebook. "They have a pretty regular conference call with Joe Harris every Friday morning. He's the PR guy."

"Oh, yeah." *Yup.* I'd conned him, too. "Okay, thanks." I retreated through the bathroom wondering how anyone here could speak to me. I'd messed with them all in my little revenge plot last summer. *What was I thinking?*

I grabbed my coat, hat, and scarf, as I justified a meal at the restaurant. I stopped at Karen's door and called to her. "I need to check out the restaurant, Karen. I'll just be a little while. I've got my phone with me if anyone needs me."

"Okay." She barely looked up.

The frigid wind was ferocious as I plodded along the path from the converted barn to the old farmhouse-turned-restaurant. Yet the parking lots were plenty full, and there was a crowd of women around the prayer bowl on the porch. Heartier souls than me. I hurled myself through the door and almost collided with the elderly hostess. *That's all I need today*. Nate would have me locked up.

She blessed me sweetly and profusely, then led me on a long and winding route through the dining rooms to a small table in a far corner. There was a large window and a spectacular view of wild waves crashing on the rocks. I began removing layers of clothing.

"May I bring you some coffee?"

"Yes! Black." I sunk into a comfortable cushioned seat as the coffee arrived and quickly ordered a veggie omelet. The warmth of my drink and the splashing waves relaxed me. My head started to clear. My thoughts returned to Nate, and I realized deep down somewhere I wanted him to know about Mom. Why else would I have been stupid enough to bring her here?

"Great time to move to Maine."

That Brooklyn accent rose above the ambient noise. He sat on my coat I'd draped on the opposite chair. His ski jacket collar covered his mouth and nose. His hat was pulled down over his eyebrows.

I choked. *How did he find me so fast?*

"I'm adding a surcharge. I can't be chasin' you all the way to Maine for my money."

"Yeah … okay." I imagine my croaking voice sounded terrified enough for him. The fact that he found me so quickly scared me out of my mind. "I … uh … I'll write you a check every week … every week if you want."

"Cash. Every week. Hal'll pick it up at the old folks' home. Add an extra five hundred for his trouble."

I could feel my eyes pop. "Five hundred!"

"He'll meet you on the bench near the back entrance tomorrow morning, 8:00 sharp. Don't be late. And don't be short."

"Okay." I watched him leave the restaurant. *I bet he didn't leave a prayer in the bowl*. He didn't need one. He had all my money. Well, all his boss's money that I'd been recycling.

The waitress arrived with my breakfast. It took time to get it down, along with the fear I was swallowing. I watched one wave after another crash and die on those rocks. *Insanity is doing the same thing over and over.* I'd been paying that creep for as long as I could remember, and somehow there'd always be some penalty and interest added for something else I did wrong.

And don't be short. I started snickering into my coffee. I'd make sure to take an extra thousand from his online accounts for *my* trouble. I'd made it my business to rob his boss of more money than I paid him. And, so far, he didn't have a clue.

I considered myself a Robin Hood. Nate would have considered me a cybercriminal. Or maybe a racketeer.

FOUR

~ *Lena* ~

I spent most of the day in the Customer Service Center with the manager, Tracey. Even though she'd witnessed firsthand my threat to destroy The Golden Bowl, and all the cyber-mischief prior to that last summer, she was nice as pie to me. I couldn't understand it. So I acted like it never happened either.

By 6:00 p.m. she'd had enough, so I headed back to my office. I met Annie in the hall. "There you are," she said.

Uh oh. "Hi, Annie. Is there a problem?"

"No problem. I'm hoping you and your mom can join us for dinner tomorrow night."

"Uh . . ." I was dumbfounded.

"I know it's your first weekend in Maine, and you're probably still settling in, but I'd love to do a little welcome dinner for you both. I'm sure it took a lot of effort for you to get here on such short notice. Buck and I really appreciate that, Lena."

"Oh. No problem. I appreciate the job. And Mom loves it here."

"Come by around 5:00 tomorrow. Does that suit your mom?"

"Sure, it's just that she can be a handful sometimes. But we'll leave if that happens. I promise I'll do my best not to ruin your dinner."

Annie smiled. "Sounds like a plan, but I'm sure she'll be fine. I hear she has a little crush on Roger."

It was hard not to like her.

I crawled out of bed Saturday morning in time to bundle layers over my pajamas and meet my new friend, Hal, on the designated bench promptly at 8:00 a.m. I paid him the exorbitant amount of money required to keep me and Mom alive and intact then crawled back to bed.

The aide was amazingly quiet getting Mom dressed and out to her breakfast and activities. When the apartment door clicked, I put the pillow over my head and nestled under my covers.

My phone woke me up at 10:45. "Lena, I need to talk to you. I'm in the lobby."

"Nate?" I rubbed hair out of my face.

"Yeah."

"Uh … okay … I'll be right there." I stumbled out of bed and threw on the wrinkled woolen pantsuit I'd left on a nearby chair. I grabbed my bag and down coat and flung open my bedroom window, grateful I had a first floor apartment. I landed on my feet and turned to run. Nate was blocking me. I stifled a shocked curse.

"Is there somewhere we can talk?" His eyes were unreadable. "I take it you don't want me in your apartment."

I shook with the aggravation. "Just give me a leg back up."

He tossed me back through the window. I kicked off my boots, dumped my coat and bag on the bed, then went to the kitchen to make some hot coffee. He followed me, checking the place out as we went. Once he was satisfied we were alone, he leaned on the counter, blocking the doorway. I wasn't going anywhere until he was done with me.

He casually flipped through an envelope full of Mom's multicolored tickets. "Pearson's retired, and the organization has pretty much evaporated. I couldn't just go look you up. It took a little bit of effort and some luck to piece things together. For what it's worth, I do believe your story about Pearson's son-in-law. I don't think you cheated on me."

I poured two coffees and put them on the table. I croaked, "Okay." I cleared my throat of the emotion. "You want some breakfast?"

He took a seat. "No, thanks."

"Lunch?"

He shook his head. "I want some answers. Why did you lie to me about your parents? How did you get mixed up with the mob?"

"You'd probably say I come by it naturally." I went for a box of lemon bars that had been included in my gift basket from The Golden Bowl.

Nate had obviously been observing me. With all the security

cameras everywhere that would be no problem. It took him no time at all to identify my unwanted associates.

"Lena." Nate had his no-nonsense face on.

I took a bite. "Yum. No wonder Cat told the media about these. Sure you don't want a lemon bar? These are seriously great."

If looks could kill. "Okay, Nate, I'll lay it out for ya. With two part-time jobs as a hairdressing assistant and boutique sales clerk, I wasn't exactly rolling in money. The banker wasn't impressed with my non-existent savings account and spotty work history—thanks to Pearson. Although it did look like I was a pretty ambitious teenager, if you thoroughly checked my record." I took another bite and let the lemony sugar seduce me.

"But Pearson recruited me right out of high school. I was almost fifteen, so I didn't have many years to impress a banker. Or anyone else." It occurred to me that I was lucky Pearson didn't expunge my college education from my record. *Small favors.*

"Bottom line, Nate, I needed money. So a friend of a friend recommended Gil. And now that I'm in Maine, I also owe Hal. So now it's Gilandhal. That's my new code name for my little problem."

His eyes actually softened a bit, and he took a sip of coffee.

I stuffed the rest of the lemon bar in. "Dementia and Alzheimer's isn't cheap. Mom needs constant care, and I'm not up for it. I have to work somewhere. This has been going on for years, maybe fifteen or so since she started to get confused and absent-minded. Early onset." I swallowed some coffee. "Ya know The Golden Bowl has the best coffee. Buck was smart to package it for sale. They make a fortune just off their coffee." I swept powdered sugar from my hands and face.

"Maybe I could start my own nonprofit and ask them for money. The only problem is my checkered past. Some investigative reporter'd have that on the news in a hurry. Then I'd probably lose my job."

Nate made a face. He was sick of the foolishness. How else could I distract him? I reached for another lemon bar. "Mom loves these things. Too bad I'm eating them all. Maybe I can make a quick stop at the bakery before we go to Annie's today." That comment seemed to disturb us both.

Nate took a swallow of coffee, and I stared at the table.

His voice was strangely soft. "Roger will be there today to help take care of your mom."

Tears clouded the table. "Thanks."

"What happened to your father, Lena?"

"He's dead. That's the truth." I wiped my eyes with sticky, sugary fingers and made the blur worse. "I know you couldn't find him. He's not listed on my birth certificate, and he's dead." I got up and rinsed my hands in the sink.

"I'm sorry."

"Me, too."

"What happened?" Nate was a dog with a bone.

The apartment door opened, and I could see Mom make a run for her room, the aide behind her. "Your pocketbook is by your bed, Kay."

I threw my towel on the counter. "Here we go," I said to Nate, like I was sorry his question wasn't going to be answered. I headed for Mom's room.

The aide sat on the bed watching as Mom sat in her comfy chair rummaging through her bag. I knelt on the floor in front of her, conscious of Nate in the doorway. He wasn't going to leave us alone.

"Whatcha looking for, Mom?"

She pulled out an envelope full of fake tickets and took a few. "Going to see Ricky."

"Okay, Mom, later today."

When she pulled out her lipstick and compact mirror, I couldn't help it. I started to cry.

~ *Nathan* ~

Deep down, Lena was probably a good person. That thought came to me as I drove down Annie's driveway and into the garage. I swallowed the lump in my throat that had developed as I watched her with her mother and realized I wouldn't have married Lena if I'd known about Kay.

I stared at the wall ahead of me. *I never cheated on you, Nate. I loved you. I loved you so much I lied to you. But I never cheated on you.*

I thought Lena was cheating because she spent blocks of time away from me without a reasonable excuse. It's not like I was home that often. My job took me around the world for long stretches at a time.

She was good about calling, but often hung up quickly, like someone was interfering. Some of it I chalked up to working for Pearson. But the phone rang once too often with Lena rushing off with an excuse. When Pearson finally called, I immediately believed him. I felt like a fool for putting up with Lena's behavior for so long.

She'd lied about Kay, knowing I wouldn't have wanted to deal with all that on top of my stressful job. I felt about two inches tall. Maybe Lena was not the perfect wife, but I was a lousy husband.

Uncomfortable with that thought, I decided Lena was no innocent. I still had no explanation of what happened to her father. *Maybe she didn't know.*

As I exited the garage, a cold blast of air changed my focus. Doc and Billy stood in animated conversation on the back snow-covered lawn. I headed over. "What's up?"

Billy smirked. "Doc's helping me visualize our wedding set-up. We're gonna put a tent up over there. Pastor Mike is gonna marry Lisa and me. Then we'll have a party right here on the lawn and the beach. It's gonna be awesome."

Doc took out his phone. "Yes … It's going to be awesome. This summer. But right now, I'm freezing. I'm calling Annie to make sure the coast is clear. She and Buck are having another love fest in there producing tonight's dinner. I don't want to walk in at an inopportune time."

Billy shrugged. "Newlyweds!"

~ *Lena* ~

Mom was a little over the top with her halleluiahs, probably because she was all excited about visiting "Ricky," so I decided to forgo the lemon bars and headed to the florist for a quick stop. I bought a nice bouquet for Annie in record time. Back in the car, I understood Mom wouldn't want to share them, so I ran back again for a duplicate bouquet.

By the time we got through security at the entrance to the driveway, I was a little frazzled. Billy escorted us to Annie's front door step. Mom had petals all over the snow and her halleluiahs were way too loud. Billy didn't seem to mind the nonsense.

Annie met us at the door and graciously accepted the flowers. "Come on in, it's freezing out there."

Mom rushed past Annie, stepped on Buck's foot, and threw herself into Roger's arms. Even my mouth was open in shock. I repeated, "I'm so sorry," a hundred times as I tried to pry her off of him. Petals and pieces of leaves and stems coated the foyer and us. I only wanted to go home.

Somehow Roger calmed her down, and got the coat and boots off her. Annie ushered us all into the living room for drinks and appetizers. That's where we found Tracey, Karen, Ashleigh, and Lisa, all employees at The Golden Bowl, all women who would have no reason to like me after the hassles I'd created for them last summer. Mom smiled in response to their hellos and settled with her pocketbook in a comfortable chair beside Roger. I took a seat beside her.

I almost thought it would be okay until Mom rummaged through her bag and came out with a fistful of construction paper tickets. She began sorting them and handing them off to Roger, one by one. No one could understand what she was saying, including me.

Annie took a seat on an ottoman in front of me and reached for my hand. "Don't worry, your mom is fine. Roger's fine."

I looked into kind eyes and remembered why Nate had said Annie was way better than me. It was true. "Thanks. Maybe I can stay here with Mom while you have dinner. You'll lose your appetites if she comes to the dining room table."

She half laughed. "Tell you what, Roger can stay here with Kay and help her with her dinner. He's perfectly happy to do that. And you're only one room away if you want to check on her. What do you think? It'll give you a little break."

"Sounds good, if you're sure it's okay."

"Absolutely."

Dinner was ready, and we took our seats at the table after Annie served Mom and Roger in the living room. Mom was in heaven with her lobster bisque, and she was reasonably neat about eating it. She insisted on taking Roger's crackers and gave him a piece of green construction paper in exchange. I was so relieved he took all this in stride.

Doc, Annie's birth father, patted my back and encouraged me to the table. "They'll be fine. Let's eat."

When Nate appeared and pulled a chair out for me, my stomach flipped. He took a seat beside me, and I wondered what the evening had in store.

Talk at the table was fun, which I was not used to. Mostly, I listened as everyone asked Annie and Buck about their honeymoon trip to Hawaii, and then Ashleigh, the restaurant's first shift manager, and Lisa, a dishwasher, talked about their excitement over the success of the Super Club product line. Then Karen, the confections manager, told us all about how the Clementes, everyone's favorite rock stars, were skyrocketing sales of their favorite Golden Bowl treats.

It became apparent to me that Tracey and Nate had a comfortable friendship. I felt a twinge as I remembered they occupied adjacent offices on the second floor of our building. Nate was handsome and eligible, why would I be surprised he'd be popular with the single ladies? *Get over it.*

Laughter and happy voices helped that lobster bisque glide down my throat. Then Annie served a surf and turf entrée that was to die for. Doc told us that one of Annie and Buck's favorite pastimes was creating out-of-this-world meals together. I never dared say it since he'd hired me, but Buck was definitely the "cutie" I'd called him when I scammed him last summer.

I was glad he was happily married.

As Karen asked me about how I could help get our products to market faster, Nate's phone buzzed, and he left the table to take the call. I started in on my explanation.

~ *Nathan* ~

Cat Clemente wanted to speak to me, and I was concerned, since it was after 2:00 a.m. in Salzburg, Austria. I strode through the parlor and noted Kay sound asleep on the couch. Roger lingered over dessert as he read in a nearby chair. I headed through the foyer and downstairs to my private office. I took her call on a secure line.

Her voice was heavy. "Nathan, I'm sorry to interrupt your Saturday evening, but I need your help."

"Of course."

"I don't know anything about him, really. His name is Uncle Teddy, and I believe he's Lena's uncle. He and his family are in terrible danger. Tickets—he has tickets, but I don't know his destination. I think there's supposed to be a family reunion. They'll be killed if you don't stop it."

If it were anyone else but Cat who told me this, I would have laughed them out of the room. But I knew she was for real—a modern-day prophet is what Annie called her.

I exhaled frustration into the phone. "That's all you know?"

"Yes. Please tell Lena how important it is that she tells you everything she knows. You need to stop this reunion."

"Well, that's the trick. Since the day we met, she told me she's alone in the world. Now I see she has a mother. She still claims her father is dead. She told Roger she's named after an aunt, but I couldn't find anything on the woman. This is the first I've heard of an uncle. And so far, all my searching and conversations with people from the organization are dead ends."

"Nathan, please understand Lena has had a troubled life. I'm sure it's difficult for her to confide in anyone. But if she wants to help her uncle and his family, she has no choice. Please tell her to call me any time of day or night. This is her time to trust God."

Good luck with that. "All right, Cat. I'll do my best." I jotted her number on a notepaper.

I returned to the table as everyone was finishing dessert, and chose a large slice of wild blueberry pie with honey vanilla ice cream. Lena had settled into the group pretty well, and her mother was still asleep. I should have skipped the dessert, but I was at a loss. Uncle Teddy would be a goner. Lena was incapable of telling the truth. To anyone.

I wondered exactly what Cat knew of her troubled past. She certainly knew everything about mine—without my input.

Lena carefully scraped the last of her dessert from her plate. "Uh … Annie, this meal was the best one I've had in forever. Thank you so much. And thanks for understanding and inviting Mom."

As Annie graciously accepted the compliments and thanked her for coming, they rose from the table and headed toward the parlor. I waited for all the pleasantries to be exchanged before I gave up on my pie.

I swept Lena to the foyer and explained to Buck that I needed to speak with her privately. As Lena sputtered excuses, I escorted her downstairs to my office. I pointed her to a leather chair. Her beautiful dark eyes were wide and fearfully curious.

She dropped into the chair. "What's this all about, Nate?"

I took a seat behind my desk in an effort to be professional. How could I seriously discuss Uncle Teddy's certain doom? Who the heck was Uncle Teddy? I hoped Lena would believe that Cat was more than a prayerful rock star who was credited with healing people from time to time.

"I just got a call from Cat Clemente."

"Cat?" She almost came out of the seat. "What's going on? Is it about Mom?"

"It's about someone called Uncle Teddy and his family."

Her face went white.

"You have an Uncle Teddy?"

I noticed her gripping the arms of the chair. She looked shocked. Her voice was weak. "Is he okay?"

"He needs your help. Cat had a vision about him and his family. It sounds like they're traveling to a family reunion, and they'll be killed when they get there. You … we need to stop that reunion."

"Okay." She stood up and fainted.

She came to as I lifted her off the floor. My concern sounded too aggravated. "What's with all this fainting?"

She tried to shake me off and reached for the chair. I sat her down. "Can I get you some water?"

She had her face in her hands. "I'm fine. I don't need water." I heard her sob. "He's lasted longer than most."

"What?"

She sat up to face me and inhaled the tears. "Uncle Teddy's the best. You need a document forged … he's your guy. He worked for the mob. Still sharp as a tack, and he's into his seventies."

I stared at her. "For the first time in your life … You're telling me the truth … It's crazy enough to be true."

"I'm telling you the truth, Nate."

"And what about the aunt you're named after?"

"My Aunt Helena is Mom's older sister." To my surprise, she was forthcoming with the information. "Uncle Teddy is married to Aunt Helena."

"Okay." I handed her Cat's phone number. "Cat told me to tell you to call her. She wants you to trust God. Her words."

Lena looked at the paper and stashed it in her pocket. "Thanks."

FIVE

~ *Lena* ~

There was no point in arguing with Nate, though I wasted precious time trying. Uncle Teddy was a sweet old man who'd done his time for forgery, but he insisted on going to work in his print shop every day. Retirement was a dirty word to him. And like anyone involved with the mob, he was good at keeping his mouth shut. So I had no idea what he was really up to these days.

Nate said he'd call a friend at the FBI. But I had no intention of standing by while the authorities apprehended Uncle Teddy for whatever charges they'd likely cook up. And I had no doubt that the FBI would be very interested in whatever Teddy was up to, even if it was only a family reunion. Teddy was an important cog in the wheel of a pretty notorious family.

In the end, I admitted Nate was right, then gave him false information that would lead them on a wild goose chase.

I accepted Nate's order to go home with Mom, and Roger would stay and guard us. I thanked him for his help and concern and went to get Mom up and ready for the cold trip home. It was surprisingly simple when Mom learned she'd be going for a drive with "Ricky."

Once we had Mom loaded into Roger's SUV, an overwhelming urge to visit the prayer bowl at the restaurant overtook me. "Roger, I need to stop at The Golden Bowl. I just want to put a prayer in, okay?"

"Sure. I'll follow you there."

"Thanks." I felt like kind of a goof as I careened into the empty parking lot and ran up the stairs. The porch was softly lit with tiny white lights, and the bowl glowed like the light in the concert hall in Philadelphia. I reached into my bag for a pen and grabbed one of Mom's tickets to write on. "God help me." I said it aloud as I threw the paper into the bowl. *It couldn't hurt to say it over the bowl*. "God help Mom. God help Uncle Teddy and Aunt Helena."

I turned on my heel and remembered the sign read: *Leave a Prayer, Take a Prayer*. I spun back and grabbed a paper. Roger's headlights caught the prayer.

Don't blame us for the sins of our parents. Hurry up and help us; we're at the end of our rope. You're famous for helping; God, give us a break. Psalm 79: 8-10 The Message

I did a double take. *Roger must think I'm insane.* I blinked to un-pop my eyes and shut my mouth. I waved the prayer at him and rushed to my car. *Maybe God heard me*. Then I thought, maybe I should call Cat.

It was close to midnight, but I sat sipping decaf coffee with Mom and Roger at the kitchen table. I'd made up the couch for Roger, and Mom was ecstatic to have him there. He did resemble old pictures of my dad. Straight dark hair and eyes. Handsome face, Roman nose, strong chin. A strapping six feet. I had only glimpses of memories of my dad.

Mom had found my extra stash of fake tickets and graced Roger with one after the other. I was so impressed with how patient and kind he was with her. Her speech was especially poor tonight, and I chalked that up to overexcitement.

Finally, I managed to get her to bed with the promise that Roger would join us for breakfast tomorrow. I made sure the alarm was on, and said goodnight to Roger.

As soon as I was alone in my room, I took out my laptop and sent a covert warning to Uncle Teddy. Then I removed all my information from my phone and tossed it on the bed. I took my Glock from the nightstand drawer, bundled up, and clutched my laptop and overnight bag in a careful exit from my window. No Nate this time.

I ran for my car and headed to a nice neighborhood nearby where I abandoned my rental and picked a comfortable sedan that was not even locked. Then I drove south to a neighboring town, replaced the license plates, and continued south.

Sunday morning, I parked in a Manhattan garage not far from Brooke, Lewis & Wynn. I cleaned the car, tightened my scarf around my face, pulled my woolen hat down over my forehead, took my briefcase and bag, and unrecognizable, headed into wind-whipping cold. The subway was a block away. After a short wait, I was on my way to Queens.

When I left the train, I walked a block and then down an alleyway past an old garage behind Uncle Teddy's modest brick house. I had my key inside my glove to quickly let myself in the back door. I stepped into an empty kitchen, dropped my bag, and put my briefcase on the table. "Uncle Teddy? Auntie?"

I heard, "oh," coming from the living room. Helena was in her chair in front of the TV. I took off my coat and dropped it on a couch, as she began to work her way out of her seat. Her hair was completely gray and pulled back in a frizzy bun. She'd obviously put on more weight since I'd last seen her. A fuzzy old beige sweater clung to her housedress.

"Hi, Auntie." I wrapped her in a big hug, catching her on the edge of the chair.

"You all right, honey?" She reached for her cane.

"I'm fine. Where's Uncle Teddy?"

"He went for a crumb cake. He knows that's my favorite, and I was so disappointed he cancelled Vegas."

I breathed a sigh of relief. "It was too dangerous, Auntie. I heard a bad rumor."

She settled back in her seat. "Where's Kay?"

"She's safe at the nursing home."

Auntie shook her cane at me. "You shouldn't have come back here."

"No one saw me. I had to make sure you cancelled that reunion." I heard a key in the front door and peered through the window curtain. Uncle Teddy came through the door with a cake box and a newspaper. He looked to be a little more stooped than the last time I'd seen him.

"Lena!" He dropped the stuff on an old wooden credenza and hugged me. "You shouldn't have come all this way. I cancelled Vegas. The boys have their eyes open. We're fine. Where's Kay?"

Auntie answered, "She's fine. Still in Maine."

He looked concerned.

I walked him to his well-worn recliner. "Don't worry. Mom's fine. She's got Annie's guard looking after her ... a Navy SEAL."

"Annie?"

I tried to soothe him. "Annie doesn't know anything. She was just being nice to lend me the guard so I'd have a little break."

Uncle Teddy dropped into the recliner. "Don't be careless, Lena. You never know when Kay might come out with something she shouldn't."

What could I say to that? "No one takes anything she says seriously. She mostly talks gibberish. Don't worry, okay?"

Auntie pointed her cane at me. "You put my boys in danger. Now we're missing our reunion because of you."

"Excuse me? I got the tip."

She took a framed photo of her grandsons from the table beside her. "Your mother's always been spoiled, and you're the same. We fed you both the whole time you were growing up. You owe Teddy everything. He taught you everything you needed to know. Then you got that job. You shouldn't even be alive."

By now Uncle Teddy had taken the cake and me in hand, urging me to the kitchen table. "She's upset about Vegas. Misses the boys. Losing her filters, like Kay did."

"It's okay." I took a seat at the old Formica table.

He put the cake on the counter and turned to me. "Why did you come all the way back from Maine?"

That choking feeling started in my throat again. "You're the only link to my past. Mom's lost it. Auntie's going down the same path."

He sat and faced me. "Usually, Lena, it's best to let go of the past. Don't go dredging things up. It's over, and there's nothing you can do to change it."

"I need to see where I died."

He rubbed his gray head in frustration, and I watched flakes of dandruff fall to his shirt. "Lena!"

"I need you to take me there. I need to see that place before I die."

"You're not gonna die. Not unless you go and do something stupid."

"Everyone dies, Uncle Teddy. Sooner or later."

He turned in his seat, arm on the back of his chair, head buried in his elbow.

I knew I was pushing him too hard. But I had to. That's where it all started, when it all started. It was time to face it, before I lost Uncle Teddy. Then it'd just be me, all alone with no past. I needed to make sense of my life sometime.

It was a silent couple of minutes before he faced me. "I don't even know where it is."

"You were there. You can help me find it."

"No."

"We can leave tomorrow."

"Too much going on at the print shop. I'm on vacation

Wednesday."

"Okay, we'll leave Wednesday morning."

~ *Nathan* ~

Lena had left her car in an upscale neighborhood near her apartment, then made off with a luxury sedan. It was Tuesday when someone in another town discovered they had the wrong license plates on their vehicle. Lena could have been anywhere by then.

Of course, my friend at the FBI quickly learned Lena had given me bad information on "Uncle Teddy." He told me he'd continue his search and keep me updated.

Wednesday morning, I sat sipping coffee with Annie and Buck at the conference table in Lena's office. "I should've known she'd take off once she had someone to take care of Kay. Why didn't I see that coming?"

Buck shook his head. "Gerald was expecting her report this morning on the Super Club numbers ... and it was in his inbox at 6:00 a.m. Apparently she's still working." He slid his tablet to me.

"Hmm ... not that we'll find out her location." I returned his tablet. "I'll go have a talk with Gerald." That would be pointless, of course, but at least it would be doing something. There'd been no word from the FBI since the license plate discovery. And I couldn't bring myself to visit with Kay.

As I stood, Annie spoke. "Cat would know if something bad happened, Nathan. I know she would. She hasn't had another inkling since that first vision. That's a good sign to me that Lena and her uncle's family must be alive and well. Thank God."

I couldn't help noticing Buck's smirk as he patted Annie's hand. "As long as she's not on some island somewhere robbing us blind."

I left the bakery building to check in at the restaurant before leaving for the food prep location. Annie was so incredibly trusting of people. At least Buck had a healthy skepticism.

I remembered handing Lena Cat's number. It didn't surprise me that she had decided not to call. Apparently, she didn't realize it was her time to trust God, as Cat had recommended.

Climbing the stairs, I noticed the gold bowl overflowing with paper. So many people needed so much help. I hovered there, guilt building.

My only encounter with the prayer bowl had been to throw Lena's engagement ring in there the day I arrived to begin work as Annie's director of security. That was well over a year ago. My sarcastic prayer—something like, "I hope you have better luck with this than me"—wrapped the ring.

It occurred to me that some good did come from it. Lisa Quinn, the dishwasher, had picked it out and sold it to help her family. Now she was engaged to be married to Billy. I hoped he'd be more successful at marriage than I'd been. It was plain to see that Lisa thought the world of him.

I scanned the bowl and spotted a beige linen paper sticking out of the pile. It had to be one of Cat's. I grabbed the prayer. *Never walk away from someone who deserves help; your hand is God's hand for that person. Proverbs 3:27-29 The Message*

Yeah, that was Cat's all right. A message for me from God.

I drew in a chilly breath. *God help me*. I reached for a pen and paper. I wrote, "God help L. and her family. Help me help them." I tossed it into the bowl.

The sound of the restaurant's door closing spun me around to see Tracey holding a takeout cup of coffee. Sudden embarrassment that she'd probably witnessed me leaving a prayer gave way to curiosity at the glint in her eye. Her quirky smile made me wonder if she'd be wife number four.

"You okay, Nathan?"

"Yeah. You?" I wouldn't let myself entertain the idea of a wife number four. Three strikes and you're out.

"Yeah. Just getting my caffeine for the trip to the food prep facility. Vendor feedback meeting with Gerald."

"Yeah, I saw that on the schedule." I rubbed the last of my discomfort about the prayer out of my mind. "Look, I need to check in with Billy, but then I'm going to talk to Gerald, too. I can drive you if you want."

"Works for me." A smile lit up her face as she stepped back through the door. "I'll wait for you by the coffee pot."

After putting Billy in charge at the restaurant, we headed to my SUV and discussed most everything but Lena on the six-mile drive to the food prep building. As I dropped Tracey at the door, my phone buzzed.

It was my friend at the FBI. "We've got the car, Nathan. It was in a parking garage in Manhattan, near Wynn's office. No sign of Ms. Goodwin. Just a piece of paper stuck under the passenger seat … Looks to be a prayer from your bowl."

"What does it say?"

I heard him sigh. "Let's see ... *Don't blame us for the sins of our parents. Hurry up and help us; we're at the end of our rope. You're famous for helping; God, give us a break.* Psalm 79: 8-10 The Message."

I scribbled it on a pad. "Okay, thanks. Is that a cream color paper— high quality?"

"Uh, yeah. Why?"

"I know it's from our prayer bowl. Keep me posted." I wasn't about to tell him Cat's prayers were on cream color linen, and those words may well have some insight.

I reread the prayer and wondered if it was meant for me. It certainly applied to me. And considering Lena's refusal to discuss her parents—or even admit they were alive during our marriage—it sounded like that prayer was meant for her. My instinctive need to learn about her parents was, no doubt, correct.

~ *Lena* ~

Wednesday morning was dry and cold in New York. Uncle Teddy left Auntie Helena with plenty of crumb cake and endless directions.

She held up her phone, her face etched in a frown. "I'm all set. Go, if you're going."

I kissed Auntie goodbye and fired up my uncle's old Cadillac. We were on our way to the Catskills.

I glanced over at my uncle. "I know this isn't the way you wanted to spend your vacation."

"I don't like you missing work. You need this job."

"I know. I feel bad. Annie and Buck've been so nice to me. But this is important. I need to see the place. I need to know what happened."

He took a long, rattling breath. "You know what happened, Lena."

"It was thirty years ago. It was my fourth birthday. What does a four-year-old remember?"

"Kay needs you."

"I promise I'll be back in Maine on Friday."

His head fell back against the headrest.

I took a couple of glances his way, but he wasn't engaging. "Uh, Teddy, I don't know the way."

He sighed again. "Just drive to the Catskills. Maybe I'll remember when we get there."

It wasn't a long drive to the Catskills. That's why it was so popular with tourists. January was not the time to go, though. Winding back roads, some steep and icy, reminded me of Maine. I remembered Mom broke into a song she used to sing to me as a child, as we encountered the back roads of Maine heading to Marberry for the first time. *Country Roads.*

Maybe she sang it to me in the Catskills, all those years ago. I wanted to sing a verse, but my croak was back. Maybe this wasn't a good idea after all.

"Uncle Teddy, do you know where we are?"

I think my croaking startled him. He sat up. "No."

I pointed to the sign for an old diner, happy that the "open" light was on. "Let's stop here. Maybe someone'll know something."

He didn't look pleased with that idea. "We'll just get some lunch."

I'd guess the place had been around since the fifties, maybe even before. There was only one other patron, an old man munching on a burger and fries. I helped Teddy get his coat off and get seated in a booth. The green plastic cushions were worn, torn, and lumpy. But it didn't matter what booth you chose, they were all like that.

The waitress was on me before I could take a seat. "Coffee?"

"Two, please. Black."

Teddy craned his stiff neck, taking a good look around. He raised a canister, as the waitress delivered the coffee.

She nodded at him. "That's a fundraiser for a local family ... lost everything in a terrible fire."

I shuddered. She looked old enough to ask, "Sounds like there's been a number of bad fires around here ... going way back. Do you remember any of them?"

She gave me a funny look, then lifted her eyes to the ceiling. She focused back on me. "Come to think of it, we have had some big fires over the years. I suppose it's the woodstoves ... problems with heating, that kind of thing."

I tried to sound nonchalant. "You probably even get them in the summer."

"Yeah, camp fires, I guess." She refilled Teddy's cup, surprised he'd drunk half of his so quickly. "Yeah, there was a real bad one years and years ago. Big family killed—parents and a bunch of kids. No one made it out. That was the worst."

"Wow. That's awful." I stuffed a twenty dollar bill into the slot.

She nodded her approval. "Our specials are on the board. I'll get you some menus."

Uncle Teddy gave me the eye, but the waitress was back before he could say a word.

I took the menu. "Look, I'm doing a project for a class. Do you happen to remember anything more about that fire, or where exactly it happened? I'm researching how we can prevent these tragedies … gathering some historical data … you know … so I can make some kind of a difference here." I was sucking her in. "Actually, it's for my thesis."

"Let me think." She tapped her pencil against the order pad. "That one was about a mile, mile-and-a-half, from here."

I had a tuna sandwich, but don't remember anything other than that. My mind was too preoccupied. Teddy never uttered a word until he paid the waitress and thanked her.

I helped him with his coat, and the other elderly patron approached us. He sounded as old as Methuselah. "I fought that fire. I was chief then. Horrible tragedy. All the kids. Everyone died, even the dog. It was arson."

The shock of it clouded my eyes. *Peppy*! I'd forgotten my dog. How could I forget Peppy?

SIX

~ *Lena* ~

Uncle Teddy steered me out the door to the edge of the parking lot where the fire chief gave us detailed directions. It was now just a wooded lot. The owner never rebuilt.

We thanked him and returned to our car.

"Let's go home, Lena." Uncle Teddy was now visibly shaking.

I probably was, too. "I have to do this." I helped him into the passenger seat and stumbled around the car to the driver's side.

His hand over his eyes, he began to sob. I patted his arm. Confusion and questions tossed in my head, along with fear and mounting anger. I turned the motor on to keep us warm and stared straight ahead. I'd never seen my uncle cry before. When the sobs turned to loud breaths and finally softened, I turned out of the lot.

"You have to help me find this place. It's just woods now." I looked over at him.

"I remember this street ... this rock ledge." A guttural sound I'd never heard from him made me jam my foot on the brake. I could see the woods straight ahead led down to the frozen pond. I'd chased Peppy down there that very afternoon. I could almost see him. I heard his bark . . .

It was nighttime, and the barking dog woke me. I was huddled on the couch with Mom and Dad. Mom told me I'd had a sick stomach that day, and it'd kept my parents up with me. My older brother and sisters, my cousin, and my aunt had all been asleep upstairs.

I heard Mom say, "Ricky, where are the kids?" The dog wouldn't stop barking.

"Smoke," Dad said. He grabbed Mom off the couch. I remembered the feel of her fingers tight on my back, gripping me as we ran through

fire. *It was everywhere. We made it outside into the dark.* My stomach jolted in pain as I heard Dad's last words. *"Julia! Run!" He turned back and disappeared into the house. Mom was screaming. No one came out.*

I could still see the fire against the night. I plastered my body to the steering wheel, trying to see everything. I needed to see everything. *There was nothing but fire, deep orange and yellow in blazing towers. No more barking. Just the strange sound of all-consuming fire.*

Mom started to run. I bounced in her arms. We landed in the pond.

Uncle Teddy's cry brought me back to reality. "I killed Kay. I killed her."

"Huh?" My foot had squeezed the brake pedal so tightly I noticed a painful cramp. Teddy was wailing. My heart was hammering. "It's okay, Uncle Teddy. It's okay. It's over. Over and done."

It wasn't okay. Not by a long shot. But his meltdown was worse than mine. I turned the car back toward the diner and pulled to the side of the road. I worried he'd have a heart attack.

"Uncle Teddy?"

"I killed Kay. I killed Lena. I killed them." He was out of his mind.

I remembered there'd been a motel that looked open about ten or twelve miles back. I wiped the tears off my face and put my foot on the gas.

By the time I checked into the motel and returned to the car, Uncle Teddy was staring silently into space. I opened his passenger door. "Let's get to the room, and I'll come back for our bags. It's a good thing we decided to pack them."

He didn't say a word, but got out of the car and walked with me to a first floor room. It had two full beds and was reasonably clean. That was about all I could hope for. I turned the heat up, and it made a racket.

"I'll fix that noise once we get some heat. I'm goin' to get the bags."

Uncle Teddy sat motionless on the bed. I ran out and grabbed some coffees in the lobby, then went for the bags. Teddy's listlessness was scaring me. I turned the heater down to a tolerable noise level, closed all the curtains, and sat beside him.

"I'm sorry I stressed you like that." I gulped my coffee. "This stuff isn't bad."

He didn't answer me.

"I ... I needed to see it, Uncle Teddy. It was awful, but I needed to see it. I'm sorry I upset you." I sucked in the emotion. *I need to go back tomorrow. Even if it's by myself.*

"I was in love with Kay ... from the first time I saw her." His voice was scratchy, and I wasn't sure I really heard him.

"In love with Kay?" I was confused. Surely Teddy was.

"We had a daughter."

Now I understood. Teddy wasn't talking about my mother. *Is he? No!*

Uncle Teddy rolled forward, and I dropped my coffee to grab him. He fell back on the bed, eyes closed. He was still breathing.

"Uncle Teddy?"

"I'm tired, Lena. Too tired."

I put a pillow under his head, then found some tissues in my pockets to soak up coffee off the rug. I dug deeper for another, and pulled out the paper Nate had given me. *Cat's phone number.* How many times had I seriously wanted to call her? Nate said she said to trust God. That's what she'd said in Philadelphia. *Love is what is important.*

I left the pile of damp tissues on the coffee stain, went to the bathroom, and sat there for a long time. Thinking. I couldn't put Uncle Teddy through anymore. But I couldn't leave this place without knowing the truth about that day, the truth about my family. Was Teddy even capable of telling the truth at this point?

I wasn't sure I was capable of hearing it.

~ *Annie* ~

There was a quick knock at my office door, and Buck poked his head in to find me sprawled on the couch, notebook in hand. "How's the cookbook coming?"

I looked down at the blank page. "I've been thinking about Lena and Nathan."

He sat beside me and put his arm around me. "No worries, my dear. Brooke, Lewis & Wynn has three outstanding IT people on our case. Not that they can keep up with Lena, but I don't think she wants to take us down."

I often amazed myself with my lack of a "business mind." I was thinking about Nathan and Lena's relationship. It hadn't occurred to me that Lena would want to do The Golden Bowl harm at this point. No need to make that painfully obvious to Buck—again. "Agreed. I don't think she intends to do us harm, either ... But you'd think with all the experts at the FBI, they'd be able to figure out who Uncle Teddy is. How many Uncle Teddies have been to prison for forgery?"

Buck laughed. "You make a good point, my dear. They're certainly taking their time with the investigation."

"Well, I called Cat, and I have to say, I'm surprised she knows nothing about Uncle Teddy or Lena's whereabouts. God gave her one little glimpse of a vision, and Cat's okay with that. She's totally fine because she knows God's in charge, and she's being used for his purposes. She doesn't need to know what God doesn't show her. Wow. I wonder how I could ever get to that depth of trust."

I turned to get his reaction. Buck's eyes were intense. "Sometimes you need time to figure things out for yourself. Perhaps God is giving Lena some time and space."

Joy welled up. It wasn't so long ago when Buck had a time of figuring himself, and it changed both of our lives. "You're a smart man, Buck Wynn." I kissed his cheek. "Maybe he is giving her time to figure. But I keep thinking of that scripture Cat quotes from Revelation. God stands at the door and knocks. If we choose to answer that call, he comes in to join us for a meal. I bet God is tapping on Lena's door now ... and Nathan's."

~ *Lena* ~

I'm not sure how long I sat on that hard toilet seat before I took a towel and sat on the rim of the tub. That wasn't any more comfortable. I opened the door to check on Uncle Teddy. He was curled in a fetal position asleep on his bed. I took a seat on the only chair in the room.

I'd stressed him to the max. It wasn't fair. He'd watched out for me from the word go. He loved me even more than Auntie Helena loved me, and she was Mom's sister. I was selfish. That's one thing I had in common with my aunt.

My Aunt Helena and her two sisters—in their younger days often referred to as "the three Goodwin girls"—were special. That's what I was always told. That's about all I was told. My past was a jumble of truth and lies. The truths I clung to could have been lies, too.

Did Uncle Teddy fall in love with Mom? She'd told me Teddy introduced her to Dad when he'd worked for him at the print shop.

I noticed Teddy stirring, then he sat up in the bed facing away from me. I went around and sat on the edge of the bed with him. He gave me a groggy hug and a kiss on the side of my head.

I spoke softly near his ear. "Can I get you something? Are you warm enough?"

"I'm okay."

"We need to stay here tonight. I need to sort some things out. Auntie should be fine."

He nodded.

"I'm going for coffee. Want some?"

"Okay."

When I got back he was stashing his phone in his pocket. He replied to my accusatory glare. "Helena is fine. I didn't want her to worry."

"All right." I handed him a cup and sat with mine on the edge of my bed, facing him. "It's not bad out there, maybe twenty degrees. Want some takeout from that diner for supper?"

"Fine." He rubbed his face so hard I was afraid he'd scrape his skin off. "Lena, we need to talk."

I swallowed the coffee in an uncomfortable gulp. "Okay. Talk." *Love is what is important.* I softened my voice. "When you're ready, Uncle Teddy."

He put his cup on the nightstand and lifted mournful brown eyes to meet mine. "When could I ever be ready to tell you what a miserable excuse for a human being I am?"

"It's not that bad." The pit of my stomach told me it was. *God help me.*

"I met the Goodwin girls not long after I'd set up my shop. I watched your mother practically skipping from one merchant to the other, up and down the street. I couldn't take my eyes off her. She was barely out of high school and looking for a job. I hired her on the spot. That afternoon I found her and Ricky in the back room making out. He stole her right out from under my nose. They were madly in love from that day." He looked around for his coffee cup and took a sip.

A sad, sick feeling oozed up from my stomach. "They still are."

Teddy stared at his coffee. "Yeah. I could see those two were meant for each other. So I didn't interfere." Shaky hands returned it to the nightstand.

He looked at me with a weak laugh. "I was jealous though."

I attempted a smile. "I can understand that."

"Next day I met your mother's sisters—Helena and Kay. Six months later I was married to Helena. But I was in love with Kay." He rubbed his face again. "I don't really know how that happened."

"Oh." The truth tumbled through me, burning my insides, as hot as the fire that killed my family. I didn't need Uncle Teddy to fill in the blanks.

But he did. "There were pressures, Lena. The guys I worked for … like I said … miserable excuses for human beings. And I was one of them. Ricky, too, but he was true to his wife, his kids. They could only push him so far. It started to scare me. I took up with Kay. My wife didn't know, or I didn't think she knew."

I handed him a box of tissues. My voice bubbled with acid. "Baby Lena was your daughter."

He nodded. "Yes."

I could hardly see him through the tears. "Well, at least she has a father. I bet Auntie knew baby Lena was yours." I bit my lip, wishing I hadn't said it. But I wanted to hurt him. In that moment, I wanted to hurt him.

Love is what is important. Cat's accent made the phrase indelible in my brain. I wailed. "Why wouldn't you ever tell me *my* name? Everyone else has a real name. Didn't I deserve a real name?"

He got to his feet, landed on the bed beside me, and held me to his side, somehow trying to comfort me. "We were afraid you'd slip. You were just a baby. You were … you *are* … Lena."

I don't know how long it was before I calmed myself down, but the room was dark when I took my hands off my face. He was still beside me, gripping me, looking straight ahead at nothing.

I couldn't remember my cousin Lena's face to save my life. She'd lived almost five years. But her face was gone in the terror of that night.

I spoke straight ahead into the dark, not daring to look at my uncle. "That very next morning you called me Lena. You called me Lena until I couldn't remember my real name. I was six years old before I dared ask Mom about my real name."

My voice was a croak again, but I forced the words out. "The minute I had my first computer, I looked up my name. Grace. The name no one could ever say. Grace was dead and buried. Along with her mother, Julia. Dead and buried."

But they aren't. I'm Grace, and Mom is Julia. Aunt Kay and baby Lena are dead and buried.

Uncle Teddy burst into sobs. I'm sure he wished Mom and I had died in that fire instead—as intended. Even if it meant revealing his infidelity with my Aunt Kay.

I was the one who crashed into oblivion, waking up scrunched in the fetal position. Uncle Teddy was shaving at the bathroom sink. I decided it was good he did everything in slow motion these days. Maybe I'd have a chance of keeping up today.

I stretched in the bed, realizing it was Thursday. "Uncle Teddy, you want some breakfast at the diner?"

He stepped out of the bathroom, rubbing his face with a towel. "Okay. There's a cup of coffee on the table for you. Still warm."

I guzzled the coffee, then took over the bathroom and dressed in a fresh set of clothes. I started to feel human again. Teddy was in front of the TV.

"I'm going to visit that lot again. Do you want to stay here? I can drop you back after breakfast."

"I'll go with you."

It was a brisk winter day, but at least there was sun. We were both quiet as we pulled up to that woodsy lot. There was patchy snow covering the ground, but with warm boots, I wasn't concerned. I walked the considerable length of the property. The two homes on either side were closed down for the season. Not a soul in sight. Thinking back thirty years, I understood that the neighbors wouldn't have seen a fire next door until it was massive.

Teddy had gone down to the pond then back up to sit on a pile of rocks. As I approached him, I could see it was the remains of an old foundation. I caught his watery brown eyes.

"Hardly anything left, huh?"

"Just memories." He pulled his collar up around his chin. "They would've come back to finish the job if they'd found out you and your mother were alive, Lena. You know that."

"Yeah." I took a seat on some rubble. "Who did it?" I had my suspicions but never dared ask that question.

"They're long dead. Joey B ordered it."

I shook my head. "Thirty years is a long time. It's Joey B2 now."

Teddy snickered a bit. "Yeah." He rubbed the expression off his face. "I'm pretty sure you're already doing battle with him. A different world now. A cyber-battle. Right?"

"Right." I surveyed the patches of snow that used to be the basement and focused on a tiny pine tree that had pushed through the packed dirt. "I'm winning, Uncle Teddy. And I'm gonna win even bigger. That guy's gonna be cyber-dust." *Time to take the gloves off.*

He nodded and took out a half-used napkin he had at the diner to mop his face.

Childhood memories flooded back. How many times had I been at Teddy's shop, soaking up everything he had to teach me, when Joey B and his associates ambled in? My uncle would wipe his face with a handkerchief, almost like he was absolving himself from the whole thing. Then he'd give me ice cream money and send me on my way.

Too many times I hid in the back room and listened to that ugly voice telling ugly stories, giving terrible orders. He was only in his twenties, but he'd inherited his father's mean gene. That was obvious. I knew deep down inside Joey B and his father were behind my family's massacre. I couldn't face it until now.

I got up and headed down to the pond. *Yeah.* It was time to take the gloves off. Why had I tried to straddle two opposite worlds my entire life? All that struggle with stupid hairdressing assistant and sales clerk jobs when I was a world-class hacker playing Robin Hood. I could have been fabulously rich instead of living hand-to-mouth in Brooklyn. Why not give in to my natural talents?

My immediate answer was Mom and Uncle Teddy. Neither one of them wanted me involved in criminal activity. Mom had told me as soon as I was old enough to understand that my dad had agreed to leave the mob. She'd pressured him for years, more and more the older my brother got. He was ten when my dad acquiesced. No doubt that decision cost him and our family their lives.

I almost laughed out loud. Despite Mom's efforts, everyone around me was up to something criminal. Then General Pearson came calling. Uncle Teddy thought that was an upstanding job I could be proud of, and he told Mom so. Not that I could ever breathe a word about it. That should've been his clue that it wasn't all that upstanding.

I noticed paw prints on the snow-skimmed ice. I could hear Peppy, still barking thirty years later. I went for the bottle of aspirin at the bottom of my handbag and pulled out a handful of paper—the prayers Mom had taken out of the golden bowl the day we arrived in Maine. I grabbed one and the others fell back into the bag.

"For I know the plans I have for you," declares the Lord, "plans to prosper you and not to harm you, plans to give you hope and a future. Then you will call upon me and come and pray to me, and I will listen to you. You will seek me and find me when you seek me with all your heart. I will be found by you." Jeremiah 29:11-14 NIV

I fell on my knees reading the prayer. I looked up. There was no more barking, just the comforting quiet of a winter afternoon.

Uncle Teddy approached hesitantly. "Lena?"

I stood and wiped slush and mud from my jeans. "Mind if we stay here another day? I need some quiet time."

SEVEN

~ *Lena* ~

It was too cold for my uncle to stay outside, so we warmed up with lunch at the diner, then I dropped him back at the motel with some coffee and various slices of pie. After we spoke with Auntie, I left him content in front of the TV.

I drove back to the lot and parked facing it, keeping the engine running and the heat blasting. Sporadic sunshine glistened on the icy pond. I fumbled through my bag for the prayers Mom had grabbed from the golden bowl. Reading through them, I was blown away. Each and every one fit with me and my situation. I needed to call Cat.

Was it Cat who was beckoning me to God? Or was it Mom? Her voice came to me in a whisper of lucidity she'd had a while ago. She was talking to the window and telling Dad how his life of crime had destroyed everything good in their lives. Maybe she saw his ghost there. I don't know. The heat in the car did nothing to stop cold shivers.

Scrambling through the papers, I remembered the one about the sins of our parents that I'd pulled out of the bowl myself. It wasn't in my pile, so I dumped the contents out of my bag and onto the passenger seat. It wasn't there. I ran my hand through all the compartments. "Give me a break … Oh, that's the prayer … God, give me a break." Then it came to me. *Don't blame us for the sins of our parents. Hurry up and help us; we're at the end of our rope. You're famous for helping; God, give us a break.*

Where the paper ended up was anybody's guess. Maybe someone else needed it. I noticed sunlight on the pile of rocks—the remains of a basement where Teddy and I had sat earlier. I thought about my promise to get Joey B. I'd already been stealing from him in dribs and drabs. I guess the sins of the parents were working their way through a new generation. *You're famous for helping; God, give us a break.*

Cousin Lena's face appeared in the sunshine, and I gasped with the shock. I knew her face. She was always smiling, always fun-loving. I missed her. I looked up to her. What would she think of me? Pretending to be her, yet nothing like her. I needed to make somebody pay for the suffering and loss that happened that day. Joey B would pay for his sins and his father's.

I wondered at her sweet young face smiling right at me like an angel. Like everything would be okay, despite that horrific suffering.

I picked up a prayer paper. *Revenge belongs to God.* A shiver went through me. It was like I was being set up. Who could have replaced every prayer in the bowl to speak only to me?

I picked another one. *For the Lord is our Judge, the Lord is our lawgiver, the lord is our King; it is he who will save us. Isaiah 33:22, NIV.*

Somehow, God was going to save us. According to Cat, all I had to do was focus on love. That's what's important. *Not revenge, huh?* That was a tough one to swallow today.

I picked up the Jeremiah prayer. I had hope and a future. All I had to do was seek God, and he'd take care of the rest. Could I really believe that?

Doing things my way wasn't working out great. One minute a world-class cybercriminal, the other a lowly hairdressing assistant. I could try believing in God and see if it worked. A little voice inside said I obviously wanted to, since I'd spent so much time and effort to meet Cat Clemente.

The people at The Golden Bowl came to mind. I'd given every one of them trouble they didn't deserve. Just because I was mad at Nate and jealous of Annie. I'd created every form of chaos you could think of for those poor people. Short supplies, unhappy, screwed up vendors, lies upon lies, you name it. Almost every email I'd sent out named the dishwasher, Lisa Quinn, as the one in charge of whatever ridiculous order I'd written. It's a wonder she hadn't given me a piece of her mind or a tub of dirty dishwater over my head.

I'd blown everything out of proportion. Just because I'd had no life, and I was jealous of my ex-husband's interest in his boss. I'd been willing to ruin lives, ruin a whole business for stupid revenge.

And then they embraced me. It was incomprehensible. *Love is what is important.* I guess they walked their talk. That was the only explanation.

Buck hired me at Brooke, Lewis & Wynn despite the fact I'd tried to ruin his business, his relationship with Annie, and her business. Then he hired me at The Golden Bowl, where I basically had no oversight whatsoever. He knew I could do that job with one hand tied behind my back, but he also knew what I was capable of in the crazy-revenge-lady department.

Sparkling in the snow caught my attention. I turned off the car and bundled up. Heading toward the rock pile, I could see the light reflecting. It was an old chain with a big gold pendant that looked like the elements had given it a strange sheen. I pried the heart-shaped pendant from the ground, and looked it over. Dirt covered some writing, and I used my glove to clean it off. A flash in my mind showed me Cousin Lena with her tricycle, decked out in a little yellow sun suit, the big heart hanging to her waist.

I read the word aloud, "Love." Pain darted through me, and I jogged toward the pond, tears clouding my vision. Her mom must have let Lena take it. It was the kind of jewelry my Aunt Kay would wear. In every picture I'd ever seen of her, she had jewelry everywhere. The bigger and bolder, the better.

I clutched the pendant and stood staring at the ice, the trees in the distance, the colorless winter sky. *Love is what is important.* I'd been draining money from Joey B's online businesses to pay Mom's expenses, and mine, too. I knew my morals were screwed up. I'd been brought up without a clear sense of right and wrong.

As a matter of fact, that was one of the traits that General Pearson liked most in me. *Blurry lines.* I was happy to agree with his version of right and wrong.

Like I told Nate, I had lost myself along the way. I lost myself the day I lost my family, and the loss only spiraled from there.

Today I knew Cat was right. My heart could agree that love is what is important. It was worth working through the pain it would take to make my life reflect that. It was probably the only way to find my real self—to find Grace.

I stared at the sky, the colorlessness now appeared as soft shades of gray, blue, pink, and purple clouds melding into each other. *Things aren't always as they seem at first glance.* Cat had to be right about trusting God. I sure wasn't able to fix things on my own.

I couldn't ignore Joey B and the sins of his family against mine. I'd see him brought to justice. I'd need to use his ill-gotten money to do it. *God will understand ... Maybe.*

Uncle Teddy? Loving him—and Aunt Helena—would mean

overlooking past mistakes. His infidelity was in the past, dead and buried with Kay and Lena. Why they called their illegitimate child Lena, after Kay's older sister and Teddy's wife, I couldn't imagine.

But, except for that big indiscretion, Uncle Teddy had been a good husband to Auntie Helena, a good father to his boys, and a good grandfather. At least from my perspective.

I walked along the shore, the chain of the pendant tight around my wrist and hand, anchoring me thirty years in the past.

I'd inherited the name that was convenient. I was almost the same age and coloring as my cousin. In pictures, I'd always thought Mom and Aunt Kay could have been twins. Mom was less than two years younger than her sister. Add a little bling and you couldn't tell the difference. Lena and her mother were the perfect substitute bodies for me and Mom.

After Uncle Teddy found us wandering in the woods that night, it was a no brainer for him to switch documents and hide us in plain sight in Brooklyn. No one knew that Kay and Lena were in the Catskills with my family that day. No one cared that they were alive. Auntie Helena made sure Mom had all Kay's jewelry—and that she wore it for quite a few years. It was a simple matter for Mom and me to assume their identities.

A simple matter that has messed me up to this day.

I went into my coat pocket for a tissue and came out with a prayer.

For the Lord is our Judge, the Lord is our lawgiver, the lord is our King; it is he who will save us. Isaiah 33:22 NIV

Maybe God was telling me I was right. I was okay. Joey B would be brought to justice with God's help. I sniffled and laughed out loud, then yelled up at the sky, "God is the judge." It echoed on the pond. "Let him be the judge."

It was late Friday night when Uncle Teddy and I rolled into his garage in Queens. The house was in darkness. As I ran through every room calling for Auntie Helena, Teddy remained in the kitchen. I returned to find him at the table reading a note, his head buried in his arm.

"Where'd you find that?"

He didn't look up. "In the toaster. We have a certain protocol. When the toaster is unplugged, I look for a note in the crumb tray."

I shook my head. "Of course." I couldn't resist. "What does a crumb cake mean?"

He looked up at me. "It means your aunt is mad, and I need to appease her."

Laughter tumbled out of me in involuntary streams—until my uncle told me Auntie Helena was en route to Maine.

I dropped into a kitchen chair. "This isn't good. What happens when Nate and the FBI get hold of her?"

Uncle Teddy was straight-faced. "God help them." He put his hand up to stop me from launching into a tirade. "She knows how to handle herself, Lena. Don't worry. I'm not surprised she left. She does worry about Kay. And when we stayed away for days—"

I interrupted. "Uncle Teddy, we left Wednesday morning. It's Friday night. Mom has aides to take care of her and a Navy SEAL guard she thinks is her husband. She's as fine as she's gonna be."

"Nevertheless, she worries. I had all I could do to convince her not to go visit the boys. She was looking forward to a vacation ... away from this New York weather."

"Okay ... yeah ... then heading to Maine is like jumping from the frying pan into the fire." I put my head in my hands. "Now what am I gonna do?"

~ *Nathan* ~

I hadn't seen Kay since Roger drove off with her last Saturday evening. Since I expected Lena's loan shark, Hal, would be visiting Washington Gardens this morning promptly at 8:00 a.m., I decided to check in with Kay before confronting Hal. I arrived in the apartment at 7:30.

Roger met me at the door. I could see Kay and her aide at the kitchen table. Kay wasn't paying much attention to breakfast. She seemed more concerned with her colorful tickets.

I took Roger aside. "What's that all about?"

He shrugged. "From what I can understand, which isn't much, she's telling us about Julia and how much she needs tickets. I don't know what the tickets are for. But she wants them for this Julia person. Sometimes desperately. We try and distract her by giving her those tickets Lena made. Sometimes it works. Sometimes it doesn't."

What could I do but shake my head? "No idea how to help with that."

I met two FBI agents in the lobby, and we proceeded to the bench near the back door in time to witness a silver-haired woman knock Hal off that bench with her cane. As we ran to them, she cursed up a storm. He was out cold. My colleagues burst into laughter.

I approached her with caution. "Ma'am?"

She straightened her long coat, her cane at the ready. "I'm here to visit Kay. Kay Goodwin."

"Of course you are."

Aunt Helena resembled her niece only in her stubborn personality. She carried no identification, would not give us her full name, and insisted on making sure Kay was all right before answering our many questions. She deflected us with the same chorus. "He had a gun, and he threatened me."

We did find a gun on Hal's unconscious body, but it was tucked in his belt at his back. It would have taken some doing for Helena to see it or for him to get to it under the zippered ski jacket stretched tight over his belly.

Regardless, Helena got what she wanted. The FBI decided not to take her into custody. Instead, I ushered her to her sister's apartment. Kay rushed to her, all smiles. "Nana!"

Helena embraced her, comforted her, and eventually took her to sit on the couch with her. She looked up at Roger and me, a bit teary. "Kay's called me her mother for a while now. This is the first time she thinks I'm her grandmother. It's been months since I've seen her. It's getting worse."

"I'm sorry to hear that." What else could I say?

I suppose all the emotion tuckered them out. It wasn't long before Kay fell asleep, and then Helena dozed off on the couch.

Roger and I went to a conference room off the lobby to meet with the administrator for Washington Gardens. We'd left an aide in the apartment with them. The administrator wasn't much help, but she did comment on Kay's declining condition.

I could see Roger welling up at the news. The woman took him by the hand and coaxed his childhood memories of his grandmother out of him. Apparently, she'd died of Alzheimer's.

As I checked the time, vaguely annoyed at the nosy administrator, I realized how hard my heart was.

Helena appeared in the doorway. "Kay's wandered off. She's not in the apartment."

The aide came up behind her before we could speak. "I can see her from the back window—outside. I'll go grab her coat."

I let Roger approach her because we could hear Kay singing, swinging her arms, and staring up into a leafless tree. "Julia and Ricky up in a tree . . ."

"Kay?" Roger took her by her shoulder.

"Ricky!" She hugged him, and he threw her coat over her. She didn't let go as he escorted her back to the apartment.

Her sister followed her, bawling into an oversized handkerchief. I was at a loss. No wonder my ex-wife ran.

As soon as we entered the lobby, the aide appeared with a towel, dry socks, and slippers. Roger placed his charge in a winged-back chair and carefully attended to her.

When they entered the apartment, Kay tugged Roger to sit on the couch with her. Her expression was suddenly serious, and it stopped her sister and me in the doorway.

Kay spoke clearly to Roger's face. "I gave up things for you I'd never give up for anyone else."

Roger looked startled. "I know."

She patted his hand. "Love is all important. Gracie needs to know. Her whole life ahead. She needs love. She needs be loved."

He took her hand. "Yes."

Kay rolled back and stared at the ceiling, a strange smile on her face. When her sister went to speak with her, Kay returned to her gibberish. Roger disappeared into the bathroom. I think he had a good cry.

After lunch I returned to my office in the basement of Annie's farmhouse and began a search of records that might reveal Uncle Teddy and his family. Friends at the FBI had not been forthcoming. My hunt thus far had been half-hearted and fruitless. For a brief moment, I wondered why that was.

When it came to the women I married, I'd vetted them more quickly than a visitor at Annie's gate. Lena was a snap judgment. I took her at face value and soon came to regret that. What was it in me that was so careful about everything else in my life, but allowed me to gloss over her questionable background? To *marry* the woman.

Now we were divorced and rightly so. She wasn't the right one for me. But I had a nagging feeling deep inside. Something inside that couldn't let her go. I needed to detach myself and think rationally.

It occurred to me that Lena might not have her father's name. *Duh.*

I'd been influenced by her past stories of her parents' fondness for bus trips and their deaths in that vacation accident. Any time we'd discussed her parents she'd told me they were Kay and Rick Goodwin. She was an effective liar, to say the least. It was entirely possible Lena was the result of a brief relationship.

I'd stupidly overlooked the fact that there was no father listed on Lena's birth certificate. What my friends at the FBI were doing was beyond me. What was their excuse?

What if Kay and Aunt Helena were Goodwin? Sure enough, a genealogy website showed me they were. They'd grown up in Queens, New York, and they had a sister, Julia, who was deceased. I was vaguely surprised Lena hadn't wiped the entire internet clean.

I dug deeper and located a marriage record for Aunt Helena. *Bingo.* Her husband was Edward Nardone. Uncle Teddy was *the* Teddy Nardone. Lena wasn't kidding when she said Uncle Teddy was the best. Nardone was a legend, and the fact that he was still alive was as incredible as his counterfeiting skills.

My phone buzzed. "Hi Billy, what's up?"

"Lena's here to see Annie and Buck. I'm in possession of her Glock. I'll escort her to the house."

Julia and Ricky up in a tree ... "Okay." Why would Kay be singing about her dead sister, Julia, with her husband?

And why would Lena attempt to visit her employers with a weapon?

EIGHT

~ *Lena* ~

Annie was out the front door before Billy and I climbed the stairs. "Lena! Are you okay? We've been worried sick about you."

"I'm sorry about the gun, Annie. I forgot I had it." She looked a bit taken aback, but that didn't stop her from pulling me into the foyer and hugging me the second I was through the door.

Buck came from the kitchen. "Lena. Are you all right?"

I spoke into his wife's shoulder. "I'm fine." Annie finally let go. "I had to take care of my Uncle Teddy. Time got away from me. I think everything's okay now. I need to call Cat to see if she has any updates. I'm so sorry I missed work."

Buck took the coat that Annie had peeled off me. "Well, I'm pleased you sent the reports we needed. I understand about your family issues. Annie and I were concerned for you."

Annie pointed me in the direction of the parlor. "Come sit down, and I'll get you some coffee and something to eat."

I looked back in time to see Billy hand my Glock to Nate. "Okay." I fled to the parlor. "Coffee'd be great, Annie."

Nate strode toward me, my weapon in his belt. "I need a word with you."

Annie made a face. "I'll get that coffee."

I wrung my hands. "Thanks. Nate, I've gotta get to Washington Gardens to see Mom. It's been a week."

Without a word, he grabbed me and pulled me downstairs to his office, then closed the door. He pointed to the chair, and I sat. Shivers of fear ran through me, but I set my jaw in defiance.

"I imagine you've been pretty busy this week. You did a remarkable job of avoiding the FBI ... made yourself a needle in the haystack of New York." He took out his phone. "We've been recording everything that goes on in your apartment, on the off chance that your mother or your aunt might say something helpful. You'll want to hear this from today."

He started a recording of Mom sounding more herself than she had in years. "I gave up things for you I'd never give up for anyone else."

Roger's voice said, "I know."

"Love is all important. Gracie needs to know. Her whole life ahead. She needs love. She needs be loved."

Roger said, "Yes."

I quickly wiped my eyes to remove the emotion.

Nate's expression was sad, but his voice even. "Your father was involved with the mob. His name was Ricky Cavalieri. Your mother is Julia Goodwin Cavalieri. You're Gracie."

My mouth was bone dry, but I swallowed my anger and sorrow. "I … I know Mom's not long for this world, but if you breathe a word to *anyone*, FBI or anyone else, she's dead. It wasn't pretty for my Auntie Kay or my cousin, Lena, or my dad, or my brother, or my two sisters. Or my dog." A strange pleading sound squeaked up through my throat. "I'm begging you not to breathe a word."

There was some emotion going on inside Nate, but I couldn't read it. He sat back in his seat. "This place is a fortress, and there are rooms that go unused all winter. I'll see that Roger and some of my other staff safely transport your mother and your aunt here—with approval from Annie and Buck. That will give you and your family protection while we sort everything out. Wait here." He left.

~ *Nathan* ~

I found Annie in the kitchen making roast turkey sandwiches, Buck assisting with the cranberry sauce as he spoke to her in a soothing voice. They both went quiet as I pushed through the swinging door.

Annie turned to me. "Is Lena okay?"

I headed to the coffeepot and poured myself a cup. "We have some issues going on, and I'm asking you both if it's all right to bring Lena, Kay, and Lena's aunt here to stay for a while. I believe their lives are in danger."

Buck's eyes bulged a bit, but the only sound came out of Annie. "Oh."

"I have no doubt that we can easily protect everyone here. But I understand if you don't want to bring that threat into your home."

Buck leaned back on the counter. "What exactly is this threat?"

I took a breath. "I'm still sorting out the issues, but Lena has had some associations with the mob. That explains Cat's vision about Lena's uncle and his family being in danger. I don't think she did herself any favors by running to New York to try and help her uncle, but that's what happened, and now we'll deal with it."

Annie faced her husband. "Um … Buck … I think we need to help them."

"Of course, my dear." He turned to me. "Rhodes, do what you think is necessary."

Billy and Keith joined Roger at Washington Gardens to pack up and transport Lena's mother and aunt. I notified my friend at the FBI that Lena was safely back in Maine and returned to my office to find turkey sandwiches on the desk with a pot of hot coffee and two mugs. Lena ignored it all, her head down on the edge of my desk.

"You should eat something." I poured the coffee. "Your mother and aunt are on the way. You'll be staying here until we get this all figured out."

Lena was slow to raise her head. "Thanks, Nate." She pushed her hair out of her face and took a sip of coffee. "Annie and Buck are so sweet for taking us in."

I took a seat and pushed the sandwich around the plate. "Yeah. We need to talk."

"Okay." She sat back in her chair, letting the mug warm her hands.

"Were you born Grace Cavalieri?"

She nodded. "Please don't do this to Mom. Let her die of natural causes."

"I have no intention of hurting your mother—or you. I need to know the truth so I can help you. You once trusted me enough to marry me." I took a gulp of coffee to clear the lump in my throat. "Trust me now to do the best for you and your mom."

I was surprised she didn't burst into derisive laughter. Instead she stared quietly at her cup.

Memories of conversations last summer with Cat and her family came to mind. "Cat's always talking about grace and mercy. When I realized your given name is Grace, it made me smile."

Lena looked up. "Grace and mercy. Reminds me of one of the prayers Mom pulled out of the bowl our first day here. 'And what does the Lord require of you? To act justly and to love mercy and to walk humbly with your God. Micah 6:8' I thought it was pretty cool, so I memorized it. I found it in my bag when I went to the old lot where my family burned to death." She put the mug on the desk to wipe the tear dripping down her face.

"So I intend to act justly, Nate. I'm gonna get the guy that did that to them—bring him to justice so you can fry him for what he did." She heaved more tears. "He even killed Peppy … my dog, Peppy."

As I stood, I wondered if my shaky legs would hold me, but I made it around the desk. I pulled Lena out of her seat and held her, cried with her.

~ *Lena* ~

I told Nate the truth about my family, how they died, and how Uncle Teddy had arranged everything for Mom to live as my dead Aunt Kay and for me to assume the identity of my cousin, Lena. Nate had probably put the pieces together pretty quickly, but he let me tell the story my way. I was grateful for that. I guess it was therapeutic in a way.

When that emotional tale was done, he made me eat half a sandwich.

Then we went outside to find Mom playing on the beach with Roger and Billy overseeing. Auntie Helena yelled her disapproval into the wind, as Mom jumped into the water lapping up on shore. Mom laughed like a kid and stomped around in the wet sand. Roger stayed right by her side to help her with her balance. She had boots and a heavy jacket on, so I don't know why Auntie was so worried.

I noticed Nate got a kick out of watching her.

"She thinks she's on Fire Island, I guess," I said.

When Mom finally noticed me, she threw up her arms and smiled. "Gracie!"

I turned to Nate. "Yeah, Mom's secret-keeping days are over."

He grinned at me.

Roger helped her through the sand to the stairs where we stood. "Gracie!"

"Hi, Mom."

Auntie Helena gripped the railing and turned to me. "You left your wedding photo in an old plastic album. She found it today. She remembers Gracie and Nate."

Mom smiled up at Nate. "Gracie and Nate."

Those stupid tears started again. I didn't want Nate to feel like he had to comfort me again. I needed to be strong. So I went off to my room.

By the time I unpacked everything, settled everyone in our rooms, and had some dinner, I was exhausted. Annie and Buck couldn't have been more gracious. I excused myself from the dinner table as Mom nodded off, and Auntie Helena finished her cake. "Thanks so much for everything. I'll finish all my reports tomorrow. We'll be up to date. Don't worry. I know the Valentine rush is underway, but I'll meet with Gerald Monday morning. I'm sure we're on track."

Annie and Buck stood up to help as I grabbed Mom. "No worries, Lena," Buck said.

I wondered how long it'd be before we had an official name change—or even if Nate thought it necessary. Being an ex-SEAL director of security, I expected we'd have to do everything the hard way. But truthfully, at this point, I didn't know which—Lena or Grace—would be harder to be. And I was way too tired to figure it out now.

Sunday morning, I was up early to work on my reports for The Golden Bowl, but the sun shining on the waves lured me out for a jog on the packed sand of low tide. Cold temperatures and a brisk wind cut my outing short, and as I turned back, I faced Nate maybe fifty yards down the beach. He headed toward me, and I raised my voice as he approached. "Morning, Nate. Don't worry, I'm not trying to escape."

He smirked. "The aide is here to work with your mother."

I exhaled a heavy breath. "Good. I didn't think you guys'd have security issues with her aides. Now I should be able to get some work done."

"Good." His face was unreadable.

I grabbed his arm as he turned back for the house. "I'm betting you're keeping us here because you think you'll get more information from us than the FBI would."

His face was serious. "And?"

"And … you're right. If you give me a little time, I'll bring down Joey B. I've already been snooping around some of his online businesses. I can really put some energy into it. The FBI will have more than they need to put him and his guys away forever. Just keep Mom and Auntie safe. And keep Uncle Teddy and his family out of it. What do you say?"

"It's not up to me. My opinion—you're better off leaving things alone right now. Keep pushing and you might end up having to cut some deal for yourself and for Uncle Teddy."

"The guy's in his seventies—and he *looks* like he's a good ten years older. Really? They still want to put him away?"

Nate shook his head. "I don't know. He's done his time, but if he's been up to something since, they'll be after him."

"Look, if I come up with Joey B, can you push them to overlook Teddy?"

Nate took me by the shoulders and his brown eyes bored into mine. "I have exactly *zero* say in any of this. I need you to take a break. Just breathe and relax and think about your mother and your job at The Golden Bowl. That's more than enough for you right now. I'll make some calls. But our first priority is to keep you and your family safe and out of prison. Got it?"

I smiled at the concern in his voice, in his eyes. "Thanks."

Nate tightened his grip on my shoulders, his face turned even more dead serious. "I mean it. Keep on the straight and narrow, Lena. This isn't the time to run off the rails. Got it?"

Butterflies in my stomach became nervous tingling throughout my body. Nate wasn't going to let go. "Got it."

Living at Annie's was like living at a five star resort. Breakfast was incredible. After a quick visit with Mom and Helena, I left them in the capable hands of the aide and went to my room to work. By lunchtime I had all my reports done for The Golden Bowl. Business had skyrocketed over the past year. Super Club was a major hit. Valentine's Day would be outstanding.

Attractive packaging invited people to donate to the various charities they supported. Donations were at an all-time high.

I gave Buck a summary over lunch. Not that Annie wasn't involved, but I could see her eyes glaze over when I talked numbers. She was definitely the creative side of the business. But it was more than that. She oozed care and concern—love—from every pore. Annie was a "love is what is important" person. You couldn't resist her. She and Buck made an invincible team.

Once Buck approved, he translated the financials to Annie in terms of the benefits to their charities. That perked her up. It was pretty funny.

And it was pretty strange heading back to my room thinking about

Joey B, who only cared about lining his own pockets. He'd think Annie was a total fool.

I spent the rest of the day researching some of the pump and dump deals he'd been involved with on Wall Street and his interest in New York real estate. I was pretty sure Uncle Teddy knew about Joey B's shenanigans but was on the periphery of most of it. Ideas were beginning to gel. His greed would be his undoing.

Nate will understand. I needed to get Joey B.

NINE

~ *Lena* ~

Cat's husband, Cisco, was not only a billionaire, but a financial genius who oversaw his business, Clemente Asset Management, and the various foundations and businesses his family members were involved with. Cisco's youngest brother, Paulo, was a rock star and the musical genius who composed all his band's music. Cat created most of the lyrics. It was quite a family business. They gave fortunes to charity, but kept an eye on making every penny count.

I decided Cisco, Paulo, and their fabulous wealth and celebrity would make an irresistible target for Joey B. I began to poke around their websites. As I dug deeper, I found their cybersecurity to be "top class," as Buck would say. I quickly recognized the guy in charge as a teammate of mine from Pearson's group. No big surprise, considering Cisco's other brother had worked for Pearson, too. Small world.

Hack, pump, and dump might still be an option, but I'd need their cooperation. Since Cisco was such a kind, generous person, I thought maybe he'd be in favor of putting Joey B out of business. But then again, would he risk tainting his squeaky-clean image and financial empire? After all, the SEC would be none too pleased with anyone involved in a pump and dump scheme. Fraud is fraud, and the Clementes were no frauds.

Hmm. I'd have to start with a call to Cat to see if I could possibly make this happen.

I'd been avoiding calling her. I guess I really didn't want to hear what God had to say about all of this. That would certainly be Cat's primary concern.

There I was with my blurry lines again. What was right and wrong here?

And what does the Lord require of you? To act justly and to love mercy and to walk humbly with your God. That was the verse I could throw in Cat's face if she gave me grief. One of the very verses she'd quoted herself.

We'd be acting justly to get Joey B behind bars. Okay, so it's not acting *justly*. But the ends justify the means. *No.* That would be Pearson's take on it. *Too bad I'm not with the organization anymore. Thank God, I'm not with the organization anymore.*

I quickly skipped to mercy. We'd be showing mercy to all his victims, including me. And I'd be humble, because it wouldn't benefit me financially or professionally. It'd be helping to get justice. It'd help keep me and my family alive. How could Cat quibble with that?

Something deep down told me I was wrong. Not only could I destroy Cisco Clemente, I could bring down the rock star celebrities, all their businesses and all their charities, including The Golden Bowl.

I couldn't call Cat.

First thing Monday morning I checked on Mom and Auntie Helena. The aide had breakfast well underway. After a brief visit, I went to the kitchen and pushed through the swinging door just as Annie was leaving a videoconference call with her sister.

She stayed at the table, nodded her hello to me, closed the computer, and directed her concern to her husband. "Buck, they might not get to wind up The Golden Bowl Tour in Portland this October. They're having problems with Providence, too."

Buck was at the stove, creating some scrumptious-looking omelets. "No worries, my dear, I'm sure Joe Harris will handle the dispute with his usual aplomb. The tickets will be on sale straight away."

Nate grabbed a cinnamon roll from a pan cooling nearby, chuckling. "Cisco should buy the ticket company. That'd solve that problem." He winked at me and popped half the bun into his mouth.

The sweet cinnamon smell was too wonderful to ignore. I ran for the pan, aware Buck's eyes were tracking me.

Buck's gaze went to Nate. "That's not a bad idea. This isn't the first tussle for Ticket Depot. They've had some very prominent artists complaining about them before. Not to mention the fans. Cisco could buy them with his pin money. It might be worth it."

Annie slid the laptop aside and addressed Buck. "I'd never think to buy a company to solve a problem like that. But that's probably why I'm not a billionaire. Whatever they do, I sure hope we have that concert in Portland. People are excited already." She got up and headed toward me. "Did you sleep well, Lena?"

"Good, thanks." I licked the last of the cinnamon off my fingers and steered out of her way as she went for the silverware drawer. "Let me wash my hands, and I'll help you set the table."

I couldn't wait to get to my office. I was ready to burst by the time I rushed through the door. This Ticket Depot thing could be just the ticket for me. I didn't even throw off my coat before I was online investigating the company. It took me thirty seconds to realize this was the perfect set up. Ticket Depot was a badly beaten down stock—and it was traded on the New York Stock Exchange.

I muffled my cheers. This'd be the most elegant pump and dump ever. Joey B was going down.

I considered the possibilities as I wriggled out of my coat. I really did need Cisco's cooperation to get the best result. I bet the SEC wouldn't mind giving the billionaire a little leeway for a good cause. I tossed the coat. Shaking in my boots, I called Cat.

I was a little shocked when she answered immediately. "Lena, I wondered when I'd hear from you."

"I've been praying more than ever. I've been trying to put love first. It's not easy, but I'm making progress. And about Uncle Teddy … he's alive, and they didn't do the family reunion. So that's good."

"I'm glad to hear the good news."

"Yeah. Now Annie's a little worried about The Golden Bowl Tour. She said the big finale in Portland might not happen. We were saying the easiest solution might be to have Cisco or Paulo just buy Ticket Depot. The stock's a bargain at this point. You think Cisco is interested?"

There was a little giggle on the other end. Scamming a woman everyone called a prophet was probably not going to happen. I guess my old self had to give it a try.

"Tell me more about your idea, Lena."

I gulped. "Okay … well, I'm … I'm really interested in bringing Joey B and his gang to justice. I think it's a good idea for me to work on it. I mean, maybe they'll leave Uncle Teddy in peace if we help the FBI on this one." I started to choke. "Also, it might keep Mom alive long enough to die of natural causes." I found a tissue on my desk.

Cat obviously picked up my emotion. "It sounds as though you've got some good ideas on solving some very diverse problems. I'm afraid I'm not the best one to discuss this with. Perhaps we could arrange a call with Cisco, David, and Nathan. That would be quickest and simplest."

My teeth chattered. "Uh … David? The assassin, David?" Nothing good could come of that. I still had nightmares about the day he stopped me and my plot to obliterate Annie's business.

Cat's voice roused me from my downward spiral. "As you know, David worked for General Pearson. I'm sure he can be of help."

"Yeah." I swallowed a big bubble of fear. "And Cisco's brother . . ." I couldn't come out with his name to save my life. "He could help … instead . . ." This wasn't going so good.

"Eduardo is on holiday with his family."

"Oh. Eduardo. Yeah." Fat lot of help he'd be. "Okay." I was up to my eyebrows now. Cat obviously knew I'd worked for Pearson. She probably knew everything about me. What did she know about me and David? I took a deep breath. "Well, it's really gonna be an elegant pump and dump. No need for actual, you know, *physical* violence."

"I'm happy to hear that. I'll be sure to tell David."

My voice was a croak again. "Okay, good."

"Lena, I'll phone you back shortly to let you know a time. Cisco will probably be breaking in a couple of hours. Perhaps we could do the call then."

"Okay, thanks, Cat." *I'm doomed.*

I didn't stop to think things through. I felt alone—and vulnerable—to say the least. Uncle Teddy was my closest confidant, so I called him. He was at work at his print shop but said he had time to talk.

Something in me was determined to make this scheme work. I let loose. "Uncle Teddy, if ever there was a perfect pump and dump, it's Ticket Depot. I have a stock tip I can't resist. It's badly beaten down with a big dispute with musicians, fans, and all sorts of controversy. Haven't had time to really look into it, but it's traded on the New York Stock Exchange, and today it's well below five bucks. The rock star, Paulo Clemente and his band, might not be able to do their final Golden Bowl Tour appearance in Portland because of it."

I could hear Uncle Teddy's smile. "Okay."

"The best part. I heard Paulo or his brother, Cisco, might buy the company. It's cheap for them, and they'd get their way. What do you think?"

"Just a minute," Teddy said.

I heard Joey B in the background. There was no mistaking that voice. I froze. Then I disconnected the call.

"What have I done?" My mind was in a tumult.

I stood up to hang my coat on the rack. The room spun.

I woke up staring into Nate's brown eyes, a little confused. "I'm on the floor." My coat was twisted around me.

"Yeah. Again." He picked me up and put me back in my chair. "What happened? I'll get you some water."

"I don't need water. I need you to talk to David Lambrecht and make sure he stays in Austria."

"Huh?"

"He's too scary. I can't think straight when he's around."

Nate shook his head. "Okay. Whatever. We're going back to my office for the conference call you instigated. Are you all right to talk?"

"Yeah. Just keep him in Austria."

Nate reheated some of Annie's leftover chicken soup while I sipped water at her kitchen table. "Isn't it a little early for chicken soup?"

He turned to me. "Nope. It's supposed to cure everything, so you're having some. You need to see a doctor … find out what this fainting is all about."

"It's nothing. When Cat said David Lambrecht would be on the call, I freaked a little. I was scared out of my wits that day when he grabbed me. I know I sassed him, but that was raw fear on autopilot."

Nate delivered a large cup of soup and handed me a spoon. "David told me you were instrumental in saving lives, even entire missions. He was impressed with you. And he was sorry Pearson treated you so badly."

I tried to keep my face and my voice emotionless. "Okay." I took a spoonful of soup, hoping to change the subject. "Delicious! Thanks, Nate."

His grin told me he'd go along with me.

"Finish this up. Then you'll go sell your plan to Cisco. But I know he's gonna say no if he has a brain in his head. And judging by where he is in life, he does."

"Okay, I'll focus on his blue eyes."

Nate laughed.

"It's worth a try. That's all I've heard in the short time I've been at The Golden Bowl. Cisco and Paulo have the same *amazing* blue eyes, and all the women from the teenage waitresses to the elderly hostess go gaga over them. That's what they say ... *amazing* blue eyes."

I drank the last of the broth. "Let's just keep David out of it. He'd scare the crap out of Joey B. No shooting or killing necessary. This'll be a nice big pump and dump. Joey B won't be able to resist."

I guess Nate didn't trust the chicken soup. He took my briefcase, put his arm around me as I rose from the table, and escorted me downstairs to his office. We settled at his desk with my laptop, and Cat and Cisco appeared on the large screen on the wall in front of us. They were seated together on a couch, probably in his home office. He had a laptop with him.

We exchanged pleasantries, but nerves pushed me to my business. His blue eyes and handsome smile weren't helping. I knew David had to be around there somewhere listening in. He knew full well why I didn't want him involved. But it was out of my hands. I met Cat's eyes. *God help me.*

I jumped in. "As you know, many pump and dump schemes involve penny stocks. Joey B and all his mobster friends have been involved in the stock market for years. They'd buy a penny stock and manipulate it, promote it to go higher and higher in value, then sell it, making a good profit. Of course, all the buyers they sucked in would lose everything."

I fooled with my laptop, trying to get up my nerve to meet those blue eyes. "I realized that Ticket Depot would be an ideal stock to use in a plan to bring Joey B and his gang to justice. Especially because it's not a penny stock. What would the likes of Cisco Clemente have to do with a penny stock? But it *is* a very badly beaten down stock, if you check the market today." I wiped a bead of sweat off my forehead and scrolled on my laptop.

"You can see it's traded on the New York Stock Exchange, and today it's falling again ... below four dollars now. That's probably because of all the woes with Paulo and his band, and some other musicians ... You probably know better than I what their business and stock pressures are."

I looked up to see Cisco smile. "I see where you're going, Lena. Interesting."

I started to breathe again. "Well, it was Nate's idea for you or Paulo to just buy the company so you don't have any more hassles with your Golden Bowl Tour."

"Excellent idea. I've been distracted lately with so much volatility in currencies. I hadn't thought to look at Ticket Depot's stock."

My giggle was automatic. "That's not being distracted. It takes a lot of focus to trade currencies." I guess I was taken in by his charm. The guy defined charisma.

He kept the smile on his face. "Unfortunately, the Securities and Exchange Commission would be unhappy with anyone who undermines the New York Stock Exchange in any way."

I took a breath. "Uh … yeah … but they don't have to know, do they?"

"I'm afraid so, Lena." The sideways glance he gave told me David was most definitely in on the conversation. But there was not a sound from him. Cisco's face said it all. In *his* world, we don't mess with the SEC.

I went for a sip of water. In General Pearson's world, we messed with anyone he wanted. I couldn't bring David Lambrecht into this.

I knew I should keep my mouth shut, but I didn't. "I understand." My stomach twisted in knots, and I thought the water would come back up. "Uh … I guess part of me knew you wouldn't be able to work it out my way … which, I understand, is illegal. But I … I called my Uncle Teddy and gave him the stock tip. I … I just want you to know in case buying the company would be a problem now. I think I messed up. I'm sorry."

"It's okay, Lena. Thanks for telling me. Don't worry about it. We have people working on the concert venue. It will work out."

My eyes filled, and I could hardly see the screen. "The show must go on, right?"

"Right."

I thought his blue eyes really were amazing. I could still see them, despite the clouds in my eyes.

Nate disconnected the call, and I put my head down on the desk. Why did I have to blab to Cisco? Now it'd be even tougher for me to execute my plan to get Joey B. And I put Uncle Teddy under more suspicion. I needed to contact him right away.

I pushed myself up from the desk. "Thanks, Nate, I'm gonna go take a nap. It's already been a very long day."

He stood to face me. "What is it with you and Lambrecht?"

"I don't want to discuss it."

"You were so worked up over keeping him in Austria, it's obvious something happened when you worked for Pearson. What happened?"

"I can't say."

"You won't say. Did you screw up one of his missions?"

I let out a breath. "No."

"So I should ask him?"

"No!"

"Did he hurt you?"

"Uh … no." My voice was a croak.

Nate let out one of his mile-long expletives, and I knew he knew.

I grabbed my laptop and rushed out of his office and up the stairs to my room on the second floor. I couldn't face this today.

It was mere months ago when Nate told me I was the worst of the worst because I was about to obliterate Annie's business. Now he'd have even more cruel names for me.

TEN

~ *Lena* ~

Despite the fact that I was a cauldron of emotion and nerves, I tagged along with Billy to The Golden Bowl and headed to my office. I was half surprised Nate hadn't tried to continue our conversation. Hoping we were done for the day, I slinked out to the beach and contacted Teddy with a disposable cell phone.

"Uncle Teddy, I need you to get to Maine ASAP. You and Auntie can stay here at Annie's with Mom and me, or I'll get you an apartment where you can lay low."

"I'm fine, Lena. You keep your aunt right there with you. I'll be fine here … need to keep the shop going."

How could I explain he didn't need to do anything at his age?

"Look—"

Teddy wasn't going to have it. "Listen to me. Joey B heard what he needed to hear. He's going for it. Ticket Depot's his new project. Too juicy to ignore. You can bring him down, Lena. If that's what you want, you can go for it. I'll do whatever you want."

"Uncle Teddy, it's time for you to retire and enjoy life. Not get mixed up in the middle of more mob business. I don't want you in prison."

"I'm an old man. It doesn't matter what happens to me. I want what's best for my family. I've done prison before. I survived. I can do it again if I need to."

I exhaled a breath of frigid air. "Why was Joey B even at your shop today?"

"I do his photo books—all the kids, the vacations, you know. He likes to keep them organized, so he can display them in his bookcase. He won't trust anyone else with them."

I squinted into the wind. "You're kidding."

"No." Teddy coughed. "So he's not gonna see anything unusual with me. I'll be here. You do what you need to do."

~ *Nathan* ~

I met my employer's eyes on the screen. David Lambrecht would only let you see what he wanted you to see. At this moment, it was nothing.

"You know Lena won't stop with her plans to get Joey B just because Cisco wasn't in agreement."

A faint curl crossed his lips. "I'm not surprised to hear that. Having worked for Pearson, she knows there's a way around everything. We'll be keeping track and do our best to keep her out of trouble. You have my support, Nathan."

"Thanks." I decided to take the risk. "I need to know about your history with my wife." I disregarded the urge to clarify: with my ex-wife.

"We discussed that a while back."

"I mean your personal history."

There was a warning in his voice. "Until that incident a few months ago, I hadn't seen or heard from Lena in years … since she left Pearson's organization. There's no more to say."

There was more to say. But it would have to come from Lena.

~ *Lena* ~

Since Joey B had taken the accidental bait, I decided I needed to run with this. Really, all I'd need to do is let the mobster do his usual thing. It'd be obvious to Cisco and everyone else what had happened.

And since I was in up to my eyebrows, I might as well go for the gold. I started spending my free time increasing my take from Joey B's various online ventures. The money was going to be eye-popping. I had my salary from The Golden Bowl and now the spoils of my game. Since Hal and Gil were out of the picture, I'd have quite the surplus.

I decided to donate money to Annie's charities. A quarter million dollars distributed in dribs and drabs to the entire list of Golden Bowl charities was transferred from a clueless Joey B before the Valentine's rush turned into a tsunami. Then it was all hands on deck, and I joined in the holiday insanity.

Valentine's Day was madness at The Golden Bowl. I'd never seen anything like it. Customers overflowed the place, and there wasn't a product of any kind left on any shelf anywhere by the end of the day.

My head was whirling by the time I returned to Annie's. Mom had a collage of valentines taped to her bedroom door, and several vases full of flowers on her bureau. She slept soundly in her bed. *Thank God.*

I went to my room and dumped my stuff in a corner. All I wanted was a hot shower and a warm bed. But once I got out of the shower, I realized I was starving. I don't think any of the staff had eaten a thing all day. Everyone was going a million miles an hour.

I wrapped myself in my long fluffy white robe and slouchy slippers, then padded downstairs to the kitchen. The smell of coffee summoned me, and I poured a cup. As I opened the refrigerator, the swinging door startled me.

Nate held a bouquet of red roses. His face turned the same shade. "I … uh… the florist brought these to the wrong office. I … uh … wanted you to have these this morning."

I almost dropped my coffee cup. "Uh … thanks, Nate, that's so sweet." I butted the door closed and leaned back against the cold metal. Then I remembered my damp hair must have been curling up everywhere around my head. Not my best moment. I pulled the robe tight as I could with one useful hand. "Uh … want something to eat?"

"Yeah. I'm starved."

"Me, too."

He put the roses on the table and went looking for a vase while I found Annie's leftover beef stew and served that with some of her "homemade at The Golden Bowl" bread and butter.

I took a whiff of the roses as I clumsily sat. "That's sweet of you, Nate. Thanks."

"Happy Valentine's Day. A little late." He dove into the stew.

"Happy Valentine's." I wondered if I should have gotten him a card.

Conversation wasn't scintillating. But considering we were both exhausted, it wasn't so bad. Sad to say, it was one of my better Valentine's Days.

February 15th was a day to take a close look at what had transpired in the restaurant, Bakery & Sweet Shop, and online and phone orders for the holiday. That meant a meeting with Tracey, who was in charge of customer service at The Golden Bowl.

I stepped into her office and, after exchanging chipper "good mornings," immediately noticed the two Valentine bouquets on her desk. One was a pretty variety of flowers you'd get from a business associate and the other was a seriously romantic collection of perfect roses in a heavy crystal vase, complete with all the baby's breath and whatnot that made it plain she had a suitor. *Hmm.* I had to know who'd sent them.

"Gorgeous flowers!"

It was impossible not to like Tracey when she smiled. "I've got some fresh coffee brewing. How about a cup?"

"Sure."

She stepped into the call center to get the coffee, and I spun the gift card on the roses. "Love, Stefano." My heart resumed its normal beat. I caressed the other arrangement. It was signed by Nate and all his men. *I can live with that.* My fantasy was intact.

When she returned with our drinks, I made a point to comment on Stefano's excellent taste. Tracey was happy to tell me all about him.

~ *Nathan* ~

Annie and Buck took a brief London vacation to celebrate Annie's birthday on the first of March, and to deal with some business Buck had with a university. Since business was robust, and we were still harboring Lena, her mother, and aunt, Buck preferred I stay in Maine to handle things. I felt comfortable sending Billy and Keith to protect the newlyweds.

When I thought about it, I decided not to push Lena about her past relationship with David Lambrecht. We were divorced, and at this point, it was none of my business. He'd been happily married for years, so it wasn't as though there were any real feelings there. Prying would only lead to more pain.

Instead, I tried to conduct myself as a friend who had a duty to protect Lena and family, which is exactly what I was. Unfortunately, I found myself dwelling on Lena, wondering if we should try again as a couple. I knew that was not rational.

But there was something about our mundane Valentine's dinner that had heightened my preoccupation with her. Maybe it was the way her hair curled wildly around her face. Or the way she blushed when I gave her the roses. Whatever it was, it wasn't rational.

I wanted to believe Lena was a genuine, good person, the kind of woman a man in my position would be proud to have as a wife. She was certainly brilliant, but her moral compass was askew. No doubt she'd purposely lured Joey B into perpetrating fraud, putting her own family at risk.

Who knows what else she'd done. Anyone who could work for Pearson would be capable of all kinds of unpalatable things. I'd learned that years ago. Why set myself up for more?

There was no doubt Lena's scheme was working. Ticket Depot stock was now steadily rising. Even Buck had heard from a friend in New York that he should invest. And I had heard from my friends at the FBI that Joey B was being investigated for possible fraud.

Lena's name had not been mentioned, but her uncle had been picked up for questioning. He'd told them Joey B had overheard a rumor that Cisco Clemente was about to buy Ticket Depot. He admitted discussing that rumor with Joey in his shop the day Lena had contacted him.

They were both on thin ice as far as I could tell. But so far, Lena was free. And surprisingly, there was no word from Cisco or David about Cisco's interest—or lack of interest—in buying Ticket Depot.

I chalked that up to David's influence. He was one of Pearson's top agents, and once that organization disbanded, David and his associates became independent and very valuable assets to presidents and kings of allied countries around the globe. I didn't know a tenth of what they were involved in.

At this point, I wanted to keep it that way.

I guess it was partly in tribute to Annie's birthday, and partly the unexpectedly mild weather that brought me out to the Adirondack chairs in the back yard overlooking the Atlantic. The sun was newly risen when Lena joined me and handed me a coffee.

"Morning." Lena looked as though she hadn't slept. She took a seat beside me. "I've been thinking about how Cat said to trust God."

I shook my head. "It's not easy."

"I don't know how. I read the prayers she left in the bowl and ask God to help me every day. Sometimes I sing along with Mom when she does her halleluiahs or amens. But I'm not sure if it's helping … I feel really lousy, Nate."

She passed out, and I caught her before her head hit the wooden chair.

Lena didn't argue when the ambulance arrived. Her blood pressure was low, heart rate high, and her breathing was shallow. She repeated to the EMT, "I feel like crap."

I paced the hospital's hallway and waiting room until the ER doctor appeared. She looked concerned.

"Mr. Rhodes? You look very pale."

"Is she all right?"

"Lena's going to be okay. But I'm sorry—she's had a rupture of an ectopic pregnancy. We're taking her to surgery right now."

Ectopic pregnancy? "Surgery?"

"The embryo embedded in the fallopian tube. When it ruptured it caused some serious bleeding. But I believe Lena will be fine."

I dropped into a chair and put my head in my hands. When I managed to tamp down my anxiety, I took out my phone to find out what an ectopic pregnancy was.

Hours later they finally let me see her. Lena's eyes were open wide, sad, and fearfully silent. I stumbled over my words. "I'm sorry."

Her eyes filled. "Why does God hate me?"

The pit of my stomach ached. "God doesn't hate you. That much I know." I squeezed her hand and swallowed my confusion. It was probably wrong to pry, but I had to know. "The baby?"

She averted her eyes. "Not yours, Nate … I wish it could've been."

I couldn't let go of her hand. "Me, too."

I wiped a rush of her tears with a washcloth and stood there frozen. I'd spent the past hours wondering if and how it could have been the result of our lapse of judgment last fall after Lena had attempted to destroy The Golden Bowl. It had to have been too many months ago. But I had no idea what the "ectopic" in ectopic pregnancy meant. Maybe a nonviable fetus could linger for months. From my meager research, it seemed an unlikely scenario.

Her shaky voice brought my stare from her hand to her face.

"A New Year's gift from Carter Lewis. He wouldn't take no for an answer … I needed to keep my job."

I could feel my blood boil. "It's over. He won't bother you again. Get some rest now."

She gripped my hand with surprising strength. "Nate, leave the guy alone. I'm in Maine now. I don't have to see him again. Just let it be … Please." She ran out of steam.

"It's okay. Get some rest." I watched Lena's eyes close and thought about revenge. Carter Lewis was born with a silver spoon. I could make him dig his own grave with it.

~ *Lena* ~

I woke up in a sweat from a bad dream. I'd been expelled from The

Golden Bowl and Joey B was after me. I had nowhere to run. No one to help me. Suddenly, I was in Carter's office, and he turned into a monster demon from the depths of fiery hell. I came to, struggling with the bed sheet as he came around the desk after me.

Where did that come from? I used the sheet to dry off, hoping to whisk away the fright as well.

Nate came through the door. "Annie called. I didn't want to disturb your nap, so I told her I'd relay her get-well wishes. And prayers. And Buck, too."

As I looked up, Karen smiled at me and tapped the door. "Knock, knock. It's visiting hour." A contingent of women from The Golden Bowl stood behind her.

Nate squeezed my hand and spoke to the group. "Don't wear her out." He left with a smile that said he'd keep track of their time.

I was genuinely thrilled to see them. I never thought any of my coworkers could like me enough to visit me in the hospital. The flowers, candies, and crowd made me feel like I was wanted. For the first time, I truly felt like a part of The Golden Bowl. But I was worn out.

The nurse ducked into the room and invited everyone to leave so I could take a call from Cat. Nate appeared with the phone.

"It must be the middle of the night in Austria. Cat must go 24/7, huh?" My brain was still in a fog, but I really needed to talk to Cat. I took the phone. "Hi."

"Lena, I'm so sorry."

"How'd you hear all the way in Austria? It's not like I'm dead."

"I had a dream about your distress. God loves you, Lena, and you must know that. Fear, doubt, and insecurity are not from God."

"Oh." That nightmare I had was all about fear, doubt and insecurity. And the fact that I was very much alone in this. I'd insisted the doctor not go into detail with Nate, because he was not my husband, but it sounded like he did anyway.

Nate told everyone else I had internal bleeding and left it at that. Which was fine with me. I didn't want everyone to know my business.

Did Cat know about that nightmare? "You had a dream about my distress? Did we have the same dream?"

Cat sounded tired. "It doesn't matter. What matters is that you know God loves you, Lena. God will never leave you or abandon you."

The thought of God still loving me was a relief, but only because Cat's voice was so certain. I couldn't really believe it. And the fear, doubt, and insecurity thing would be a little too much to handle right now.

"I know you must be exhausted. We'll talk soon when you're feeling better. For now, please remember to keep your eyes on God. Trust."

I couldn't keep my eyes open. "I will, Cat. Love is what is important."

Nate caught the phone.

The next morning, Nate was standing in the doorway speaking with one of his men when I woke up. Concern about why I'd have a guard buzzed in my brain along with wondering how bad my hair looked. My inner voice went right to—because you're a criminal and Nate would never want you back anyway. When he stepped back into the room, all I could think was how much I wished we had a child.

He came to my bedside and took my hand. "How are you feeling?"

"I'm fine. I should be able to go home today."

"The doctor told me they're keeping you another day, just to make sure."

I batted at the bed to help drag myself up. "I'm fine."

Nate grabbed me and settled me back on the pillow. "I know, but another day here won't hurt."

"Mom and Auntie need me. Not to mention my job."

"No problem, they'll all be there when you get back. Breakfast is on the way, then you can rest up."

With that the nurse arrived to get me up to the bathroom. Yeah, my hair was as messy as I'd thought, and I looked sickly pale.

They let me leave the next morning, after lengthy instructions that I was to take it easy. My doctor decided to ignore my request and brought Nate up to speed on my recovery plan. I had zero energy, so I gave them no argument. Dr. Nate took over and treated me like a piece of glass.

We arrived home to a massive brunch prepared by Doc. I tried to joke with him about Annie inheriting her culinary skills from him, but he was too busy encouraging me to eat to hear a word I said. Nate got a kick out of it.

I was relieved to finally get to the peace and quiet of my room. After napping for an hour or so, I peered out my window to see Nate standing by the low hedge at the edge of the lawn, staring out to sea. I pulled on some sweats, a coat, and boots and went out to meet him. Snow had melted, leaving the lawn mushy and muddy. I made it to the Adirondack chairs before he turned and made a face. I lowered myself into the seat. It'd been enough of a trip for me.

Nate strode up the lawn toward me. His face was unreadable, as it often was, so I decided to deflect any potential upsetting comment. "Hi Nate. I hear it's sixty degrees in New York today."

He shook his head, but a vague smirk told me we were okay. "It's no sixty here. What are you doin' out of bed?"

"I think I need to circulate whatever blood I have left. That little walk did it."

He let out half a laugh. "You never did follow directions."

I refused to be insulted. "You know I was usually smarter than the people giving the orders."

His eyes were smiling now. "True." He took a blanket from the other chair and draped it over me, then took a seat beside me. "Word is Paulo and his band are flying in May first for their concert in Massachusetts. Then they'll be settling in here afterward—using this as a base for their summer tour."

"I bet Annie's all excited."

"She is. She lives for her family—and The Golden Bowl."

"Nate, you don't have to worry about me. I can move Mom and Auntie back to Washington Gardens with me, no problem. I'm not going anywhere. I'll stay there till the FBI shows up. I … I just need your help to keep my family protected. That's it. Recommend someone. I'll pay them."

"I've got enough staff. We'll see to it you're safe. Don't worry about it now." Nate rubbed his hand over his head and exhaled loudly. "Lena, why did you tell me your parents died in a bus accident?"

Did I need this now? My stomach wrenched. For a smart person, I did some dumb things. I stared at the ground. "If you know about my father, then you know why. I didn't want to sully your reputation and get you mixed up in all that. I went to a lot of trouble to make sure my version of my parents' death was the official one."

I couldn't help a chuckle. "It turned out Pearson didn't even care. As long as I had the smarts, the skills he wanted, I could've been the vampire daughter of Satan, and he wouldn't have cared."

Nate laughed. "True."

"And I had a feeling you wouldn't want Mom for a mother-in-law. Your life was tough enough. It was easier for you not to have in-laws, so it was easy for me to lie."

Nate shook his head, a strange look in his eye. "Why would you keep up those crazy antics? Hiding your mother? You had to have noticed it wasn't working. Wouldn't it have been easier to just tell the truth?"

"Uh … yeah." How could I tell him lies were really much more comfortable for me?

ELEVEN

~ *Lena* ~

March was snowy, slushy, damp, and dreary. I took ten days off from work to recover, but unless I was working on my laptop, forcing myself to focus on business, I was miserable reliving my mistake. Guilt and torment were worse at night when I tried to sleep.

It was bad enough I'd messed up my own life, but I'd created a brand new life and snuffed that out, too. I couldn't even get that baby into the right spot for it to grow. How useless was I?

The monster demon was back when my phone woke me up from the nightmare. "Cat?"

"It's me, Lena, I've wanted to check in more often, but we're touring Europe before we arrive in the U.S. I'm afraid we're keeping much too busy. We did have a nice break to have dinner in London with Annie and Buck last night."

I pushed myself to smile at the phone so I'd sound human. "That sounds like fun." My voice sure didn't. I gave up trying to be cheerful.

I let out a long, weepy sigh. "I'm sorry, I haven't trusted God or done anything worthwhile lately. No prayers, nothing. I'm wondering about myself. Why would I get drunk and let someone take advantage of me just to keep a job? Why can't I stop thinking about who that little baby could've been? Why did I live and my brother and sisters and cousin die? If my parents were upstairs where they should've been at that hour, we might've all gotten out in time. All I've done with my life is mess up everyone else's."

When I realized I was spewing out all kinds of nastiness about myself to someone I barely knew, I practically swallowed my tongue.

Cat's voice was firm and sure. "Lena, you're here for a reason. Know that you are a precious child of God, and you have a purpose.

Know that you're free from condemnation. God will heal your broken heart if you let him in. These awful nightmares are not of God."

I sat up in the bed. "So this fear, doubt, and insecurity you told me about in the hospital—that's coming from that monster in my dreams?"

"You're under attack—" Sudden baby cries stopped Cat midsentence, and she quickly ended the call with the advice to "reach out to the Lord."

I dragged myself to the shower and repeated my prayer. "God help me." I soon realized I was yelling it and then broke down wailing.

There was a knock at the bathroom door. "Lena, are you okay?"

"Fine, Nate, thanks." I shut off the water and grabbed a towel.

"I'm gonna get some chicken soup for you."

"Uh … it's three in the morning." By the time I dried off and pulled the nightgown on, Nate had disappeared.

I scorned my red eyes in the bathroom mirror while twisting my wet hair into a ponytail. As I trudged back to bed, Nate knocked and came through the door with a tray. Despite my feeble protest, he was determined the soup would save me. Just like he was the day I fainted at the prospect of dealing with David on the Ticket Depot scheme. I had to admit though, once I started on the soup, it was good to the last spoonful.

"Thanks, Nate."

He took the tray and put it on the dresser. "You're welcome." He returned and fluffed my pillows against the headboard. Then he landed on the bed and took me in his arms. I couldn't help it. I let him hold me and cried myself to sleep.

The next morning I decided a walk on the beach would help, and laughed out loud when I opened the kitchen door to thick fog. The perfect metaphor for my thoughts. I headed toward the Adirondack chairs.

"Lena?"

"Annie, you're back."

We stumbled into each other's arms, and she gave me a long hug. After settling in the chairs with thermal pillows and blankets, Buck appeared with some tea and well-wishes. He went off to deal with The Golden Bowl.

I pulled the blanket tighter around me against the chill. "I didn't know you sit out here when you can't even see your hand in front of you."

Annie chuckled. "It takes a lot to keep me away. We had a

wonderful two weeks in England, but I was ready to get home."

I took a sip from the thermos. "Seems like you bought some delicious tea while you were there."

"It hits the spot, doesn't it? I'm not so sure it'll keep me from my morning coffee, but it's a nice change." Annie set her tea on the arm of the chair and faced me. "How are you, Lena? I've been concerned for you."

"I'm fine, thanks."

"Okay … I'm glad to hear it." She stared into the fog.

My mind jumbled with random thoughts. I wanted to confide in Annie, but it didn't seem like the best idea to air my dirty laundry to my employer. She'd already been too kind to me as it was.

The silence was getting uncomfortable.

"I'll be back to work in a few days. But I'm keeping on top of everything from here. No need to worry, Annie."

"You take all the time you need. Healing takes time."

The last week of April was unseasonably warm in Marberry. Temperatures topped out in the eighties two days in a row. Very strange for Maine. People walked around in shorts, and the weather was pretty much the topic of conversation. I was happy to have a sunny, hot Saturday off from work.

I put my short shorts and a T-shirt on and sat on the beach soaking up the sun, watching Mom and Auntie ambling arm in arm along the water's edge, dozing in my lounge chair. It was great to have Roger overlooking the scene, rescuing the ladies when their toes got too far into the still-frigid ocean. Or when Auntie waved her cane at the seagulls and lost her balance. *Perfect peace.*

I'd had plenty of time to myself since coming home from the hospital, and with several quick but encouraging phone calls from Cat, I'd gotten through some of the grief. The turning point came when Cat told me my baby was in heaven, and I'd see her someday. I cried with relief, to the point that Karen heard me next door. She came into my office and sat with me, patting my hand, but she never pried into my affairs.

And I never asked Cat how she knew I had a girl. But I'd had that feeling before she told me.

Nodding off to the sounds of the surf, it took me a second or two to realize the rat-a-tat-tat I heard was gunfire. I opened my eyes as

Nate grabbed me and dragged me to the cover of an overturned beach chair and nearby rock. But not before I saw a guy grab Mom from behind. "Mom!" Nate had me pinned in the sand.

Mom's horror was plain. "Ricky ... Ricky!"

I fought to lift my head.

"Stay down!" Nate was about to shoot.

I saw Roger face down on top of Auntie. They weren't moving. Mom was struggling with the stranger. Nate wouldn't get a clean shot.

The grinding sound of a loud motor turned my head, and we were blasted with sand as a helicopter rose over Annie's house and swooped down to the beach. My jaw dropped open in amazement, and I choked on the sand that flew into my mouth. David was perched in the doorway, somehow avoiding automatic gunfire. He neatly shot the bad guy right between the eyes. The guy dropped. Mom jerked and fell onto the packed wet sand.

The helicopter pitched up. I could see David and his cohorts peppering the water with gunfire as the chopper headed out to sea.

"Are you all right?" Nate pulled me to a sitting position.

I spat sand. "Mom?" I let him tug me to my feet. "Mom? Auntie?" There was a crowd of security around them. A medic began working on Roger, and my heart sank. Mom and Auntie were okay. The guards quickly took them up the stairs toward the house.

When the dust settled, I saw two dead guys. Nate confirmed they'd come up from the water. Roger was vertical by now with a bloody neck bandage. Nate escorted me up to the house before I had a chance to vomit.

By the time we got through the kitchen door, Annie was at the counter.

Buck was laughing. "Food doesn't solve every problem, my dear."

"Well, it's gonna solve this one. We're starting with gazpacho." In seconds the blender was whirring.

Nate rolled his eyes and directed me into the living room. "Let's get that scraped knee attended to."

I looked down, unaware of my injury. "Practically no blood. I'm fine."

He directed me to the couch and grabbed antiseptic and a bandage from the medic. I let Nate work on my knee without further comment. He'd been overly attentive to my needs recently. I'd eaten more chicken soup in the past month than I had in my entire life. Not that we'd discussed anything, but it was kind of nice to have someone care. He did the first aid job in short order and headed off downstairs to his office.

Mom was smiling with the activity in the room, but she'd probably forgotten everything that had happened, even though her sundress was wet and caked with sand. Auntie Helena was happy to fill her in. She repeated everything she remembered and then some. Over and over. I needed an aspirin.

Fortunately, the aides got them both upstairs. The sudden quiet was a relief. I noticed Annie in the dining room, so I went in to talk. I grabbed some of the silverware she had in a pile and began to help set the table.

My mouth started running. "Do you know what's going on? Why were those guys attacking us? Why was David shooting from a helicopter? How'd he know we were being attacked? I thought he wasn't even coming to the U.S. till the first."

Annie stood straight and stopped what she was doing. "Lena, I'm as clueless as you are right now. It's some crazy secret agent battle that's always going on around us, and sometimes it invades our territory, and it's like we're not even supposed to notice. I don't know what to make of it. But I do know we'll never get a straight answer unless it suits them." Her face deepened red with every word.

"Oh." I didn't know what to say. It felt like I was back working for Pearson.

Silverware clattered and she started to shake. I watched her smooth her hair, but the shaking didn't stop. "Three men are dead on my beach. I have no idea who they are, how they got there, or what they were trying to do. I'll probably never know."

She poured herself a glass of lemon and mint water from a heavy crystal vase then took a sip. "I thought that helicopter was gonna hit us. Buck and I were right there in the Adirondack chairs when it plunged down out of the sky."

Her blue eyes met mine, and I knew she'd blame me for the whole thing.

"Lena, would you like some gazpacho?"

I almost lost my balance. "Uh … okay … sounds delicious."

She put the glass down and headed to the kitchen. "I'll get us some."

I enjoyed a bowl of the best gazpacho ever, as Annie related all her concerns about her sister being married to a secret agent. She was completely in love with him, but Annie felt his job put the entire family at risk. Annie wasn't wrong, but I wouldn't tell her that.

As Annie concluded there wasn't anything she could do, and it really wasn't any of her business, and despite him being an assassin she really did like—love—him as a brother-in-law, I picked up our bowls and took them to the dishwasher. "Thanks for the gazpacho. Best I've ever had. Settled my nerves, too."

She braced herself on the counter. "Glad you liked it. Thanks for listening. Sorry I bent your ear, I needed to vent."

"No problem. I understand. It was scary out there today. I need to go check on Mom." With that, I went upstairs and stopped short at Mom's door.

It was ajar, and I saw Auntie Helena facing Mom, seated knee to knee. Auntie's voice always carried. "Teddy asked me for a divorce. That was on Lena's third birthday, and I said no. I knew he'd been fooling around with Kay all along ... All along, I knew it. I'm no dummy."

Mom rocked back and forth, nodding, but I don't think she really understood my aunt. She seemed content to be close to Auntie, holding her hands.

I was shocked, but when it sank in, I wasn't surprised that Auntie knew what Uncle Teddy had been doing.

Auntie's sudden sob startled me from my thoughts. "I can't blame you, Julia, I can't blame you for wanting Ricky out. I can't blame you for falling in love with him in the first place. I loved Teddy like that, too. I did. Until he didn't love me anymore. They were bad ... but there was a spark of good there ... There was." Auntie drew Mom closer, searching her face. "I was just as bad ... worse ... I betrayed you ... I betrayed Kay ... my own sisters ... my little sisters."

Auntie Helena began bawling, gripping Mom tighter. Mom was confused, but sympathetic in a way. I wasn't sure if she could really feel sympathy. But she seemed to be trying to comfort her sister. My heart broke watching them.

Auntie stared Mom in the eye. "Joey B was burnin' mad with you, Julia ... burnin' mad. He knew you were behind it. Ricky told him he was done. How could he think Joey wouldn't find him up there? How could he think that? You couldn't shake the likes of Joey B if you went to the ends of the earth. You couldn't!"

Auntie was now shaking Mom, and I had to stop it. I walked in and shut the door behind me. Auntie jumped in her seat, and her mouth fell open as she gawked at me. Her hands and knees remained around Mom.

"Gracie." Mom looked up and smiled at me.

"Hi Mom. Hi Auntie." I wrapped my arms around Mom's shoulders and kissed her cheek, then faced my aunt. "I'd like to hear the rest of your story, Auntie."

Her eyes were blank. "I'm tired. I need my nap. I'll tell you my story later." She grabbed for her cane, and I helped her out of the seat.

Mom's aide appeared with fresh towels. "I'm going to help Kay with her shower, now."

"Thanks." I escorted Auntie to her room. "You need to finish your story, Auntie. With me." *Love is what is important.* "Don't fret about any of this stuff. It's all water under the bridge. Okay?"

Her brows arched in surprise, but nothing came out of her mouth.

I sat her in a comfy chair by the window. "I need to know everything about that night my family died. It's time you come clean."

She sat forward in the chair, leaning on her cane, staring at the floor.

I sat on an ottoman and rested my hand on her arm. "How did Uncle Teddy know to come find us that night? It's not like he just happened to be in the neighborhood. All these years and that simple question has never been answered."

Her voice was much softer than usual. "I told him to go."

My stomach twisted in knots. I'd been comfortable with half-truths, lies, omissions, and platitudes all my life. Facing reality, coping with it, might be too hard. I wondered if prying this door open would be a death blow to my sanity. "How did you know to tell him to go?"

I watched a tear drip onto her cotton dress.

"Auntie?"

"I was mad at your Aunt Kay ... mad at Teddy. They ruined my life ... my marriage. He wanted to leave me alone ... take the boys and leave me. He loved her all along. Not me." Her face was set like stone, eyes blinking away the tears.

I handed her a tissue and cleared my throat. My voice was still a croak. "I'm sorry, Auntie."

"You were a baby, it's not your fault. But I held a grudge against you and your whole family. Julia and Ricky were deep in love the day they met. I never saw anything like it. I was jealous ... jealous of your mother—my baby sister. And she was so strong. She didn't care what Joey B said, she wanted her husband out—her kids out of harm's way.

He kept promising her. Finally, he walked away."

She wiped her face with the back of her hand. "There's no gettin' outta harm's way for us. She couldn't understand, but she put us all smack in front of harm's way."

My mind was back in the flames, Peppy barking. "Joey B wasn't gonna let my dad get away with that."

"No." Auntie let out a deep sigh. "Joey came into the shop lookin' for Teddy. He knew Teddy'd know where Ricky was. But I was there by myself. Teddy was off on a delivery. Joey hardly lifted his hand to me before I told him. I gave him the exact address of that summer house."

She found the tissue in her lap and wiped it over her face. "I wanted Kay and the baby dead. I spent two years thinkin' how I'd do it myself, I was so mad. That's the truth. I'm sorry, Lena."

I bit my lip to stop myself from saying something I'd regret. "You didn't have a choice. Joey B would've killed you right there … Anyway, you told Uncle Teddy to come help us."

She shook in her seat. "I was hopin' Joey'd kill him, too. That's the truth. I wanted him dead, too. God help me."

TWELVE

~ Annie ~

After sputtering all my family business to Lena, I decided to distract myself with dinner preparations. Buck was off with Nathan, and the kitchen was quiet. I resisted an impulse to call my sister. With her husband in the middle of whatever he was doing in Maine, I couldn't trust myself. I could end up blurting something he wouldn't want her to know. It'd devastate me to hurt Debbie.

As I stared at my phone, it rang. It was David, his voice cool, calm, and collected, as always.

"I'm sorry for the disturbance today, Annie."

I took a deep breath and exhaled. "It's okay. We haven't had a … disturbance … since … well, since you were here last time." I pictured the sarcastic curve of his lip.

"I'm sorry you had to see that. We got there as soon as we could. Unfortunately, I didn't alert Nathan to the danger soon enough. It won't happen again."

His voice was sincere, but how could I believe it wouldn't happen again? "Well, I appreciate that, David, but I know you can't guarantee that. It seems to be just another day at the office for you. But I know you lay your life on the line for your family every day. You do the best you can do under the circumstances." I needed to change the subject before I became more emotional. "Will you be able to come and stay here at the house tonight?"

"Does that mean we're invited for dinner?"

A din arose in the background as David's colleagues complained that they were starving to death. I had to smile at these crackerjack covert agents who devolved into rowdy boys once their job was done. I suppose the ruckus helped them let off steam after the tension of the day. "Yes, of course you're invited. How many in your party?"

"Seven. The usual suspects plus two."

"Debbie?"

"Debbie's at home. You'll see her in a few days."

"Okay ... just hoping."

David was matter of fact. "We'll have our IT person and Lena's uncle with us."

"Oh ... okay." Lena was mixed up in something big, for certain. David wouldn't have been involved if she wasn't.

The racket on the other end of the phone escalated. All I could make out was "fish and chips." "You want fish and chips for dinner?"

"As you can hear, Cookie's in the mood for some proper fish and chips." There was a crescendo of agreement around him.

I giggled. "Well, this is the place. I've been using his wife's recipe ever since she first made it for us. It gets rave reviews."

"Keep the pilot happy."

"When will you be here? I'll have it all ready to go."

"Thirty minutes."

Buck arrived in the kitchen in time to overhear my call to The Golden Bowl for the haddock I'd need. I put down the phone and let him scoop me into his arms. "Someone's hungry," he said.

"David and his crew are joining us for dinner. They're bringing Lena's uncle."

"Hmm. Perhaps we'll find out what's been going on all this while. Lena's uncle was involved with some dangerous characters according to Rhodes ... spent time in prison for forgery. And then we have the strange situation with Ticket Depot. I wouldn't be surprised if they were entwined."

"That's sad."

"Indeed. But it seems whatever happened is coming to a conclusion. Hopefully we're all out of danger now."

"We better be, Buck. With my family here for the summer, the last thing we need is some mobster after us."

The same drone of the helicopter I'd heard hours ago overtook the house again. I checked the clock. David was nothing if not precise. *Thirty minutes.*

Buck took my hand, and we headed out to the landing area on the far side of the house.

~ *Lena* ~

The sound of a helicopter brought Auntie out of her chair. She tottered in the window, balancing on her cane, cursing the military helicopter landing in the yard, well to the side of the house. "Are they comin' for us?"

"Don't worry. You're fine. I think it's Annie's brother-in-law ... Yeah, that's him." I did a double take as he helped Uncle Teddy onto solid ground.

Auntie let out another round of curses. I silently hoped Teddy had a crumb cake or two with him. I turned Auntie's chair to face the window and put her in it. "I'm going to see Uncle Teddy and make sure he's okay. You wait here."

I ran down the stairs, preoccupied with how I'd cope with Uncle Teddy and the secret agents. I slipped on the bottom stair and landed clumsily in front of Nate. I stifled an ouch. "What's going on?"

He picked me up. "I suggest putting on some jeans before greeting our guests. We'll have some conversation then dinner with the family."

I'd forgotten I was half-dressed, considering it was April. With everything going on, it never occurred to me I was cold. "Conversation, huh?"

"Yeah." He put his hand to my back to guide me upstairs to my room.

There was no escaping. "It's been a long day, Nate. Can't I just beg out of this one? I've been traumatized enough." I lifted my knee, pointing out the bandage.

He smirked as he opened my bedroom door. "A skinned knee doesn't qualify as trauma." He pushed me inside and closed the door.

I briefly considered shimmying down the gutter pipe.

THIRTEEN

~ *Lena* ~

After cleaning up and dressing in appropriate clothes, I poked my head out the door. Nate was there.

"We need to talk." He pushed the door and pulled me out by the waist.

Panic stopped me like a stubborn donkey. My heels tried in vain to dig into the hardwood. "What are we talking about now?"

"I expect we have several topics. Let's go." He escorted me downstairs to his basement office.

Uncle Teddy sat sipping tea, looking every bit a disheveled centenarian. He pulled himself up and over to me, tears in his eyes. "I thought we'd all end up in the drink. I thought I'd never see you again."

I kissed his cheek and smoothed his hair, frowning at the flakes of dandruff falling to his shoulders. "Are you okay? What happened?"

"They got Joey B. They got all of them." Teddy started to shake and Nate interceded to put him back in his seat.

David nodded. "Hello, Lena."

I shook his hand. "What's going on?"

David turned to his IT guy, Cole Michelson. "You remember Cole."

"Of course. Hi, Cole." I shook his hand and returned his chitchat about how long it had been since the good old days with Pearson. Cole hadn't changed a bit. Prematurely gray hair had always given him that air of maturity and authority, but Cole was only in his early forties.

I refused Nate's offer of tea or coffee and took the seat I was directed to. "So what's going on?" I tried to sound confident, but it probably came out more like a nervous, broken record.

Nate sat behind his desk, but David took control of the meeting. He looked me straight in the eye. "I'm sorry things went so badly for you with General Pearson. You're extremely talented, and I hope you'll be able to go forward with Annie and The Golden Bowl. I have no doubt you'll be a great asset to their business and charities. Despite the numerous crimes you and your family have been involved with, I believe you can turn things around starting today. If you choose."

The look on Cole's face showed me he knew every last thing I was up to online. I looked back at David. "Uh … okay … what do I need to choose?" *Blurry lines.* I'd be happy to go along with their ideas if it'd keep me and Teddy alive and out of prison.

I watched David's lip curl. "We have your nemesis in custody. He'll be behind bars for the rest of his life."

Uncle Teddy spoke with a burst of enthusiasm. "All of them. Joey B. All his guys … they got them all."

I took Teddy's hand. "What happened?"

"The plan worked. They were all on the boat. They were comin' after you, Lena. They found out you were hacking them. They were sneaking up the coast in Joey's yacht."

"And you were with them?"

"They were gonna kill me as soon as they had you."

I squeezed his hand. "I'm so sorry, Uncle Teddy." I could feel my heart squeezing in my chest.

He patted my arm with his free hand. "It's okay. I was part of the plan."

"Huh?" I caught David's eye.

"Your uncle and his two sons are FBI informants."

"What?"

Uncle Teddy shrugged. "I wanted out, too, Lena. Just like your dad. When the boys told me they were done, we took the offer. We're honorary FBI."

Everyone thought that was funny but me.

Uncle Teddy probably saw the daggers in my eyes. "It's okay, Lena." He patted my arm again. "They know you're a good person. They know about all the money you gave to charity. The money you spent for your mother's care. It's not like you really stole it. And you got back at Joey B the only way you could. You used your brain." He wiped a tear. "I'm so proud of you."

I felt like sinking through the floor. I couldn't look David or Cole in the eye. I glanced over at Nate, hoping he'd save me. He had the strangest smile on his face. "Me, too. I'm proud of you."

"Huh?"

David stood. "You must be exhausted, Lena. I know your uncle is. Annie has dinner for us. Tomorrow Cole can discuss a few things with you, and we'll arrange for proper accommodations for you and your family." He encouraged Uncle Teddy to his feet and out of the office. Cole followed.

I sat, stunned. "What just happened here?"

Nate came around the desk, a grin still in place. "You're off the hook. You and your family are free. David will see to it you have protection, but they've got pretty much every New York mobster you can name. No one's left to bother you."

"You're kidding."

"No kidding. Between David and his associates, and the FBI, they rounded up boatloads of them. Let's just say it was a pretty massive operation." Nate hoisted me from the chair. "Let's go get some dinner. Fish and chips, I hear."

Catching the laughter from the dining room, I knew I'd need to regroup before facing dinner with the guys from Pearson's organization. I continued up the stairs to the second floor. "Nate, I'll be down in a few."

He nodded. "Okay."

I stood at my bedroom window glimpsing the last light of day. Joey B was no match for David and his cohorts. Sarcastic laughter bubbled up as I wondered how Uncle Teddy would explain his affiliation with the FBI to Auntie. She'd need a hundred crumb cakes for that.

My head went back to Auntie and Mom's conversation. No wonder it felt like my heart was skipping beats. Too much reality for one day. Too much to deal with.

My phone rang, and I pulled it out of my pocket. I let it go to voice mail. It was message 371 from Carter Lewis. Since January. A dull ache started deep down inside. *He's got some screws loose all right.* Less than a minute later, he called again.

When I left my room, I saw the cart with the remnants of Mom's and Auntie's dinner in the hallway. At least there'd be no knock-down-drag-out between Uncle Teddy and Auntie Helena at the dinner table. I proceeded downstairs in a better frame of mind. Once I hit the foyer,

I was grateful to hear Cookie, the British helicopter pilot, enthusiastically reviewing London's restaurants with Buck. Before long they had a list of them for Annie to try. At least they weren't discussing me.

I slipped into my seat beside Uncle Teddy to more fanfare than I wanted. But everyone was nice, even David's normally brash associates. I said little as conversation turned to Joey B's arrest on the boat and Ticket Depot's purchase by a consortium of musicians that did not include Paulo Clemente. Annie was thrilled that The Golden Bowl Tour would conclude in Portland, Maine.

The fish and chips were fantastic, as usual, and dessert was an irresistible strawberry shortcake, loaded with sweet berries and whipped cream. I could see Uncle Teddy's eyes beginning to close as I took my last bite. Nate noticed, too, and escorted him upstairs. I was happy I wouldn't have to referee a discussion between my aunt and uncle at this hour.

As soon as I could, I excused myself to take a walk on the beach. I needed to decompress, and there was nowhere better to do that. It was still incredibly mild and calm for April on the Maine coast. My jacket kept me cozy warm as I ambled along the packed sand admiring the moonlit sky.

On top of everything else, I had 372 messages from Carter Lewis to review and respond to—or not. It's not that I hated the guy. He could be sweet in a puppy-dog way, at least now that he was sober. He had more than enough money for one lifetime. And Cat's message of being a good person—a child of God—he called it, seemed to be at least on his mind, if not totally working in his life.

But Carter wasn't the man I wanted. He probably wasn't any good for me either. He definitely needed the year his sponsor told him he should have to work on himself. I probably needed that, too.

But what about the baby we could have had? Should I even tell him about it? There wasn't anything he could do except propose to me again. That wouldn't do either one of us any good.

When I thought of the baby, all I could do was cry wishing things were different. Wishing it was a normal pregnancy, wishing it was Nate's, the one good thing that could bring us together.

Here it was the end of April, well over a month since I was hospitalized, and I still had a long way to go. When I thought about that baby, that whole situation, I shoved it to the back of my mind. No one at work ever asked me about it—only how I was feeling. Of course, I'd tell them I was fine. Nate probably was as clueless as I was about what to say.

He'd been attentive to me, like a good friend. But we'd both made a point to discuss anything but that baby girl.

Although the nightmares had stopped, I'd ignored some texts and emails from Cat. I couldn't go to that "fear, doubt, and insecurity" and deal with it. Maybe now that Joey B was in custody it was time to cope with the rest of my life. *God help me.*

I stopped and looked up at the black sky. Tiny stars gleamed back at me, thousands of them. I'd never seen so many stars as here in Marberry. New York lights blotted them all out of view.

I decided my unknown little baby could be one of those stars. Maybe my cousin Lena was one of those stars, too. My mind spiraled with the possibilities. My brother, my sisters, my dog Peppy. I picked out stars for all of them. My neck ached, and my misty eyes dimmed the sky.

David's words came to me. *You can turn things around starting today. If you choose.*

I moved on and pictured all my stress and anxiety gushing out of me with every exhaled breath. I inhaled peace and tranquility. After maybe half a mile, I turned to head back.

~ *Nathan* ~

I sat in the shelter of the rocky ledge, looking out to sea, waiting for Lena. Despite today's very good news, I fought a sense of uneasiness.

Things had gone well enough in the take-down of Joey B and his gang. But David had confided in me afterward that he'd made a last minute discovery. General John Pearson, his former boss, had an alliance with Joey B. As shocking as that was, it explained quite a bit about the attack on Annie's estate.

David had made me aware of the operation to apprehend Joey B and his associates only hours before. As far as the FBI knew, Joey B was the only ringleader in the cruise up the coast to take revenge on Lena. The FBI planned to take them out at sea with the help of David and his team. They had no plans to let them get anywhere near Annie's beach. They had no idea Joey B had the covert resources he did. No idea Pearson had anything to do with the mobster.

Knowing the operation would be happening at sea, somewhere off the coast of New Hampshire or southern Maine, I'd decided to take a short break on the beach then head back to my office. As I looked out over the water from the top of the stone staircase, Billy alerted me to what looked like lost and wandering campers at the far north end of our wooded acreage.

At the same time the guards at the front gate reported a group of confused Danish tourists who spoke minimal English. They seemed intent on visiting Paulo.

Before I had a chance to turn toward the house, my men in the woods confronted the campers and shots were fired. They quickly realized they were up against a formidable foe. Then I noticed what had to be traitorous SEALs arriving on the beach.

In the midst of the chaos on the beach and in the woods, the intruders at the front gate grabbed unsuspecting tourists as shields and drew weapons. Then a new attack launched at the opposite end of Annie's property. I was grateful my team proved their worth. We suffered only a few relatively minor injuries. All of the hostages escaped unharmed.

Somehow David had learned about Pearson and was in the process of contacting me as the attack began. It was a minor miracle that he and his team were based near Bangor and able to help us take out Pearson's men in time.

Poor Annie was beside herself. Who could blame her? Her home was attacked by a unit of highly trained agents—every bit as capable as any on my team. I didn't have the heart to tell Annie there were far more fatalities than she'd seen—all around her property. Buck and Keith had ushered her into the house before she could realize the extent of the assault.

The thought that Pearson was still out there nagged at me. David was not forthcoming on his plans to deal with him. He asked me not to give Annie any further details or inform Lena about Pearson's involvement at this time. I wondered about that, but what good would it do? It would only worry them more.

As to the scuffle at the front gate, I knew it would be only a matter of time before one or all of the unfortunate tourists told their story to the press. David had that handled as well. Paulo's manager, Joe Harris, immediately arranged exclusive interviews for them by star reporter, Amanda James. They were whisked away to a posh and private New York hotel to wait in comfort and secrecy, where they would be well paid for the pleasure.

I had to hand it to David. He had every angle covered. Though I revealed some of the facts to Buck, Annie might never know the extent of the trouble today.

The incident at the front gate would be credited to some crazies.

After Amanda's interview, it would be the sensation of the daily news then blow over. The incident on the beach would never be discussed publicly. The incidents in the woods … well, they never happened.

FOURTEEN

~ Nathan ~

I needed to clear my head, but instead my mind filled with Lena and what the future might hold for us. The events of the day brought to mind the frailty of life. If things had gone differently, one or both of us could have been killed. How much time did we have to waste?

Like so many important topics, Lena and I had not discussed her ill-fated pregnancy or her thoughts on Carter Lewis since the day she left the hospital. It was only one of the significant matters we'd never fully dealt with, one of the chasms between us.

It was as much my fault as hers. I shone my flashlight on the verse she'd taken from the Golden Bowl and left in the stolen car.

Don't blame us for the sins of our parents. Hurry up and help us; we're at the end of our rope. You're famous for helping; God, give us a break.

For some reason, it had never occurred to me the sins of our parents had anything to do with me and God. Sitting here now, I realized my parents' life experiences, their "sins," had strongly influenced mine.

I read the paper I'd taken out of the prayer bowl. *Never walk away from someone who deserves help; your hand is God's hand for that person. Proverbs 3:27-29*

God was trying to tell me something here. Maybe it was time to listen—truly listen—to my ex-wife. To try and understand. To communicate. To trust. I'd learned early on never to trust anyone. My parents had set a poor example in that department. Looking back now, it was probably the root of the trouble in all three of my marriages.

Maybe Cat was right about turning things over to God. I decided to give it an effort. To trust God with this entire situation and see what happened.

I couldn't deny the incredible power Cat had. Or the "grace" as she would say. I let out half a laugh that Grace was my wife's given name. Maybe that was a sign. There were too many signs to ignore at this point.

When I looked up, I saw Lena walking at the water's edge and went to join her.

She smiled when she saw me. "Hi Nate ... again ... not trying to escape."

"Understood." I realized I was smiling too much. I cleared my throat. "This is the last place you'd want to escape ... except for having David around, I guess."

"Well, I guess it was kind of interesting, listening to all their exploits. And when Cookie went into that speech about how David would need to forgive Joey B for making him shoot those guys on the beach—it really was funny. It must be tough for him to have a cousin like Cat. An assassin and a saint—that's pretty funny."

She doesn't know the half of it. "It is." I realized then, it must have been Cat who told David that Pearson was sending his men to attack Annie's home.

She looked up at me, and I noticed how her dark eyes glistened in the moonlight. "Do you forgive me, Nate?"

"I—of course." I took her hand and started down the beach.

"For everything?"

"Yes ... not that I know what everything is." Communication and trust was a tricky thing.

She stopped, and I felt her tug all the way to my heart. "I'll tell you everything if you want, and I'll tell you the truth. At least my truth. Like I said, I grew up in a lot of lies, but I think they're mostly sorted through now."

"That's more than I can say for myself." That surprise slip shocked us both, I think.

Her face showed sympathy for my distress. "Well, Uncle Teddy and my cousins as FBI informants is the best one of all, huh?"

I appreciated her kindness in that redirect. "It is ... I've gotta say it explains a few things."

"Like?"

"Like how slow they were to give me information on your family and letting you get to New York and back without tracking you down."

"Hmm ... I guess so. But the good thing ... it gave me time to figure everything out about the night my family died. About love being what's most important. Like Cat said. Maybe God doesn't hate me."

"That much, I know."

We walked in silence a bit, and I thought about how I'd trusted my friend at the FBI. The frostiness I felt at his minor betrayal dissolved into forgiveness. Lena had had the time she needed to begin to come to terms with her life.

"What about Carter Lewis?" Another bomb slipped out. I wiped sweat from my forehead.

"Nate, you know as much about Carter Lewis as I do. The guy's a player. He spent most of his life drunk or high, and now he's trying to get clean and sober and avoid his sponsor—who tells him he can't date for a year. Everyone but Carter knows he needs to think straight before he can do anything else. Unfortunately, I got involved with him because I needed a job. I'm not in love with him. It's hard to even *like* him most days. About all I can do is feel sorry for him."

I grunted in response. Communication was hard. But words spilled out of me. "I still want to kill him."

She stopped and stared up at me. I could hardly hear her above the tide. "Thanks … I know you mean that like you're concerned about me. That means a lot. But I hope you don't harm the guy. He's a lost soul, too."

Now at a loss for words, I hugged her until I realized my grip was too tight.

"Uh … a little hard to breathe."

"Sorry." *Awkward.*

She didn't let go of me. "Nate, want to sit with me for a while? The moon and stars are gorgeous tonight." She tugged me toward the shelter of a secluded rock formation. "Uh, if you want me to be totally honest, it's beautiful here, and I like your company, and I really don't want to get in the middle of my aunt and uncle tonight."

I laughed. "Understood."

"If you think I was surprised about Uncle Teddy and my cousins being informants, wait till you hear my aunt. She'll be bellowing and swinging that cane. It's a good thing he's a little bit faster than she is."

She did an imitation that doubled us both over, laughing. It felt good.

~ *Lena* ~

I thought I'd need to pinch myself. How many times had I fantasized about snuggling on the beach with Nate? *You can turn things around starting today. If you choose.* Maybe David was right. He sure turned his life around.

"Nate, I'm just sayin' … moving to Maine, to The Golden Bowl, that's the best thing that ever happened to me, even though it didn't feel like that at the time." I felt his grip tighten around me.

"Same here."

I twisted around to see his face. "How so?"

I could see him grimace in the light of the moon. "When I took this job—it was a tough time in my life. I'd had that big argument with you, and you threw your engagement ring in my face. I'd always held out hope that we weren't done, until that day … then my mother died. I'd quit my job to take care of her. It was an ugly situation. I lost whatever hope I'd had for a good life." He closed his eyes for a minute, like he was processing it all.

My mind replayed my ring sliding off my hand and bouncing off his nose. I'd been frustrated and angrier than I'd ever been after that argument with him. Hurting him with the ring had felt great for maybe half a second.

Then I'd been sick to my stomach at the thought of losing him for good. And then I'd been even madder to lose the money I could have sold it for. It was worth a small fortune. I could have used that money. But Nate had caught the ring, so there was no getting it back.

I remembered the look on his face—almost a sneer—when he'd held it up to me and left the tiny break room of the boutique where I worked. He was like a bull in a china shop, but most of the customers enjoyed the show. A six-foot SEAL has a certain presence about him, even when he's flipping mad.

Nate's voice boomed over the sounds of the surf. "Then David called and offered me the job. I accepted it right away. I mean, who wouldn't want to work for David Lambrecht? It's a plum job." He coughed. "I felt like this was in the middle of nowhere. I guess it is. But you can't find better people."

"True." I thought about how I'd scammed Annie and Buck and wreaked havoc with their businesses. They forgave me and welcomed me with open arms. They trusted me. *Unbelievable.*

I might as well keep going. The night was conducive to truth telling. "Nate, I'm sorry I never got to meet your parents. And I'm sorry I never told you about Mom. I just couldn't … couldn't risk losing you. But hiding the truth, that's what split us up in the end."

"We both made mistakes. Now we know better."

"Yeah." I decided to keep pushing. "Was it really that you thought your parents would contaminate our wedding? Is that why you wouldn't invite them?"

He half laughed. "Yeah, I remember I used that word, contaminate."

"Yeah, you did. I remember that clear as day."

He rubbed my arm a little. I don't know if he was trying to console me or himself. "My parents, well, they should never have married. Simple as that. My father couldn't be faithful and my mother couldn't let him go. She got more bitter and twisted as the years went by. It wasn't pleasant."

"Toxic."

He grimaced again. "Yeah."

"So maybe that's why you were so quick to end your marriages. Because your parents didn't."

"Maybe." If he had an explanation for his behavior, he wasn't saying.

I settled in with my head on his chest and watched the moonlight on the waves. "We can turn things around starting today. If we choose."

I don't know if he heard me.

~ *Nathan* ~

Billy woke me at 3:00 a.m. with a request to help Lena's aunt and uncle resolve their dispute. I roused Lena and helped her off the beach while explaining their argument was disturbing some of the family. Billy had disarmed Aunt Helena, so Uncle Teddy had avoided the cane. But I could hear her harsh words spewing out their window even before we entered the house.

As we proceeded through the kitchen, Annie was making hot chocolate in hopes of pacifying her unruly guests. The aide blew through the swinging door in a huff, almost colliding with us. Annie held up a mug of cocoa, and the woman grabbed it as though it was a life preserver.

Upstairs, Buck and Billy were trying to reason with the couple, to no avail. Lena stepped between them and pushed her aunt into her chair. Her uncle retreated and sat on the edge of the bed. Buck left, thankful for the quiet, and Billy stood guard by the door.

Once there was silence, Lena turned to Billy. "Uh ... can we have some privacy? Nate and I need to talk to my aunt and uncle in private."

"Sure." He left and closed the door behind him.

I was faintly surprised that I was to be included in the conversation.

Lena sternly looked down on her aunt, her arms crossed. "Auntie, did you tell Uncle Teddy what you told me today?"

She averted her eyes.

"Auntie?"

"I told him I wanted him dead." Her voice escalated. "Imagine turning our boys into informants. It's one thing to throw your own life away. Now he's ruining our boys' lives ... and our grandchildren's. I told him I wanted him dead thirty-five years ago. That would've solved everything."

"It wouldn't have solved anything, Auntie. I know you don't mean it. You're just hurt. Hurt bad."

She started to cry. "Of course I'm hurt. My husband never loved me ... wanted to leave me ... wanted to take my boys ... then he gave them to the FBI. Put our whole family in danger."

Lena handed her a box of tissues.

Teddy sat on the bed, stooped, facing the floor, rubbing dandruff out of his hair. I couldn't see his expression. Lena turned her attention to him, and knelt on the floor looking up at him. "Uncle Teddy, this one's gonna take more than a couple of crumb cakes."

I heard him sob.

She put her hand on his knee. "You know Auntie loves you, and she always has. She's hurt, and we both understand why. You made a big mistake, and you didn't know how to deal with it. Some mistakes have consequences that never go away—I know. But there's something you both can do to get past it. Probably tonight's not the time to figure it out. It's late. No one's thinking straight. So I need you to have some hot chocolate and try and get some rest. Both of you. Tomorrow we can start to figure out what to do." Lena got up and faced her aunt.

"Do you want Uncle Teddy to take another room tonight?"

"Yes." She nodded. "No." Her head shook.

Lena grinned a sweet little grin at me. She turned back to her aunt. "Okay, if you promise not to beat Uncle Teddy with your cane, he can stay here in the other bed."

She nodded.

"Good."

I helped Teddy to his bed, and Annie arrived with cocoa to soothe her guests.

As delicious as Annie's hot chocolate was, I headed to the kitchen for coffee. I sat at the table, staring through the large bay window at the moonlit yard, mulling over events of the past day.

Lena arrived and sat beside me. She put a half-empty mug on the table. "Great hot chocolate. It hits the spot. Even settled down an ornery old couple."

I grinned. "Something tells me I'm missing pieces of the story."

"Yeah. When I told you about my family, about that night, I left out the part that Uncle Teddy was the father of my cousin, Lena. He had an affair with my aunt, Kay—the real Kay. I only learned that recently. I never thought too deeply about Aunt Kay. She was kind of a party girl—the most vivacious of the three sisters. The prettiest, too, I think. I knew she was a single mother and never pushed anyone about who could've been the father of her child. Mom and Auntie always took special care of her, from what I heard."

Sudden tears filled her eyes. "One of Auntie's lies, I guess. Until today, I didn't realize Auntie wanted her little sister and her niece dead all these years." She wiped her face. "Well, she got her wish. The real Kay Goodwin and the real Lena Goodwin are dead and buried."

I put my arm around her. I couldn't let myself sink into the enormity of this family tragedy. "I'm sorry. It's a tough thing."

"This whole urge for revenge needs to stop. We need to get over the bitterness. We need to be a family. Who knows how much longer I'll have them?"

She wrapped her hands around her mug. "I always wondered why Auntie Helena's face was so furrowed—so different from Mom's. Tonight, when she cried, it looked like water dripping out of a stone. Those furrows came from bitterness that grew in her heart over Aunt Kay and Uncle Teddy. Bitterness hardened her heart, and it hardened her face."

"Unforgiveness . . ." Cat's lessons were buried somewhere in my brain. "It can destroy people."

"It sounds like it destroyed your mother, too."

"It did." I wasn't going to go there. Not now.

Lena's voice was almost a whisper. "And love makes people thrive. Mom may have succumbed to dementia, but she still has hardly a line on her face. She's happy in her remaining memories of my dad. She still loves him thirty years after he's gone. Love is what's important."

She put her hand to her face. "Nate, I don't want to be bitter."

~ *Annie* ~

Buck had a hard time sleeping after the incident with Lena's aunt and uncle—not to mention the assault on our beach that day. When he finally dozed, I tiptoed downstairs and outside to take in the colorful sunrise from my Adirondack chair.

I wasn't surprised when David settled into the chair beside me. We exchanged greetings and fell into silence, watching the sky. But I couldn't contain my curiosity. "Are you heading back to Austria today?"

"Probably late tonight. I'm sorry for the rude interruption."

Leave it to David to call an all-out gun battle on my beach a "rude interruption." I squelched the memory. "It's okay. Just bring my sister back. I can't wait to see her … and the rest of the family, of course."

He grinned. "Of course."

Wispy clouds caught my attention. "She's like a wisp of an angel, like that bright cloud up there. Just being in her presence makes me smile. Not a day goes by that I don't think about her near-death experience, how she actually spoke to our grandmother in heaven. It had to have changed everything about her life. How could you go through an experience like that and not be changed?"

"I don't think you can."

"It happened with Cat, too, when she was even younger than Debbie. It had to have been so profound."

I watched the rising sun etch that angel cloud in gold. "I think God chose them for a special mission here, and it's all about the power of love. They carry a simple message, each in her own unique way, and it has a big impact. Look at all the good Debbie does for charity with her designs. And Cat with her music. So many lives have changed for the better because of them. It's like they both soak up God's love and radiate it to the world."

David turned to me. "You're the same, Annie, radiating love with The Golden Bowl. Look what you've accomplished. People around the world are discovering the power of prayer."

I felt my cheeks go red with embarrassment. I wasn't looking for compliments. "That's sweet. Thank you."

He was such an enigma. The fact that he concerned himself with prayer at all was shocking, considering his profession. But his wife, and his cousin Cat, had most certainly turned his life around with the power of their love and prayers.

We fell back to silence, and my self-consciousness faded as I focused on prayer. The view of sky and sea, the sound of the waves slapping the rocks, the touch of the breeze on my face carrying the scent of spring flowers filled me with joy and gratitude.

God had protected us again.

~ *Lena* ~

Cole Michelson joined me for breakfast in Nate's office. It was one of those invitations you couldn't refuse. I picked at scrambled eggs, thinking my brain was too scrambled to cope with another thing.

Chitchat about the good old days working with General Pearson progressed into a discussion of the litany of my criminal endeavors online. Cole had caught more than a few of my tricks. "You know we need to return the quarter million dollars you donated to The Golden Bowl charities."

I looked up from my plate. "Oh?"

"Afraid so, Lena. Sorry." His gray hair glistened under the lamplight in a strange way that highlighted its texture. Women at the New York salon where I'd worked paid good money to get that effect. Cole probably got out of bed looking like that.

I shook my head. "If you say so."

Out of the corner of my eye I saw David appear in the doorway, and sweat broke out on my brow. I wondered if I'd ever get over that reaction to him. It was more than fear, more than a physical attraction to his imposing presence. With any luck, I wouldn't be seeing much more of him. Hopefully, he'd be off to Austria in short order.

We all exchanged "good mornings." My voice was a croak again.

David took a seat behind Nate's desk. "Lena, if it's all right with you, I'm adding you to our payroll. In order to keep you out of trouble, we told the authorities you've been working with us."

"So ... it's either work for you or face government prosecutors?"

"Yes." His brown eyes were inscrutable.

"I don't want to go to prison, so I'll do whatever you want."

"All I ask is for you to keep The Golden Bowl operating safely, securely, and legally."

"Uh ... Buck's paying me to do that."

His lip curved. "Consider this a raise."

"Thanks." I wiped the sweat off my forehead. "So we're kind of back in Pearson's world, huh?"

He almost smiled. "Unfortunately, once we stepped into that world there was no leaving. I'm sure you knew that."

"Uh ... yeah, I did. Even though I was fifteen freakin' years old when he recruited me ... I guess that's why I thought the Ticket Depot pump and dump was such a good idea."

"It was." David poured himself a glass of orange juice. "Welcome to the team, Lena."

We all toasted with our juice glasses. Had David orchestrated this whole thing all along? Deep down, I knew there was a lot more to him than met the eye, though that was more than enough to cope with.

Who knew how many intertwining layers of grime and scum were beneath just my sad case? Never mind all his other dealings. I felt a little bit sorry for him, having to manipulate everyone from presidents on down. But that didn't stop the nagging fear in my gut.

Later that day David and his team left, after moving me and my family into secure apartments at Washington Gardens. It was weird to think I was now in the employ of David Lambrecht and his organization. I wondered what name would be on the paycheck.

A few days later a tidy sum was deposited into my bank account from Clemente and Associates. Apparently, Cisco's younger brother, Eduardo, was the new Pearson.

FIFTEEN

~ *Nathan* ~

Amanda James Now, the star reporter's news magazine show, aired on the evening of May first. Buck had told me he'd prepare Annie to watch the episode, despite the fact that Paulo's concert near Boston would be televised live at the same hour. I arrived in the doorway to the library in time to witness Annie's displeasure.

"Buck, when were you going to tell me that a half dozen tourists were almost murdered at the end of our driveway?"

He poured her some tea. "That would be now, my dear." He glanced at me then back at his wife. "Would you care for something stronger?"

Annie was beet red. With a frustrated sigh, she leapt from the couch. "This isn't funny." She began to pace, noticing me, but not acknowledging me. "David did this, didn't he?"

Buck nodded. "I'm quite sure he arranged it. Under the circumstances, I think it was the best plan. Most of the world will be watching the concert. Amanda James will give the tourists their fifteen minutes of fame, and after the news stations report on it, it will fade into the next story."

He sat on the couch and patted the spot beside him. "Have a seat, my dear. No worries. It could all work out for the best. From now on, we may have fewer tourists trying to invade our drive."

She stopped her pacing and stared at her husband.

He took the remote and pointed it. "What would you like to watch?"

"We'll watch Amanda's show and switch it during the commercials—and then after the story." She sat in a huff. "Buck, I know you were just trying to protect me. But, don't ... don't do that again. I need to know what's going on around here."

I stepped into the room. "It's my fault. I asked Buck to give you time to recover after the attack. My mistake."

She put her head in her hands. "Okay, Nathan. Please … I'm an adult … please treat me like one." She looked up at me. "I can handle it. Okay?"

I nodded. "Okay." I felt badly that Annie was so upset, but I believed David was right to shield her as much as we could. I went to the kitchen for some coffee and found Keith and Lena had beaten me to the pot.

She smirked at me. "Hi, Nate. The guards told me it'd be okay to surprise you. But Keith had to make sure I was safely escorted to the house. You never know what crazies at the gate are gonna do, huh?"

Keith smiled ear to ear, but said nothing as he disappeared out the back door.

I found a cup in the cabinet and handed it to her. "You never know."

"Yeah. That was a big coincidence, huh?" She poured my coffee.

"Yeah." She wouldn't get any more out of me on that topic. "Want to watch the concert?"

She smiled and handed me the mug full of coffee. "Let's see what Amanda James has to say first."

Amanda James played her part in David's plan well. I was interested in watching Lena watch the show, certain she attributed the attack on the front gate to Joey B.

As the credits rolled, she asked, "Why would David and his crew be involved in getting New York mobsters in the first place?"

I shrugged. "I don't know. But I do know they move in circles most people don't know exist."

"Yeah. That's the truth." She turned to me with a mischievous smile. "I thought they just wanted us out of their summer house."

I bit back a smile. "That could've been their motivation, right there."

In the early hours of May second, all of Marberry lined up along the route taking Paulo Clemente and entourage to their summer home at Annie's farmhouse. I couldn't quite understand it, but their fervor for the rock stars seemed limitless. Tourists and townies partied in the streets, cheering Paulo and the others as the motorcade inched by.

Fortunately, the agonizingly slow journey was only a few miles through town and up Shore Road to the private drive leading to the farmhouse.

Needless to say, The Golden Bowl was packed with customers, and the crowds only grew as the summer season got underway.

Cat—and all her relatives—were most gracious in their treatment of Annie's staff, including us in the family. Nevertheless, I didn't want to impose on her while she was trying to have a break between concerts, songwriting, and taking care of her husband and one-year-old son. On day two of her vacation I watched her returning from her solo meditation on the beach.

I intercepted her at the top of the stairs by the hedge. "Cat, do you have a couple minutes to talk?"

"Of course." She led me to the Adirondack chairs, dropped her backpack, and took a seat.

I took the chair facing her. "I know I didn't pay as much attention last summer as I should have."

Her giggle was the nonjudgmental response I needed. My tension began to lift.

"It's like you were saying about God knocking over and over again. I think I'm finally ready to pay attention. Maybe open the door."

Her blue eyes lit up with her smile. "I'm happy to hear that. Do you have a question?"

"Uh … well, you know things. I'm wondering if you think—if God thinks—it's a good idea for Lena and me to try … you know … marriage again."

"Wonderful!" She clapped her hands. "You know I'm going to say yes, as long as you have God in your marriage … Holy Spirit leads you into all truth."

The pit of my stomach told me that was the problem in all my relationships. No God. No trust. No truth. "Uh … yeah, that's the thing—truth is hard." I cleared my throat. "But now I think we're onto something. Lena and I've been more truthful with each other lately than ever before. But I don't want to cause any more grief by starting this up again if it's not meant to be."

~ *Lena* ~

Annie had been sure to tell me my family could visit and use the grounds and beach anytime they wanted, despite the invasion of all her extended family of celebrities with their families and employees. I used the excuse to drop off some packaging samples to Buck on my way home from the food prep facility. I was glad to do Gerald the favor, but my main intent was to run into Nate.

Buck kept me chatting for a while. The guy was on top of every detail regarding The Golden Bowl. No wonder the business was such a phenomenal success. Buck and Annie had the golden touch.

Just as I thought I'd make a break for it, he poured me a cup of tea. "How is everyone settling in to Washington Gardens?"

"Good, thanks. It's a beautiful place, and scenic, too. Mom loves it, and Auntie and Uncle Teddy are working things out. I hope." I looked over Buck's shoulder, through his home office window, and caught a glimpse of Nate and Cat in the yard. *I need to talk to Cat.*

"Excellent. I'm happy to see you and Rhodes are on friendlier terms, also."

"Uh … yeah … friendlier."

He got out of his chair and stood at the window. He grinned watching Cat and Nate out back. "Things seem to be working out for the best."

I went to the window. "Cat looks like she's glowing."

"Indeed. Perhaps she's teaching about Holy Spirit again."

I made a face at Buck. "Uh … mind if I join them?"

He pulled open his desk drawer and handed me a small notebook. "You won't want to miss a word."

I rushed out the kitchen door and stopped short at the top of the stairs. I didn't want to look too eager. Nate smiled when he saw me. Seriously, my heart skipped a beat.

Cat waved me over, so I kicked off my heels and joined them in the Adirondack chairs. Nate draped his jacket over my shoulders, and I thought I'd melt.

"I should've worn a jacket, but I thought I'd just be a couple minutes to drop off packaging samples to Buck. So I left it in the car. When I saw you out here, I had to come say hello."

Cat took my hand. "I'm so happy to see you again. It feels like it's been years. We were discussing the Vine and the Branches, John 15 in scripture."

A giggle poured out of me, and I lifted the notebook in my free hand. "Buck gave me this and told me not to miss a word." In the same instant, my eyes filled. "I need to write at the top: love is what is important."

Cat's eyes shone magnetic. "Yes, a perfect start to your notes. John

15:17 says, 'This is my command: Love each other.' It's as simple as that."

I glanced up at Nate. There was something going on inside him. I pulled his jacket tighter around me. The sea breeze was kicking up. I looked at Cat. "It's as simple as giving someone a coat when they're cold."

She smiled at me. Out of the corner of my eye, I caught Nate grinning. My words came out laboriously. "Love is simple … and difficult."

Cat nodded.

I couldn't get over how Nate's little gesture warmed me. "Cat, why are love … relationships … marriage … so hard? And who is Holy Spirit, and where does that fit in? It sounds like Buck thinks Holy Spirit is really important."

She beamed at me. "Right in the middle of your life, your relationships, your marriage, that's where Holy Spirit fits. Holy Spirit is your counselor, your conscience, your comforter. Holy Spirit leads you into truth and guides you along the path that's right for you. Holy Spirit often speaks with that still small voice deep inside of you."

"Oh." I was back in the Catskills, clutching that chain. My little cousin Lena rode through my mind on that tricycle, the love pendant swinging at her waist. Holy Spirit was guiding me through the mess to find the truth.

I blinked away tears and searched Cat's face. "Do Nate and I have any chance of making life together work?" Today I didn't care if Nate knew how much I wanted him back. Maybe it was Holy Spirit who made me realize I had no more need for games.

Her hand tightened around mine. "Of course you do, Lena."

The kitchen door slammed, and Cisco stood at the top of the stairs with their son in his arms. He was a commanding presence, for sure, even more handsome in person. As he approached us, I thought how funny it was—he was so much taller than his wife.

He politely greeted me and invited us to dinner. We headed inside where their entire extended family assembled for the meal.

I was blown away by how kind everyone was to me. They bantered back and forth on a variety of interesting and funny topics, remembering to include me. Annie had made a roast turkey dinner that was the best ever, and dessert was Paulo's favorite blueberry cake with blueberry ice cream. I soon learned, as a rock star and the baby of the family, Paulo usually got his way.

Nate invited me for a moonlit walk on the beach and offered his jacket again. As we headed out the kitchen door, Cat intercepted me. "Lena, I'd love to visit with you and your family at Washington Gardens. Would it be all right if I come along tomorrow morning?"

~ *Nathan* ~

Mother Nature cooperated and the beach was perfect. Lena drew my jacket tight around her. "Are you cold?"

"No, I just like the feel of your jacket around me. Makes me feel … safe … I guess."

I didn't know what to say to that. My voice caught in my throat. "I was a little surprised you asked Cat today if we have a chance."

She paused and looked up at me. "I never stopped loving you, Nate. I guess there's no reason to hide that. I'll put it out there. I guess it's up to you to deal with it. Not that I want you to be uncomfortable."

I cleared my throat. "I asked Cat the same thing. I was hoping we have a chance. We're older now. Maybe more understanding."

She smiled. "Cat said we have a chance. So I'm saying my prayers to Holy Spirit that I don't screw this one up."

Laughter sputtered out of me. "Okay then, I'll say my prayers, too."

"Good." She tugged at my arm. "So take me on a romantic walk on the beach, Nate. The stars are out. There's a nice soft breeze. The sky is such a pretty deep, dark blue. And look at the man in the moon. I hear it's all cream cheese up there."

"All right." I ceremoniously placed my arm around her.

She giggled. "Be still my heart."

We cracked up laughing.

Later, as we settled on the beach, stargazing, I pondered the discussion I'd had earlier with Cat. Her enthusiasm over my desire to remarry Lena gave me hope.

But then she'd reminded me of the importance and power of forgiveness. That would be daunting. No doubt I had a long and difficult list of people to forgive, starting with my parents. Lena was on that list, along with Carter Lewis, and my boss, David Lambrecht.

~ *Lena* ~

Cat arrived at our apartment door with a contingent of bodyguards. Mom rushed over and hugged her, immediately starting her "Amen Chorus." Cat was good-natured about it and did a round of amens and halleluiahs, as we slowly proceeded to the kitchen table.

Auntie was at the counter slicing a crumb cake, bitterly complaining of missing home. Unless you had crumb cake from Brooklyn, you didn't have crumb cake. Nothing else could compare. Not that she bothered to ask if they made them at The Golden Bowl. The cheap grocery store box sitting on the counter told me Auntie would rather gripe.

Uncle Teddy focused on fitting all the placemats on the table so everyone could eat breakfast. He made a few feeble and unsuccessful attempts to calm his wife.

It was only after we sat down to the meal, and Cat was so sweet and genuine, that Auntie finally smiled and told her how much she loved her music. Then she started trying to convince Cat to buy some New York real estate.

After the New York sales pitch, Mom was a little agitated. She patted Cat's hand to get her attention. "You have tickets?"

I ran for the envelope I kept in the kitchen drawer.

Cat turned to her with a smile and a hug. "We're all set, Julia. All set."

"Good." Mom was immediately calm and smiling. "Going soon."

"Yes, soon," Cat said. "Why don't we sit outdoors for a bit? It's a glorious day."

Mom and Auntie popped out of their seats, all excited at the prospect. We bundled them up to protect them from the sea breeze and headed out to the patio. It wasn't long before the two of them were dozing in the sun.

Cat walked with me down the trail to the shore. Her bodyguards kept a comfortable distance. We sat in the shelter of some massive stone cliffs, the early morning sun warming us. As Cat sat quietly for a few minutes, I became enthralled with the sight and sound of the waves churning around the rocks below, the occasional spray misting my face. The water was especially blue today.

"Lena, I wanted to continue our conversation from yesterday."

I pulled my notebook from my sweatshirt pocket. "I'm ready."

"You asked about Holy Spirit." Her blue eyes sparkled at me.

"Yeah, I think a good dose of truth is what I need these days. I think Nate is all for that, too. It's probably gonna be hard, though, and I don't know how much truth is too much." I stared down at the rock, unable to look Cat in the eye. "I try to put it out of my mind, but I keep wondering how things could've been different if that baby was Nate's, and it lived. Instead, Nate knows it was Carter's. He probably thinks I'm … well, I'm not the purest damsel in distress."

I summoned the courage to look up at her and my eyes watered. "I loved Nate when I married him, and I never stopped loving him. But if there's been too much stuff for him to get over, I need to learn how to put him in the past, and learn how to live right moving forward. I have no idea how to move forward right now."

She took my hand. "You do need to resolve your past, change the way you think about yourself, and move forward. First, you need to know your true identity. Whatever name you call yourself, know first and foremost you are a precious child of God. You must know that in your heart. Holy Spirit will help you."

"You know my real name is Grace?"

"Yes."

She prayed over me, and I let the tears roll down. They came fast and furious when she called me Grace, when she asked for "grace for Grace." I said a big amen when she was done. "I feel like doing one of Mom's amen choruses."

Cat giggled. "Let's do it then." She began and waved me in.

I was laughing and singing all at once. When we were done, I felt lighter than air. "I can see why Mom likes singing that so much."

"God is present in your praises, Lena."

That kind of floored me.

She took my little notebook with my one entry: *Love is what is important.* I handed her my pen and she wrote, *My grace is enough; it's all you need. My strength comes into its own in your weakness. 2 Cor. 12.*

She returned it to me. "My friend, Grace, remember this: My grace is enough. Capitalize the G. My Grace is enough. You are enough. Just as you are. God meets you right where you are. God is all you need."

I stared at it for a while, then wrote out Cat's words underneath the verse. *Grace with a capital G.* "I'm God's Grace."

"You are. Remember your true identity, Gracie." Cat stretched back on the rock, like she was in no hurry.

"I feel better. Thanks." I took a gulp of salt air. "Tell me about grace."

She smiled. "Grace is God's favor, kindness, mercy, a free gift to his children. You cannot earn it. It's yours for the asking."

I reached into the air and the breeze swept the sweat from my palms. A strange sensation flowed through my hands and enveloped me. I lifted my head and spoke to the sky. "Thank you for your grace, God."

Cat giggled and warm wind whipped around us. I laid down on the rock and stretched my hands up. It was like I was a lightning rod for that wind. I didn't want it to stop.

Eventually, it did, and I knew I had to ask Cat before I lost my nerve. I couldn't get the right words out. I sat up and faced her. "I don't want to be hard and bitter like my aunt. What do I do?"

"Bitterness is unforgiveness, Gracie. Give over your resentments to God. Let them go. You're forgiven. You're set free. God will help you over all of it, if you trust him. And do pray for the person you resent."

"I never thought of praying for someone I resent. I guess it makes sense, though." I shuddered.

"It might take some time to realize all the resentments you hold. Holy Spirit reveals things to you gently. Your mind is renewed day by day."

I turned toward the ocean, my mind whirling with too many bad thoughts. Was I already too bitter to overcome all these resentments? I probably needed to spend some time figuring out everyone I resented—it'd be a cast of thousands. None of them easy.

Cat's voice penetrated the din in my head. "Grace, do you resent Carter Lewis?"

A sarcastic laugh popped out of me, and I stifled it. "Uh … yeah. Nate said he wants to kill him. I'm worried that whole incident'll keep Nate and me apart. Why would he want me after that?" I gripped my stomach with the pain of that thought. "And what if we do get together, and I can't have another baby?"

She put her hand on my arm. "Nathan has already said he'd like to move forward with you. You have a start. Give this over to God. Write about it in your journal. Get it all out, and Holy Spirit will direct you."

"Thanks. I guess I don't really feel like writing right now."

"That's all right. It's a process. It can take years sometimes, even if you think you've already forgiven someone and dealt with it."

I rolled my eyes. "Years, huh? That's encouraging."

She half-giggled. "That's the way we are sometimes. We can't let go of the past so easily."

"I bet that's never happened to you. You're not that stubborn and hard-headed."

Her blue eyes bored into mine—sincere and emotional. "When I was a child, I was badly injured in a plane crash. Over and over again, the doctors repeated to my aunt and uncle that, if I recovered, I would never have children. I heard it so many times I believed them. My family believed them. Cisco believed them."

I felt her emotion racing through my body. "That's awful. And you have your son now."

"Nothing is impossible with God, Gracie. Please remember that. We think we can rely on people and on ourselves, but in the end, we have only God. I forgot that, too."

"You did?" *How could Cat forget God?*

"Yes. From the time I could remember, I loved Cisco. We were best friends, and he always watched out for me—especially after David had left home. I was crushed when Cisco became engaged to marry someone else. I knew his parents loved me very much—but Cisco is the oldest of their three boys, and they wanted grandchildren. That influenced his decision, I'm sure."

I thought I'd fall off the rock. "You two were meant for each other, if any two ever were. What happened?"

"By the grace of God, he realized he'd made a mistake and called off the wedding. But I'd gone through a terrible time. I didn't want to confront him. I seethed in silence. I railed at God, wondering why he made me suffer, why he made me this way."

It looked like she was reliving that suffering right now. We sat for a minute or so in silence, and I was conscious of that same warm breeze. It felt like Holy Spirit was embracing us. It kind of freaked me out. "Cat?"

She gazed up at me. "Yes. I had quite a list of resentments, and I thought I'd dealt with them. Years later, at a weak point, it all came back to me. So I want you to know, Gracie, forgiveness is a process, and we are flawed, weak people. Choose to forgive, and let Holy Spirit help you with the process. As long as you put your trust in God—keep your eyes on God—all will be well. He's doing his work in and through you. That work continues until the day we die."

I let out a breath. "Yeah. It's hard to keep my eyes on God when I don't even know what he looks like. Sometimes I think about what you told me when you called me at the hospital. I try to trust God, but that fear, doubt, and insecurity thing is real. It sounds like even you went through that. It's hard to remember God some days. And I have a hard time forgiving, I guess. I hold grudges—like my aunt. But if I remember today, and this warm breeze that feels like Holy Spirit, that will help."

Cat gave me an empathetic smile. "It takes time to develop trust— with people and with God. Read his Word, and ask Holy Spirit to guide you. You'll find it will come alive to you. And pray. Talk to God. Look for his response. He speaks in so many different ways that are unique to you. This lovely warm breeze is one example."

I looked down at the water roiling around the rocks, and foam sprayed up on us. My insides felt like that churning sea. My cousin Lena made another tricycle trip through my head. I realized God couldn't have spoken any clearer to me that day. *Duh.* The love pendant confirmed "love is what is important." Little Lena wasn't holding grudges. She was free.

I remembered Cat's prayer from the golden bowl. *And what does the Lord require of you? To act justly and to love mercy and to walk humbly with your God.* I'd thought I could throw "act justly" in Cat's face if she gave me grief about getting revenge. She hadn't given me grief, she showed me how I should live my life.

SIXTEEN

~ *Lena* ~

Sitting on the rock in silence, Cat stared out to sea, probably praying. I began scribbling in my notebook, and pretty soon words poured onto the pages. Catharsis, I guess.

I began rubbing my face, much like Uncle Teddy would, and stopped myself. *Miserable excuse for a human being*. I exhaled a heavy sigh. "This resentment stuff is full of that fear, doubt, and insecurity you told me about at the hospital."

"Fear, doubt, and insecurity is not of God, Gracie. Get it out … on the page or in prayer. Give it over to God. Tell Satan to leave you alone. The Precious Blood protects you now."

I dropped the journal and put my head in my hands. I could feel the embarrassment climbing up through my throat. "David's wife is really sweet." My voice was a croak. *How fast will she see right through that one?* I looked up.

Cat's smile was sympathetic. "She is."

"I … uh … I mean for a world-famous fashion designer, she sure is sweet and humble." Cat was going to make me tell. Something inside me had to tell someone. "I mean she sure is different than the women he used to know." *Yup. Stumbled right into that hole.*

"Uh … I … yeah, I have a resentment against him, and I'm afraid it could mess up things with Nate." I wiped my eyes. *No more crying.* "I met David when he came to New York for a training meeting with Pearson. There was an attraction, and I knew he was interested in just one thing. His reputation preceded him, if you know what I mean."

"I do." Cat's eyes were sympathetic.

I wanted to run away. "So I knew what I was getting into, but I was young and stupid and thought I could handle it. I cheated on my boyfriend at the time, and in one day I fell for David. So I got what was comin' to me, I guess. My boyfriend heard about it from Pearson's secretary, believe it or not. He dropped me. And to add insult to injury, the very next day Gwen Munroe walked into David's life. I don't think he remembered my name once he got a look at her."

Cat gripped her stomach. "Oh."

"You know Agent Gwen Munroe?"

"I do."

"Yeah, she and David were quite the pair. They almost blew up the Middle East. Literally."

"I know."

I gasped. How could I speak so freely about things that were supposed to stay buried in darkness? Things I hadn't even let myself *think* about for years. "It's a good thing you do know. Pearson would have me shot dead for that little remark."

Her eyes filled. "I know that, too, Gracie. I'm so sorry for all you went through."

My voice wavered. "Part of me wanted to get back at Nate for telling me Annie was so much better than me. But I knew David was related to Annie. I wanted to get back at him, too. I wanted him to feel some kind of pain. That's why I set out to destroy The Golden Bowl. But even that pain couldn't have been as bad as what I felt when he left me in the dust for Gwen."

I wiped my nose with the sleeve of my sweatshirt. "I lost my boyfriend over it. Everyone and the dog catcher heard the story. And it made it oh-so-easy for Pearson to believe that lie about me and his son-in-law. My life was a shambles. I thought revenge would be sweet. What else did I have?"

Cat handed me a tissue.

"It's been so long since I let myself even think about all that. It hurts—it's like spreading through my guts. I feel like I could cry for days."

She put her arm around me. "It's okay for you to cry. You can tell me anything, and it will go no further. We can stay here as long as you'd like. Admit all of this to God. He sees your brokenness, and he will heal you."

"Thank you, Cat … Sometimes I feel like I have a big reject stamp on my forehead."

"No more, Gracie. You're a child of God."

The warm breeze was back, and it shocked me as it swept my clammy hands dry. I pulled Cat closer to me. "I can feel your power filling me."

"It's the grace of God. Holy Spirit is in you."

I sat there in awe for a while. Holy Spirit was *in* me. I hardly knew what to make of it. "I ... uh ... I guess I need to send up some prayers for David and Gwen ... and my old boyfriend. Even though I caused it, I was mad at him for dumping me."

"That will help you overcome the bitterness ... help you heal. Use your notebook to list people you need to forgive—including yourself. Let Holy Spirit guide you in prayer. Write your prayers in your notebook, if you like. As you work through this process, you'll feel better."

I took a deep breath, feeling it expand my lungs, then a noisy exhale. "Thanks. I feel better already. It does help to get it out. And just the thought that I have tools, and I have your help ... and I have God."

"You do. We'll plan to connect often over the summer. We should be able to fit time in around your schedule. Yes?"

"Of course! I mean it's your schedule that's so busy. I can make whatever time you say."

She squeezed me to her side. There was definitely power running through her. If that was Holy Spirit, I wanted it.

"Uh, Cat ... So now what about Nate? All my ugly stuff? Do I tell him everything? Not that he doesn't already suspect."

"Pray about it, Gracie. If you and Nathan want to remarry, you'll need to be honest with each other. But first deal with your past, your issues, for your own benefit."

"You mean work on myself first?"

"Yes."

"Makes sense. I guess Nate has stuff of his own to work on."

Cat stood and extended her hand to help me up. "Remember, look to your creator, God, for your identity. He says you are fearfully and wonderfully made." Her smile was as bright as the sun. "Now, let's take a moment to enjoy this glorious view. Then perhaps you'll join us for lunch today at The Golden Bowl. It's girls' day out. I'll have my niece with me."

Within days I had my resentments list entered into my notebook, and I'd started praying about it. Although I managed some sparse prayers for some of the people on my list, I sure wasn't going to talk to anyone about forgiveness.

As I stared into space chewing my chicken salad sandwich and pondering all the amends I should probably make, there was a knock at my office door. I swallowed with the help of some iced coffee. "Come on in."

Buck shut the door behind him and wheeled over a chair. "Sorry to disturb your lunch."

"No problem. What can I do for you?"

He opened his tablet and looked up at me. "I'd like you to take charge of the expansion of the food prep facility. If you think about it, you'll realize you're the right person to oversee that project."

"Okay." I'm not sure why I sounded so agreeable, but my insides responded with an uncomfortable heave. Memories of last summer came reeling back.

I pushed back in my chair, holding my stomach. Buck's eyes were riveted on mine.

He stood. "Are you all right?"

"Buck, I'm really sorry I tried to mess up your relationship with Annie last summer. It was mean and stupid, and I'm so sorry." The words belched out of me, and then I felt fine. Like nothing had happened. But like everything was peaceful and settled.

I was confused. Buck looked confused, too, as he took his seat.

"I'm sorry, Buck, I shouldn't have brought it up … On second thought, well, I guess I needed to tell you. But now probably isn't the best time to discuss it."

He arched his brow. "It's as good a time as any, I suppose. And I do appreciate your apology."

"So you forgive me?"

"I forgave you a long time ago. Since you brought it up, I should tell you, in fact, you did me a great favor."

A giggle slipped out. "A favor?"

"Indeed. If you hadn't cancelled Annie's celebrity guest for her television show that day—and inserted me as the replacement—we may never have reconciled. Your antics were disturbing, of course, but the fact remains that Annie and I realized how very much we loved each other. How we wanted to spend our lives together. If not for you, I might have taken that position in London. We may never have married. I feel I owe you a debt of gratitude, Lena."

"Oh." That was all I could say, but from that moment I knew for sure this forgiveness idea had merit. *Cat's always right.*

It was a minute or so before I could meet his eyes. "So that's why you were so nice to give me this job? To give me a second chance? And a third?"

He smiled. "I know you're well qualified for the position. I recognize talent when I see it." He pulled up my report on his screen. "Shall we discuss the food prep facility?"

By mid-May throngs of tourists had descended on Marberry, and there was not a room to be had for miles around. The Golden Bowl was stuffed with customers everywhere from opening to close. Most of them wanted a glimpse of the rock stars, but they'd taken off for California for a series of concerts that would take them from west to east then back for vacation at Annie's.

It was Wednesday evening, and I was still at my desk. All my work was done, but I'd gotten sucked into the underbelly of the internet. There was some weird chatter, more than usual, that threatened Paulo and his band. A knock at my door startled me, and Nate walked in before I could make a sound.

He gave me the grin that would make me follow him anywhere. "Why don't we order some dinner and watch the concert on TV?"

"Sounds good, but I need to tell you I'm a little worried about them. There's a lot of chatter online that makes me wonder if there'll be a problem tonight. Especially since it's an outdoor concert, and they haven't done that for a very long time. They could be in danger, Nate."

He made a face and leaned over the desk. "Cole said the same thing. They're aware of it—even declared a no-fly zone in the area. It's an isolated place, and they think they can defend it." He straightened up and kept his eyes on me. "Cat had one of those sleeping prayer spells she has sometimes when things get tough. I'm kind of worried myself."

I didn't know what a sleeping prayer spell was, but the look on his face made me shiver. "Why don't they cancel?"

"You said it yourself. The show must go on. They're on a mission. Cat wouldn't hear of canceling. And Paulo and the others'd follow Cat anywhere." He came around the desk and lifted me from my seat. "Let's get going. I'm hungry, and there's nothing we can do from here. David's got an army of security out there. Between that and God it should work out for them."

An hour later we sat in front of the TV in the library at Annie's house with burgers from The Golden Bowl. "Nate, I think you oughta tell Annie about this threat at the concert. She'll be furious if something happens and you knew about this."

"I have my orders, and David specifically said there was no need to worry Annie about any of this. So let's just enjoy the concert." He grabbed the remote.

I put my hand over his to stop him from ignoring me with the television. "So did David specifically tell you there was no need to worry Annie or me with the assault on Annie's front gate that day? Danish tourists, my *behind*."

Nate glanced at me then hit the remote. "You know I have my orders. And nothing is going to happen tonight. Joey B is behind bars—along with the Danish tourists."

I couldn't help laughing. "Okay. Glad to hear the Danish tourists are under control. And who knew they were speaking Danish, anyway?"

Even Nate couldn't help laughing. But the aggravation gnawing underneath the joking was real. Another addition to my list of resentments. It was endless.

The celebrity announcers revved up the TV audience, the camera panned hordes of people as far as the eye could see. "Reminds me of Woodstock … without all the mud."

Nate snorted. "Leave it to you to remember Woodstock. You were just a twinkle then." He winked at me. "And they're more worried about a wildfire there in California. Bad drought … been a couple years of no rain." He opened a bottle of beer. "Want one?"

I took it. "Thanks."

In due time Aubrey Rose took the stage and gold light engulfed her. "I like the way they did the lighting. Very cool. I wondered what they'd do to make it golden bowl-like."

It was probably fifteen or twenty minutes later when Paulo and the rest of his band joined Aubrey on the stage. They were superstars, but they acted so down-to-earth. Celebrity was the last thing on their minds. No waiting for the superstars to take the stage. They were chomping at the bit to share the joy of their music and their message. Cat's words were their truth: Love is what is important. You could tell they loved the music, and they loved their audience. They were having the time of their lives out there.

Nate and I fell under their spell, even dancing around the library to our favorite songs. I was giggling and flirting after half a beer.

"Ready to practice our twirls, Nate."

He saved me from crashing into the coffee table more than a few times. But when Cat rose from her keyboard and took center stage, I pulled Nate back to the couch. "This is where it gets amazing." I landed in his lap.

He stole a kiss.

"Hey!" I cozied up beside him.

"Yeah. Amazing."

Cat looked a bit strange. I straightened in my seat. "Is she okay?"

Nate stared at the screen. The crowd was going crazy, but she wasn't in any rush to speak. It looked like some guys were trying to get the audience to quiet down. In a minute or two, there was silence.

She reached open hands to the crowd. "*Mercy unto you, and peace, and love, be multiplied.* This scripture is Jude 1:2 and inspires our song, *Grace and Mercy Rain.*" She held up her hands to the heavens and began to sing. The music had an irresistible beat.

Pretty soon I was singing along about grace, and mercy, and peace, and love is what is important. I noticed Nate gripped me closer to his side, and that same power I felt from Cat on the rock at Washington Gardens came through me. And I bet he felt it, too.

A flash of lightning and the sound of thunder made me jump. "What was that?"

Nate squeezed me. "It's storming on their stage and here at the same time."

Sure enough, sheets of rain poured down the library windows, and lightning lit them up as it did the TV screen. Thunderclaps were synchronous. I was dumfounded.

Nate shook his head. "Look at her. She's bringing rain down from the sky."

"It's God, Nate." The fire inside me didn't care how crazy I sounded.

"You're right," he said. "It's God."

Cat was sopping wet. Everyone was drenched, but no one moved from their spot. Thousands of people joined in her song, raising their hands. Thunder and lightning stopped after five minutes or so, but pouring rain continued in California and Maine. Cameras caught sheer joy on the faces of the people, the dancing, the laughter, the amazement.

The television station broke in with a news bulletin about the strange phenomena that was occurring at Paulo's concert. I yelled at the screen. "It's a miracle, you morons! A miracle."

Nate burst out laughing. "My godly girl."

We stayed by the TV as long as they broadcast. It was still raining at 4:30 a.m. when the early morning news came on.

"I'm gonna get some coffee. Want some?" I started up from the comfort of his arms.

"I'll come with you. I don't think the newscasters have anything more to report."

The kitchen window was open and there were voices above the patter of the rain and the sounds of the sea. Nate and I doubled over laughing as we saw Annie and Buck run down to the beach like a couple of kids.

SEVENTEEN

~ *Annie* ~

It was after 6:00 in the morning when Buck and I finally dozed off. My phone woke me at 9:30. I grabbed for it so it wouldn't wake my husband, but panicked a bit when I heard Amanda James on the other end.

"Annie? It's me … Amanda. Annie, I was there. I saw it all." Her voice was strange.

"Are you okay?" I stumbled out of bed and to the bathroom.

"I'm okay. You … and Cat … you were right all along."

"Oh?" I gingerly closed the door.

"God's real. I know it now. The hundred thousand people that were there with me last night know it now."

I sat at the vanity and pulled back the curtains, glimpsing shades of gray, sky blending into sea, and let a misty breeze calm me. "I'm glad, Amanda."

"They kept going—till almost 2:00 in the morning. Singing. And when they left the stage … I saw it myself … the stage was dry! Cat was out front. She was the only one doused with all that rain. The band … they were all dry. It rained *around* them—on Cat, on the crowd—but none of their instruments were wet, none of the band. I knelt down on that stage and felt it myself. Dry as a bone."

She sure didn't sound like herself. "Where are you?"

"I'm at the airport. Heading to Texas. It's raining there, too. It's raining everywhere, except on that stage in California."

I rubbed my eyes. "Everywhere?"

"All across the United States. From California to Maine. If you check the weather forecasts for yesterday—no rain in sight for the west coast. No rain in sight for the northeast. It all started with Cat.

There was a three minute thunderstorm all across the United States. Then the lightning stopped, and a steady rain's been coming down since." She broke into a giggle. "It's that new song, *Grace and Mercy Rain*. That's what it is."

I took another look out my window. Gentle rain watered the green lawn. "Praise God."

"That's what Cat said. That's *all* Cat said. I can't even get a comment out of their manager. All Joe would tell me is Cat's hoarse from singing all night. But they still plan to do all their scheduled concerts, so I'm heading to Texas. Who knows what's gonna happen there? Well, I suppose God knows."

I laughed a bit too loudly. Remembering Buck was trying to sleep, I stopped myself.

"Annie, I'm asking you as a friend first and a reporter second. What's going on?"

"I think you said it yourself. Only God knows. But I'm pretty sure he's got your attention—and everyone else's. God wants people to know him, to have a real relationship with him. So this might just be one way he's telling us he's here and he cares. It's all about love. That's what it boils down to."

"*Mercy unto you, and peace, and love, be multiplied.* I wrote down the verse Cat said inspired her. Love is being multiplied, I guess. Well, it makes sense since there's been such an awful drought in this part of the country."

"Hasn't there been an awful drought all over this country? A lack of love and caring for each other?" I swallowed the start of a lump in my throat.

There was a long pause on the other end. "I … I guess you're right. Grace and mercy are raining all around the country now. Maybe something will change."

When I opened the bathroom door, Buck was sitting in bed watching the news on TV. I pushed in beside him, and he put his arm around me. "Apparently God is unleashing Cat on the United States."

I couldn't help a giggle. "Seems to be the focus of all the media. God's getting some good press." I tucked my phone under a pillow. "I tried calling my sister, but it went to voicemail. I hope they're okay. Amanda called and said they were hoarse from singing all night, otherwise it sounds like they're all right."

"I'm sure they're fine. Every station is saying the same thing. The band—with the exception of Cat—wasn't even touched by a raindrop, so they were able to continue playing. Surely miraculous. Sounds like God has a plan."

I kissed his cheek. "He does."

"And the weather ... we were supposed to have a week of sunshine the last I checked ... although you can't rely on the weatherman around here."

"Amanda said it's raining all over the country ... raining grace and mercy, I hope."

Exactly three days later the rain stopped. That was Saturday night. Sunday morning every preacher in the world spoke on the meaning of grace and mercy and the strange phenomena around Cat. My dad's church was overflowing. News reports showed the same in every town across America.

As Cat and the band moved about the country, miracles happened all around them. Real miracles, like thousands of people being healed, crime coming to a stop in the cities they visited, rain in parched places and sun in flooded places. People were getting along. Engagements and marriages spiked to record proportions. Churches were full.

The media reported continuously on the meaning and results of *Mercy unto you, and peace, and love, be multiplied*. That prayer was on people's lips as a greeting, a good-bye, and a pronouncement in between. It was every other prayer I took out of the golden bowl.

Having recently experienced the horror of what people were capable of, in the attack on my beach and front gate, this was a welcome change. I expect people all across the country felt the same way. Life for so many was difficult, with the added threat of violence and crime in so many neighborhoods around the country. I hoped the changes I'd noticed around The Golden Bowl would be happening everywhere. From conversations with Amanda James, it sounded like it was.

Grace and Mercy Rain was everyone's new favorite song. I heard people singing it on the beach, in the restaurant, and on the grounds, and watched many of them raise their hands as Cat always did. It was strange, wonderful, and awe-inspiring to see God at work through Cat, Paulo, and the band.

I was lucky enough to be able to speak with my sister, Debbie, every day. They were keeping a grueling pace, and probably no one was more exhausted than Cat. The press now always referred to her as a prophet, which she was, but I'm sure it added stress to the team around her. Cat kept her eyes on God, and that focus directed her. But it likely confounded the entertainment industry people who wanted to run the show.

Cat and her bandmates spent whatever time they weren't performing out in the public ministering to people in hospitals, homeless shelters, and on the streets. Anywhere Cat went there were miracles waiting to happen. Debbie told me David and his security forces were exhausted trying to stay ahead of Cat's pace.

Cisco and their baby accompanied her to most of her appearances. Watching them on TV, I was inspired to see how patient Cisco was with all the commotion around them. He was as genuinely interested in helping people as Cat was. The baby took it all in, smiling and cooing at his many admirers. Just over a year old, I could tell he took after his dad.

Joe Harris, the band's manager, insisted on making the most of all the publicity. He was smart enough to understand Cat was on a mission that he could not control. But he deftly supplied local charities with our packaged meals and anyone who asked with golden bowls and instructions on using them for prayers. The entertainment and news shows had video of everything, to the point there was almost nothing else on television.

Joe was adept at negotiating, so when Cat and the band members did take the time to appear on the late night talk shows, it was apparent God took center stage. Cat wouldn't have it any other way.

~ *Lena* ~

I can't imagine what the rest of the world thought about the strange happenings around Cat and the band, but I was glad I'd had some conversations with Cat before all those miracles suddenly started happening. I think a lot of people freaked, and who could blame them? Pretty much every news story centered around all the wonders Cat was bringing to light. I couldn't wait for her to get back to Marberry so I could talk to her.

Since Annie and Buck were used to Cat, grace and mercy, and all the miracles, life seemed to be pretty much the same for them—just happier, I think. Annie took every new opportunity to inspire people to turn to prayer and God. Her face was always radiant these days. Anyone could plainly see Annie was a "love is what is important" person.

Buck was confronted with even more explosive growth in the

business, but he seemed to take it all in stride. He kept to his plan to go to New York for four days of meetings with his London and New York staffs. I was grateful I wasn't required to go, but since The Golden Bowl was Brooke, Lewis & Wynn's most prominent client, I spent a lot of time on the phone and compiling reports. More of Brooke, Lewis & Wynn's staff would be assigned to The Golden Bowl projects on both sides of the pond.

I was so engrossed in my work, I didn't check caller ID and took the call.

"Lena? Lena, don't hang up." It was Carter.

I froze.

"Lena, I'm sorry about calling so much. I'm not gonna ask you to marry me again—unless you ask me. Okay?"

I croaked. "Okay."

"It's that … I … I've been working on this thing. Well, Cat says repentance is turning away from sin, and sin is whatever offends God. So my sponsor says I need to make amends, and I have pages and pages of these amends, and I need to make amends to you. So … you don't have to forgive me if you don't want to, but it'd really help me if you'd listen to me for a minute. Just so I can make amends. Then you don't have to talk to me again if you don't want to. Okay?"

I took a breath. "Okay."

"Okay." It sounded like he'd pass out, but he went on rapid fire with his long list of amends—some really picayune stuff in the scheme of things. "I'd really like it if you forgive me."

"Okay, I forgive you."

"Really?" That sounded too hopeful.

"Really. But I'm not going to marry you—ever. So don't ask, don't even think about it."

There was a heavy sigh. "Okay."

"Uh, Carter?"

"Yeah?" Again, way too hopeful.

I told him all about my ectopic pregnancy, and I told him I'd forgiven him for his part in it. I told him I realized I had to take some of the responsibility because I purposely got drunk so I could get through that night instead of saying no in the first place. I should have realized no job was worth it.

Because there was awkward silence on the other end, I told him I regretted not telling him sooner, but I'd been conflicted about it. I asked his forgiveness about that, and I heard a mumble. Maybe he was crying. Whatever. I couldn't cope, so I took that sound as a yes and ended the call.

A little voice told me I'd need to do more writing in my notebook under "resentments—Carter Lewis."

Even though David never called on me to do any work for his organization other than taking care of The Golden Bowl, I took it upon myself to keep an eye out online for any threats or menacing chatter concerning my favorite band. Undoubtedly, Cole had that well taken care of, but I decided one could never be too careful. And I guess I was nosy.

Their Fourth of July show in New York went on for days, not to mention all their media appearances. I was exhausted just watching them.

Nate came through my office door as I watched more miracle stories from the Big Apple. "Lena, you can't be working. The fireworks are about to start."

I snickered. "Around here, that might not be such a good thing."

He came around my desk, and I closed my laptop.

"Let's go." He hoisted me from my seat and planted a kiss on my lips.

"Mmm … intoxicating."

He snorted a laugh and kissed me again, much more on purpose this time. Then he took me by the shoulders. "How was that?"

My smile came all the way up from my toes. "I guess we don't need romance lessons."

There was a glint in his eye. "Okay then, time for fireworks."

"Okay, then." I couldn't take my eyes off his.

Nate broke the spell as he pushed me to the door and ushered me to his SUV. "Are we really getting into all the crowds just to see fireworks?"

"I reserved the Adirondack chairs. We'll have a perfect view."

A wave of laughter came over me. "You *reserved* the chairs?"

"Yup."

I got into the vehicle. "So what about Annie and Buck? The chairs belong to them."

"No problem. They'll see them from the second floor. Don't worry." He slammed the door.

Mobs of people meandered the quaint streets of Marberry, and Shore Road was practically a parking lot. Mini celebrations went on all around us as people waited for the big show. With so many tourists flooding into Marberry lately, the town fathers had decided to entertain them with Fourth of July festivities beyond The Golden Bowl. Some of the small businesses that benefited from the tourist trade contributed, but most of the money came from Cisco and Paulo. It seemed to generate a ton of goodwill.

Nate used the lights and sirens that were normally reserved for emergencies to hustle everyone out of our way. I felt like a queen. He sure was intent on getting me to those Adirondack chairs.

When we arrived at Annie's house, we found a beautifully arranged table and chairs on the back lawn with wine chilling in a fancy bucket nearby. Fine china, crystal, and silverware were set out on the table. A multicolor summer bouquet sat in the center, but the lilacs still flourishing near the garage spread their heady fragrance on the sea breeze. I inhaled the sight and scent.

"Nate! You did all this for me?"

"Of course."

"You sure don't need romance lessons."

He tilted my chin up with his thumb. "I may be a little rusty, but don't put me on your resentments list." Then he kissed me, and I stretched on tip toes for more.

I was dizzy by the time the fireworks started.

EIGHTEEN

~ *Annie* ~

Buck pushed through the kitchen door as I loaded my blueberry muffins into the oven. "They're here. Just pulling up the drive, my dear."

"Oh!" I twisted around in time to receive his kiss. "Good timing."

"Indeed."

It was 5:45 a.m. on the fifth of July and my extended family was back home. With all the miracles and events of the past weeks, I couldn't wait to see them. "Well, Debbie said Paulo wants blueberry muffins for breakfast, so he'll have them." I threw my apron over a chair and followed Buck out through the front door. Doc stood in the walkway, in his glory, swarmed with kids, each with a story to tell.

Debbie blew a kiss to Doc, made her way around the kids, and we had a great big tearful hug proclaiming how much we missed each other. As we ambled back toward the door, Joe Harris appeared and shook Buck's hand. "Mind if I join you for a few days?"

"Not at all," Buck said. "I'm sure you could use a holiday. And we have some things to discuss with The Golden Bowl."

Joe smiled at me. "It's goin' good, Annie. You guys are gonna be expanding again. More exploding sales. That's what we like to see."

My momentary concern over handling another "business explosion" left when I saw Cat and Cisco coming up the walk. Baby Jack was asleep over his father's shoulder.

The family was obviously exhausted from their tour. After we had breakfast and settled them in, the day was one of rest and relaxation. They all retired to their rooms after an early dinner. Joe joined Buck in his office for some business conversation after helping us clean up the kitchen.

I put on a fresh pot of coffee and settled at the table with Doc. "You looked so cute out there today playing kickball with the kids."

He chuckled. "I was able to keep up this time. They were pretty tired when we started." He sipped his decaf. "They were all out like a light about three sentences into my bedtime story."

"I'm not surprised. I don't know how any of them are coherent after that trip. It was non-stop day and night for weeks on end. And in the middle of all that ... miracles."

He rubbed his chin. "I don't know how I'm coherent after watching it from a distance. Surreal. After all that, you've got to believe there's a God out there."

"I think you do."

Doc's hesitant faith was a topic we hadn't discussed much lately. But I had noticed he attended services at my Dad's church every week now. He made a point to join the men's Bible study group at our local church as well. But he hadn't shared much of his experience with me. Maybe he thought I was too busy between my new husband and my exploding business.

He was quiet for a few minutes, sipping his coffee, staring out the bay window at the yard dimly lit in the last light of day. My thoughts went to time spent in my Adirondack chairs connecting with God and family.

"Annie, I'm going to ask David if I can join the family on the rest of the tour this summer. I'm not busy around here, and with all the charity work they're doing, I think I can be useful to them. Who knows, I may be able to support some of their work at the hospitals or at the shelters. And I'd be around the kids more."

I smiled. "And Debbie."

He nodded. "And Debbie ... What do you think?"

"It sounds wonderful, Doc. As long as David is okay with it from a security point of view. He's got his own army at this point, so I can't imagine they'd have a problem with it."

"Good. I'll ask him about it."

Doc's eyes had a glassy look about them. I wondered if he was overtired. I reached for his hand. "Are you okay?"

He pushed his coffee aside and put his other hand over mine. "I got a call from an old friend just after I tucked the kids in. He told me one of his colleagues was very intent on meeting Cat, and he did—in Texas after all the miracles started happening. He went to a children's hospital where Cat was visiting the patients, and they even put on a little concert for them. Anyway, this surgeon managed an audience with Cat and they prayed together. Every patient he's operated on since is cancer-free after their surgery."

He tightened his grip on my hand. "No chemo … no radiation … *every one* healed from surgery alone. All healed, no matter how hopeless the case."

Tingling from head to toe told me Holy Spirit was at work. "That's amazing."

"Annie, do you think God can use me?"

The following day was to be a restful one, but I found Cat out in the Adirondack chairs with Doc at dawn. I turned on my heel so I wouldn't interrupt, but they both called to me to join them.

Doc's face was as bright as the new day. "Annie, I'm joining The Golden Bowl Tour."

I planted a kiss on his forehead and took my chair. "As a roadie?"

He pointed his cup at me. "As a medical liaison."

"Wow. That's an official title."

Cat chuckled. "I thought so when Doc pitched it to me, but as we discussed it, I think it's perfect."

He beamed. "We haven't worked out the exact job description yet, but the title is so good, David will have to approve it."

"Well, take another swig of that coffee, and we'll come up with that irresistible job description. How about documenting all those miracles?"

Cat nodded. "That's a fine idea. People everywhere will see the glory of God."

"Sounds good to me. I can get started right away."

Doc had a spring in his step that was more than all that caffeine he'd consumed. When the kids poured out of the house with a soccer ball, he was ready for them.

The game relocated to the beach and became the focus of most of the family after breakfast. I settled into the Adirondack chairs with Debbie and Cat. Baby Jack played in the grass beside his mother. A gentle sea breeze kept us cool. Conversation quickly turned to the miraculous weeks on The Golden Bowl Tour.

I sat forward in my chair so Cat would be sure to hear me. "Did you expect all that to start in California?"

"I wasn't surprised, but I wasn't expecting such an outpouring of Holy Spirit. I'm so grateful for thousands of miracles—and they're continuing still. God is drawing us. People are waking up from their slumber."

"Did Doc tell you about the surgeon that prayed with you in Texas?"

"He did, and I believe that inspired Doc, as well. He told me he's giving his life to God's work, if he'll have him." Cat giggled and pushed her hair back from those mesmerizing blue eyes. "Of course he will. We prayed about it together, and Doc knows he's a child of God."

Cat focused on me. "And you're correct, with Doc's expertise and credibility as a cardiac surgeon, he's the right person to document these medical miracles. He'll impact even more doctors, nurses, and their patients to turn to God in prayer." Cat picked up her beach bag and found a packet of tissues, which she handed to Debbie.

I noticed her tears. "Are you okay, sweetie?"

She blew her nose. "I'm fine. I'm just so happy that Doc is doing this. I'm honored to have him as my ... father."

That triggered tears of joy for me. Debbie had been reticent about embracing Doc wholeheartedly as her birth father. But Doc's step toward God would bring him the desire of his heart. He'd grow closer to his daughter and grandchildren. He had the family he'd always wanted. And he'd make a true difference in the world.

Debbie gave me the packet of tissues.

After a late afternoon cookout on the beach, we gathered for an impromptu business meeting for The Golden Bowl. Basically, my family was my board of directors, and you couldn't put Buck and Cisco together for more than a few minutes without conversation turning to business. We circled some chairs and made it official.

Buck took charge of the meeting and turned to me. "Annie, after some thought and discussion, I'd like to put forward some ideas on the expansion of The Golden Bowl."

I sat back in my seat. "Okay."

"Super Club has been a phenomenal success, and demand continues to spiral. As a matter of fact, we've created a multitude of new jobs since that product line launched last January. Our food prep facility now operates at capacity twenty-four hours a day, seven days a week. This is very good news, not only in terms of income and funding for charity. It also allows us to make some important decisions."

He turned to Cat and Cisco. "It wasn't so very long ago when you discussed Annie's vision with her and decided to keep The Golden Bowl as the base of operations here in Maine. The Golden Bowl would continue as an iconic restaurant, a quaint tourist destination on the scenic coast of Marberry."

I nodded in agreement. We'd put the franchise model on the back burner, and I was hoping it would stay there. I put my hand on Buck's arm. "I know I said we'd do whatever it takes to make The Golden Bowl everything God wants it to be. I'm just hoping we don't have to franchise to do this expansion, Buck." I noticed Cisco's smile.

"Agreed, my dear. I believe you're right to keep this Marberry property as the center of attention and attraction. I've been in touch with some highly reputable co-packers. People I've worked with for years who are capable of packaging and shipping our products to our strict specifications. Because they're located in diverse geographic areas, they'll help us expand quickly and seamlessly."

"What about our food prep facility?"

"We're proceeding with the plan to expand it as well. You'll continue to be a leading employer here in Maine, Annie." Buck addressed Cisco. "So we're keeping to a steady course as we've discussed. Joe is revving up publicity as your tour continues. I believe we'll keep up with demand for our products, keeping our quality consistent, as we bring on these co-packers."

Cisco nodded. "Perfect."

~ *Lena* ~

Once the rock stars returned to Marberry, Nate was pretty much consumed with work. Too bad. Fourth of July had some surprising fireworks. Even Mom picked up on my euphoria when I finally returned home to Washington Gardens. She started to sing again. Aunty Helena didn't appreciate that. At that point, I didn't care. I joined Mom in her amen and halleluiah choruses.

Back at work, I kept my nose to the grindstone, but found time to putter around online. The negative chatter continued, despite so many miraculous stories filling the media. I was in the middle of reading one of them when there was a knock at my door. "Come on in."

Cat walked into my office, and I jumped up and around the desk. "You're here!"

She hugged me. "How are you, Gracie?"

It thrilled me to hear my real name. "I'm fine … a little worried about you. I mean … lots of weird things going on. Getting out in public, rubbing elbows with people—it kind of makes me nervous you guys could get hurt."

By Cat's expression, you'd think that had never entered her mind.

"I mean it, Cat … lots of wackos out there."

"Evil is alive in this world—there's no doubt. But we're called to be salt and light. Have courage."

"I know … I know I'm fearfully and wonderfully made, and when I'm weak, God's strong."

Cat's smile did light up the place. "You've been working in your journal?"

I went to my desk drawer, took it out and handed it to her. "Yup."

She flipped through it, nodding. "Impressive."

"Thanks. You probably noticed I can't end my day without writing *Grace and Mercy Rain*. My new favorite song. And of course, then I remember that peace and love is multiplied. That makes me happy. I think it's coming true."

She bounced into a chair and the wheels took her featherweight body across the floor. "It is coming true." She went back to my journal.

I went back to my desk. "Even with all that, I'm still concerned about all this internet chatter."

Cat glanced up at me, but didn't have to say a word. Her face said, "Internet, schminternet." She returned to the journal. "Grace is empowerment. Remember that, Gracie."

I handed her a pen. "Write that down in there, please."

NINETEEN

~ *Lena* ~

Expansion plans for the food prep facility at The Golden Bowl required collaboration with the experts at Brooke, Lewis & Wynn. I traveled to New York, at Buck's request, to handle all that. Keith came along as my bodyguard, since I was now part of David's team. I thought it was overkill, but I didn't argue. Keith was a low-key kind of guy, and we got along fine.

I phoned Mom a couple of times a day from my hotel or the office. Sometimes the aide put her on videoconference with me. She was confused, but doing okay.

Auntie Helena and Uncle Teddy would pop onto the call and reassure me that Mom was getting the best of care. And Auntie would always tell me to make sure to bring a Brooklyn crumb cake home with me. At least she used the word "home." That was a minor miracle.

My excitement over Auntie Helena's progress led me to an old family bakery in Brooklyn where I ordered a fresh crumb cake to be shipped to Washington Gardens every single day. It was well worth the expense and Auntie's protests that it was too extravagant of me to waste my money like that. The look on Uncle Teddy's face said I was doing just fine.

Nate called me at least once a day. He visited my family at Washington Gardens most every day and reported back to me. He was so sweet to keep an eye on everyone. According to Uncle Teddy, he'd spent a fair amount of time talking through issues with them. He and Auntie were getting along better as a result.

Teddy told me, "Nate's a keeper."

Nate never told me what they discussed, but Teddy was

surprisingly forthcoming. He said Nate was obviously upset about letting lies break us up and ruining years that could've been happy. From the sound of it, Nate was almost as miserable and lonely as I was. It gave me hope that things could work out with him.

And his intervention with Auntie and Uncle Teddy was helping them see they had more reasons to stay together than to break up. They had a relationship worth working on.

I'd planned to be back home in plenty of time for Billy and Lisa's wedding, since Nate was best man, and he needed a dance partner. But that wasn't happening.

Not surprisingly, things moved at a snail's pace at Brooke, Lewis & Wynn in the summertime, and I needed way too many people on board to make the project happen. Then I'd need to confirm everything with Dominguez Construction, who would oversee the actual construction and implementation of our plan.

I was beginning to wonder if I'd make my deadline. As it was I'd extended my stay in New York. I was supposed to fly back to Maine tonight for Billy and Lisa's wedding tomorrow. Then back to the Big Apple again a few days later.

It was almost dinnertime when I picked up my phone, and Carter's voice startled me from my workaholic haze. "Lena, you need to come now. I need to see you—to talk to you … now."

Something stopped me from yelling at him. I took a breath. "Carter, cut the crap."

"It's life and death. I'm on the brink, and I need to see you now."

I exhaled into the phone. "You're not on the brink … Where are you?"

"My apartment … Come … Now. Lena … Please." His voice was so pathetic. But he was the Lewis at Brooke, Lewis & Wynn, and I was expected to listen when the partners spoke.

I looked at the time. I'd probably need to cancel my flight and rent a car to drive home tonight. "Carter, I swear I'm gonna bring a bottle of scotch and hit you over the head with it."

Keith must have been down the hall getting some dinner. I was so aggravated with Carter and preoccupied with calling the airline, I totally forgot to tell him I was leaving.

When the doorman let me into Carter's building, I regretted not bringing that bottle of scotch. I had an irresistible urge to harm Carter Lewis. *God help me.* I was supposed to be a new person, but just that man's voice was enough to eradicate all the progress I thought I'd made.

Then I realized I was upset over the baby I'd lost. *That's why he wants to see me*. My blood pressure must have hit the ceiling at the thought of dredging all that up with Carter. I'd need that bottle of scotch.

I was barely at his door when it flew open, and I was pulled inside.

It wasn't Carter doing the pulling. I tried to scream, but I couldn't.

"It's been a long time, Lena."

I looked up at General John Pearson, the man who'd ruined my life. He hadn't changed much. Same gray crew cut, same military posture, same hard eyes. The black, white, and bold red décor of Carter's posh apartment made a bizarre backdrop to the moment. Somehow I thought it lent itself to bloodletting.

Pearson's guard relieved me of my handbag, my only hope, which contained my Glock and my phone.

"I thought I dealt with you a long time ago, young lady. But you're still here, messing things up for me."

I shook my head, the only way I could tell him I wasn't messing things up, since my voice wouldn't work. Every nerve in my body was on fire.

Carter cowered by the bar with one of Pearson's goons. The one who'd grabbed me stood by the door. I wasn't going anywhere. And Carter wouldn't be any use.

And didn't Pearson get the memo that Cat—well, God—was bringing an end to crime?

The fire flaring through me was anger, and it reached a boil. I felt power surge through me. *Grace is empowerment. Remember that, Gracie.* My voice came out strong. "You sick old man, you ruined my life, and you're saying I'm messing things up for *you*? I gave up my life to work for you. Supposedly to serve my country. But I was serving you and your whims. And all these years later, I'm only starting to recover. To know who I really am. To be myself. To earn a decent living. To have a real life."

Pearson sniggered as he drew a Glock from under his jacket. "This is going to be a pleasure."

I was rage on autopilot, ignoring his weapon. "You miserable excuse for a human being! How the heck am I supposed to forgive you? Huh? How? But I have to if I'm ever gonna have a life. You mean, sick—"

"You're not going to have a life." Pearson's smirk suddenly turned to shock, and his face froze white in terror.

The goon at the bar had the same expression. Carter stared at the ceiling above me, his eyes popping, his mouth hanging open. Fiery pins and needles engulfed me—the strange sense of power I'd felt that day by the water with Cat. I could handle these thugs.

I lunged at Pearson and pushed him with all my might. The gun went off, and he struck his head on the side of a glass table as he fell backward. I heard the bullet whiz past me as the momentum landed me on my knees. Pearson hit the floor out cold.

In that instant, Carter cracked a seltzer bottle over the goon's head. I turned to see the other guy slumped in front of the door, downed by the bullet from Pearson's gun. I ran to grab my bag, then Carter.

But he caught me by the arm. "This way! Service elevator."

I rifled through my bag for my Glock and my phone as we ran. I came up with the weapon.

In no time we were in the garage, and Carter pointed me to his Bentley.

"Yeah, they'll never find us in this." I jumped in as our assailants' bullets ricocheted off the door and huddled between the seat and the dashboard.

Carter took off like a bat out of hell. When we made it out of the garage and down the street, I crawled up into the seat. "We need to ditch this thing, Carter." I noticed a bullet hole through the windshield and wondered how he was still driving. "Are you okay?"

I put the gun back in my bag and found the phone.

"We can catch a train down here," he said. The car came to a screeching halt, and we both bolted for the subway. I only vaguely wondered how much money he was leaving on the street in the form of a shining new Bentley.

Within an hour Carter and I arrived at my old apartment building in Brooklyn. I'd managed to text Keith, and he was on the way. Darkness was falling as we let ourselves into the basement. The dim light of a single bulb beckoned at the far end of the space. Feeling around in my bag, I found my weapon and the small flashlight I'd attached to my key chain to help light the way. We passed rows of storage compartments, and Carter tested each wire gate. The door to my old storage bin was hanging open.

I motioned Carter inside. "We can stay here. I'll get that light." I headed toward the bulb hanging from a beam.

Carter pulled at my sleeve. "Leave it on. There might be rodents."

I rolled my eyes. "Thanks for reminding me. Now I've got the creeps." No way could I turn the light off now.

We huddled on the floor in my old storage bin with some sports equipment and a ratty looking chair. I tried to focus in the direction of the basement door, but Carter's continuous palm slapping routine distracted me.

"Do you really need to do that?"

He stopped short. "Sorry."

In that moment, I realized he wasn't so bad. With his sandy-colored hair all disheveled, he looked like an overgrown kid in spite of his fifty-something years. He'd been pretty brave to get me out of that building, despite the gunfire. I was the one who ducked under the dashboard. "It's okay. I'm sorry I've been so … unforgiving. I don't want to be bitter. So I'm making amends over that. Over everything."

He grinned a little. "Okay. Thanks."

I noticed a hole in his shirt pocket and pointed to his chest. "Are you okay? Did that bullet get you?"

"Huh." Carter stuck his finger through the hole, then pulled out a small hardcover book. He held it up so I could see a bullet wedged inside. He balanced the book on his knee and stared at it. "The Holy Bible." Then he cried like a baby.

When Keith found us, I smiled up at him. "You're a sight for sore eyes."

He shook his head. "Leave it to you to find trouble." He turned to Carter, still heaving tears. "Are you okay?"

Carter remained mesmerized by the bullet in his Bible.

I shrugged my shoulders. "I've been trying to comfort him with words—didn't dare offer a hug. Carter would've taken that as a marriage proposal."

Keith let out a laugh and slid down to take a seat against the wall. "David and Nathan are on the way with reinforcements. We sit tight for now."

My jaw dropped. "We're okay, Keith. We don't need them to come all this way. We can just head back to Maine. They've got too much to do with the wedding. And I don't want to mess up David's holiday with his family."

Keith's smile lit up the dark space. My insides twisted up, remembering David's admonishment last summer that I was interfering with his "holiday."

"Why can't they just say, vacation?"

Keith answered with a guffaw.

I asked the terrifying question. "They're not going after Pearson, are they?"

"I don't think David Lambrecht's gonna let Pearson get away with this, do you?"

My mouth was dry as the desert. "I guess not."

I watched Carter slowly pry apart the pages of his Bible around the bullet. Keith shone a penlight on it, to try and help the poor sniveling guy.

Carter grabbed the light from him. "Psalm 91:11. That's where it stopped." Visibly shaking, Carter wiped his face with his shirtsleeve, then read aloud. "For he will order his angels to protect you wherever you go."

He inhaled tears and looked up at me deadly serious. "Did you see the angel behind you?"

"What?"

I could see him gulp. "It had to be ten feet tall. We all saw it. Right behind you."

"An angel?"

"Yeah." He broke down crying again.

Keith and I looked at each other. I remembered the power I'd felt and the surge when I pushed Pearson. *Grace is empowerment. Remember that, Gracie.* I remembered the terror on their faces. *I need to call Cat.*

With the sound of the basement door opening and closing, I heard Nate. "Gracie!"

I burst into tears and ran to him. His face was full of pain and concern, his voice was full of relief. "Thank God you're okay." He lifted me into his arms, squeezing me. I heard a rumbling sound in his chest. But he couldn't say another word.

When we finally got over our emotion, Nate and Roger accompanied us to Cisco's private plane. Carter had quickly agreed to return to Maine with us and stay until things were settled. We weren't told exactly what "settled" meant. But since David was not on the scene, I had a feeling he was in the process of settling things.

When Carter started telling Nate about the angel that saved us, I excused myself and took my time in the restroom freshening up. My knees were still knocking when I returned to my seat.

Nate dropped into the chair beside me. His face was unreadable. "I heard the demons were removed from Brooke, Lewis & Wynn sometime ago."

I bit my lip, unsure of how to take that. Was he joking? Or was he serious? "Uh … yeah. Cat did it, I hear."

Nate stroked his chin. "And the angel?"

"Um … seems like a new development. I thought I'd ask Cat."

"Good idea." It looked like the light bulb went on. "But it makes sense you'd have angels now, right?"

I nodded tentatively. "Right."

David boarded the plane with his cohort, Cisco's brother, Eduardo Clemente, the two of them dressed in menacing black. The pilot headed to the cockpit, and we were preparing to depart.

David stopped to address us. "Pearson won't be bothering you again. I don't know what you did, Lena, but you put the fear of God into him. Thank you."

"Uh … you're welcome." I spent most of the flight to Maine staring out the window into the darkness, searching for my angel.

~ *Nathan* ~

Arriving in Maine, I was wide awake in spite of all the stress and activity of the day. After settling Carter in a spare room, checking in with my security team, and ensuring Lena and her family were safe, I went to bed and stared at the ceiling. It was well before sunrise when I gave up tossing and turning and headed downstairs for coffee.

On my way down the hall, I noticed the door to the art studio was open, and a light was on. I stopped in the doorway. David slouched against the wall, staring at a large canvas on the easel in front of him. He glanced up, his lip curving slightly, recognizing my presence.

"Is everything all right?"

He stood straight and motioned me into the room.

"Your wife's been painting again?" I hadn't meant to let that sarcastic tone show in my voice.

He smirked. "She has."

I faced the canvas and the pit of my stomach burned. "Angels." There had to be a couple dozen of them surrounding the stage at that outdoor concert in California. I looked up at him. "You saw them?"

He shook his head. "No." He took a seat in the artist's chair, and I heard him exhale a loud breath. "Debbie saw them. Cat saw them. No one else that I know of—other than Carter Lewis and probably Pearson."

I wiped my eyes. "Did they see them again? I mean, at the other concerts?"

"Each and every one. Cat says they do God's bidding. I suppose they were there for protection. I don't know. Either that or they like the music."

I chuckled. "Well, maybe they got sick of harp music."

He let out half a laugh. "I hope that's all it is."

"Yesterday—Pearson had to have seen the angel Carter saw."

"It explains his behavior. He was terrified. And it wasn't just the concussion." David put his head in his hands. He looked as tired as I felt.

"I know it's probably not my business, but I thought you were done with Pearson. He's in with the mob, and it sounds like he's still holding some grudge against you. And Lena."

David sat up. "As long as he's alive, he'll be a thorn in my side. He gets greedier by the day. He was furious that Lena shortened Joey B's career. Pearson had found a way to tap into him. A finger in many pies. So he decided to keep Lena from doing any more harm to his bank account."

I looked him in the eye. "I don't know much of who or what Pearson was involved with. The mob is dangerous enough. Aside from that, he had the personnel to carry out a covert attack on Annie's property. What does he want?"

"He wanted to impress his business partner and get his revenge on us. Pearson was a brilliant man who's losing his mind. At this point, it seems his goals are rather simple. Get money and kill his enemies."

"What are you going to do?"

"Just keep an eye on him, as best we can. The President wants him alive."

TWENTY

~ *Nathan* ~

When I finally poured that cup of coffee, I headed outside and down the back lawn to the hedge overlooking the beach. The tide was out, and Lena sat in the middle of the sand facing the first light of day. As I watched her watching the sunrise, I pondered the situation with Pearson.

Why would David and his crew be involved in getting New York mobsters in the first place? Lena's question to me, the night Amanda James interviewed the victims of our "Danish tourists," came to mind. It was obvious David knew more than the FBI when it came to Joey B. And it was obvious that David was privy to information from the President of the United States. No doubt there was a supernatural connection through Cat, as well.

I surmised David had to have known Pearson was involved with the mob early on and was charged by the President with keeping him under control. It sounded as though David would've happily taken him out with a word from the President. I decided I really didn't need to know more than that. It was David's problem. And I hoped it would stay that way.

I descended the stone staircase and ambled over to Lena. "Morning."

She turned. "Hi, Nate. Get any sleep?"

"Not much." I sat in the sand. "You?"

"Not much. Pretty sunrise, though."

"Yeah." I offered her my cup.

"I just need a sip." She took some and handed it back. "What kept you awake?"

"Angels. Demons. I don't know."

"Yeah. Carter told us the psalm says the angels protect us wherever we go. That's kind of a relief, considering I'm working for David now."

I almost swallowed the coffee the wrong way, then finally cleared my throat. "When were you planning on telling me?"

She made a face. "Uh … well, Nate, I really didn't know how to tell you. And I'm really not sure it's a great idea. And after this episode with Pearson, I'm really not sure I have a choice. I think David was trying to tell me that, but I wasn't totally buying it."

She took my coffee cup and another swig, then handed it back. "I'm supposed to keep things under control at The Golden Bowl. Just doing the job Buck hired me for, but David is adding on some salary and a title to keep me out of prison. He told the authorities I was working for him on that Joey B thing. Otherwise, I'd have the feds after me. I don't want to go to prison, Nate. For sure I'd be bitter about that, and I don't ever want to be bitter again. Remember I told you?"

I don't know why, but I couldn't help a smile. I swiped it away with the back of my hand. "Gracie, what am I going to do with you?"

The sunlight caught a glint in her eye when she looked up at me. "What?"

I shoved the cup into the sand and took her into my arms. "I'm going to marry you, Gracie. If you'll have me."

"I will, Nate, if we do it right this time."

"We will."

~ *Lena* ~

I was flabbergasted that my voice was so calm while my heart pounded like a drum. *Nate wants me back.* When we started getting catcalls from our security team standing on the cliff above us, I pulled away from Nate's insistent lips. "Uh … we have an audience, in case you didn't notice."

He pulled me back. "Ignore them. They'll go away."

"I don't think so." The whistles and jeers grew louder. "See?"

Nate placed me purposefully in the sand, then stood up. I watched the big jerks scatter. "You show 'em, Nate."

"Yeah." He smiled down at me. "Let's go."

I reached up, he grabbed my hand, and I was on my feet. We headed down the beach. My heart was still going a mile a minute, so I was quiet. I decided a little silence was okay. Today was a milestone, and contemplation would be in order. I looked to the horizon. *Looks like God's got this one.* "Love is what's important."

Nate's voice startled me. "You're right. You woke me up to that fact. I guess I always thought being right was most important. I was wrong."

I wished that walk could have gone on forever, but Nate was soon called to work. Today was the big day for Billy and Lisa. As we walked up the stairs and onto the lawn, I could see the huge white tent was at the ready and most everything was set up. Tables were done in white and blue, with gorgeous summer flowers everywhere. Now that I was alert enough to notice, the scent of the flowers, the landscaping, and the decorations made it look like a fairyland. Half the town of Marberry would be there today.

Lisa Quinn stood in the middle of it, taking pictures of every little thing, chatting with her matron of honor, Annie. I took a seat in an Adirondack chair and observed them, emotion welling up from somewhere deep inside all the way up to my eyeballs.

As I'd crept out of my apartment early this morning, a security guard had presented me with an envelope. I took it out of my beach bag. It was a handwritten note on Lisa's formal wedding invitation, and I read it again. *Lena, I don't know if you got the invitation I mailed. It went to your hotel in New York, but I wasn't sure you got it. Nathan said you'd be coming to our wedding, but I want to be sure you know how much Billy and I are looking forward to seeing you there. Thanks for celebrating the best day of my life with me. Lisa*

The sea breeze carried the most gorgeous floral fragrance, and it reminded me of my Fourth of July with Nate. I broke down bawling. Lisa and I were having the best day of our lives. I covered my face with my hands so no one would notice me.

"Lena, are you okay?"

I slipped my hand down from one eye only enough to see Lisa take a seat beside me. She put her hand on my arm. "Are you okay?"

I wiped my face with the sleeve of my sweatshirt and picked up the invitation that had fallen on the grass. I held it up to her then put it in my bag. My voice croaked. "Thanks for inviting me—and for trying so hard to track me down and make sure I knew. It was so sweet of you. And I was such a jerk—I treated you so badly when I didn't even know you."

I rubbed my face again, then looked her in the eye. "I was lashing out at Annie and Nate and The Golden Bowl for no good reason. I wanted revenge, and I didn't care who I hurt. And I hurt you. For no reason at all. I put you through all kinds of aggravation and probably fear that you'd lose your job over it. I'm so sorry, Lisa."

I found a tissue in my bag and sopped up more tears. "And you never said a mean word to me. If I were you, I'd have dumped dirty dishwater over my head a long time ago. But you invited me to your wedding."

She looked a little baffled, sitting there patting my arm. She must have thought I was a lunatic. I could feel another rush of tears getting ready to go. "I'm sorry."

"It's okay." She gripped my sleeve. "Most of my life, I acted like a jerk. I'd be first in line to get revenge on people … to talk bad about them if they looked at me sideways."

"Really?"

"Yeah. But Annie gave me this dishwashing job at The Golden Bowl, and things started going better. Me and Rosie … Rosie and *I* had a new house and enough money … and I met Billy. He wants to marry me and adopt Rosie. I can't even believe it, and it's my wedding day."

"That's sweet."

"Yeah. I was a nobody … a single mom with nothing. Now I'm gonna be a nurse—I'm in *college*. I can't believe it. Rosie is awesome. And Billy Foster wants me to be his *wife*. I feel like I should pinch myself."

"I'm so happy for you, Lisa." I inhaled more water. "How did you turn things around?"

"It wasn't me. I applied for a dishwashing job and pulled a prayer out of the golden bowl. Annie says God did the rest. She says prayer and gratitude are what did it. I'm grateful every day now. I don't sweat small stuff any more … Even big stuff. I know who to take it to."

"Wow. I guess that's a good way to live. Being grateful. And I'm thankful to have you as a friend, Lisa. That must have been some prayer you pulled out of the bowl."

"I'll never forget it. It said, 'I hope you have better luck with this than me.' Then I found a gigantic diamond ring inside of the paper. It was worth a fortune, and that's how me and Rosie … Rosie and *I* got our start to our new life."

I stopped dead. I don't think I took a breath for a minute or more. My face dried in the sea breeze. Then I burst into the most gleeful laughter I'd ever experienced. When I could breathe again, I giggled into her quizzical, but amused, face. "Cat says God does have a sense of humor." I cracked up again.

Later that day, I watched Annie's dad, Pastor Mike Auclair, marry Lisa Quinn and Billy Foster. Annie was the matron of honor, and Nate was the best man. The ceremony was beautiful, and Paulo graced the attendees with a heartfelt song he and Cat wrote for the occasion. The woman beside me whispered that the proceeds from the song would pay for little Rosie's college. Since the woman was Lisa's best friend and babysitter, Peg, I presumed it was correct information. That would definitely be something the Clementes would do.

As the bride and groom led everyone to the receiving line, Peg bent my ear. To be honest, I thought Peg was Lisa's grandmother. But she quickly informed me that they'd been friends for years, ever since Lisa was born to alcoholic parents in the trailer park where Peg lived. Apparently, Peg drank a bit too much, too. But she kicked the habit, and ever since she moved to Marberry with Lisa, they'd both found God and happiness. *Chalk another one up for Annie and The Golden Bowl.*

It looked to be a long wait on line, but Peg was kind of a fascinating woman. Underneath her fragile, skeletal frame, I could tell there was a courageous and loyal heart. I took off my heels and wiggled my toes in the cool grass. "Where are Lisa's parents?"

Peg's wrinkled face was suddenly downcast. "They moved to Florida. Didn't want anything to do with Lisa and Rosie when they needed them most. Lisa was hardly squeakin' by before she got the job at The Golden Bowl. They didn't care—said goodbye one day and drove off. One o' their drinkin' buddies told us they ended up in Florida somewhere."

Don't blame us for the sins of our parents. Hurry up and help us; we're at the end of our rope. You're famous for helping; God, give us a break. "I guess God gave Lisa and Rosie a break."

Peg smiled up at the sky. "Ay-uh. He sure did."

~ *Nathan* ~

After a brief dance with Annie, Buck was there to take her into his arms. I was free to enjoy the party. I found Gracie chatting with Peg and offered my hand. "May I have this dance?"

She sprung from the chair into my arms. "You can have every dance, sir."

I don't think I ever saw her look more radiant or more relaxed. We left the dance floor when dinner was served.

"Nate, I need to ask you a question." She tugged me in the direction of the water. We stopped at the top of the stairs as many of the guests came up from the beach.

I did a double take, noticing Carter Lewis wading into the ocean, decked out in his expensive suit. I wondered if I'd need to be diving in after him shortly. But I turned back to Gracie. "Do we need privacy for this question?"

Her expression was ardent. "Nate, do you believe God works in and through you? Like ... always?"

"This is probably not the time for this conversation, but Cat says yes, so it's probably true." I might as well admit it. I glanced back at Carter, now standing in the surf, staring up at the sky. "After what I've seen since I started this job, I have to say yes."

She giggled up at me. "Cat says God can use anything."

"I don't doubt it."

Sudden emotion appeared in her eyes. "Nate, when you asked me to marry you, I thought I was gonna have a heart attack I was so ecstatic. When we were walking on the beach afterwards, one niggling thought in the back of my mind wouldn't leave me alone. So I said a little prayer about it, and I left it in God's hands. I told myself I wouldn't worry about it, because God is taking care of it."

She wiped something on her cheek. "Only hours later ... today ... I realized God solved the whole thing. And in a way that helped people who needed it. In the best possible way, that probably no one would think of."

I was confused, but it sounded like she was happy about something. I glanced back to see Carter was speaking to one of my team. In the instant of gratitude that I wouldn't need to take that dip into the ocean, compassion for Carter Lewis filled me. The guy may have been a self-centered, wealthy businessman, but he was alone in the world. Who would've truly cared if he walked into the Atlantic and didn't come out? I needed to let that grudge go.

I turned back to try and understand Gracie.

Her eyes were wide. "Nate! You threw my ring into the golden bowl. Lisa found it, and it helped her and her baby start a new life."

A lump filled my throat. "I'm sorry, Gracie. I—"

"It's okay. I was worried that you'd want me to wear that ring again. God showed me that I wouldn't have to. I mean it's a symbol of my old life to me. I don't care if I have an engagement ring now. I have a new life with you. Brand new. That's what matters. And now I know the ring was put to good use."

Relief came over me. I looked down into deep chocolate eyes that were windows to a most beautiful soul. "I didn't know how I was going to tell you that the ring was gone. It's been on my mind a lot lately. But give me time … we'll find just the right one."

"I have just the right one."

That night I sat by my open window, comfortable in my cushioned chair, a bottle of beer in my hand. My mind was too busy to go to bed.

Don't blame us for the sins of our parents. Hurry up and help us; we're at the end of our rope. You're famous for helping; God, give us a break. Rolling that verse around in my head with childhood memories, I realized my parents had shaped my life more than I'd ever imagined. I was expert at burying everything. Seeing my part in it now, I knew I'd need to forgive myself, as well as my parents. That wouldn't be easy.

A sudden gust of wind swept through my window and woke me up. Gracie's words came to me. *Love is what's important.*

I decided I'd give all of it over to God.

Me, my parents, my ex-wives, Gracie, Carter Lewis, David … we were all in his capable hands. All I'd need to do: choose to forgive them. I made that choice.

A knock at the door took me out of my contemplation. David walked in, and we had a long conversation over a beer. I could almost see Cat smiling at us. She would have said we were Spirit led.

~ *Lena* ~

That night I sat in bed staring out my window. One bright star kept my attention. I thought it must be cousin Lena's star. Little Lena in her yellow sun suit, her huge love pendant over her heart, peddled in the endless heavens. It was time to let her go. It was time to forgive and move on. Time to let Lena be Lena and Gracie be Gracie.

Cat was so right. Nothing is impossible with God. Even a diamond ring that was once so important to me was transformed into help for a destitute single mother. A new life for her and a new life for me.

I knew Nate's mother had given him that ring. It was her engagement ring that she couldn't bear to wear. Her husband had brought her so much pain. It was gorgeous and worth a lot of money.

But I also knew that Nate didn't want his parents at our wedding because they'd *contaminate* it. The way he'd used that word still made me shudder years later. I didn't want that ring to contaminate our future. I wanted our new life to be a fresh start in every way.

I took out my notebook and reviewed my first entry: *Love is what is important.* Then the verse Cat discussed with me: *My grace is enough; it's all you need. My strength comes into its own in your weakness.*

Yeah, I lived that one yesterday. I was weak, and God was strong. I wished I'd been able to talk to Cat about the angel at the wedding today. But there wasn't a minute when she wasn't mobbed with people who only wanted to be associated with her. She and her family took that all in stride. They were all so gracious and happy to help a self-described "nobody" live the life of her dreams.

And until recently, I was a nobody, too. I wasn't lying when I told Cat I had a reject stamp on my forehead. I wasn't much good at being Lena, and I wasn't allowed to be Gracie.

I scanned down the page. *My grace is enough. Capitalize the G. My Grace is enough. You are enough. Just as you are. Weak and broken. God meets you right where you are. God is all you need.*

I took out a pen and re-wrote Cat's words: *Grace with a capital G.* "I'm God's Grace." Today I knew in my heart, in my soul, that God is real. God is interested in *me.*

I spoke to the star outside my window. "God loves me—Gracie." He loved me from the start. So I'd tell Nate and then everyone else. *From now on, I'll be Gracie.* The name no one could ever say— Gracie. I'd have the courage to say it now.

I pictured myself wearing a simple white dress, my groom at my side. *Gracie Goodwin Cavelieri Rhodes. . . has a nice ring to it.* The star twinkled back at me.

I flipped the pages and my eyes rested on this: *And what does the Lord require of you? To act justly and to love mercy and to walk humbly with your God.*

If God could do all this for me—give me my life back—I could do my best to live this way. I'd trust that He'd give me a life worth living.

The following Monday I was at my desk at The Golden Bowl. Buck and everyone else was spooked enough by Pearson's antics in New York, so I was told I could wrap up the food prep facility expansion plans from the comfort of my office.

Suddenly, the people I needed surfaced from their vacations and holidays. Conference calls became doable. Things got done. Finally, Dominguez Construction had the go-ahead to put people to work at the site in Washington County.

It was Tuesday evening when I had all the i's dotted and t's crossed. Within minutes of my celebratory dance around the office, Nate knocked and walked in. "Cookout on the beach tonight. Are you in the mood for burgers?"

"Sure. Sounds good."

He took me in his arms, and we had a leisurely kiss. "Let's get out of here, Nate. I've been stuck in the office for two solid days. How about a walk on the beach?"

There was a funny quirk to his grin. "I've got just the spot."

I just about had time to gather my bag and sweater before he whisked me out of the building and to his SUV. This was a man on a mission.

"What's goin' on? You discovered a new place?"

He skillfully maneuvered around the summer crowds in the parking lots and on the streets of Marberry. Not a word out of him, just that funny grin. We sped by the entrance to Annie's driveway.

"Whoa, Nate! Where're we going?"

All of a sudden we careened onto a tiny dirt path you had to know was a road. As we bumped along, tree branches and brush swiped the vehicle. We came to a stop in a clearing overlooking the blue Atlantic. He jumped out and came around to help me out.

"This is a great place! Where are we?"

His hand to my back, he guided me to the edge of the bluff. Wind whistled around us, reminding me of the day I met Holy Spirit on the rocks near Washington Gardens.

"It's so beautiful."

"It's ours—if we want it." His smile told me he definitely wanted it.

But I wasn't sure what "it" was. "Huh?"

"It's a wedding present from Annie and her family. Raphael is gonna build us a house here. He's already got a crew at the food prep facility. They can come here when they're done."

I squinted up at him. "The land?"

"Yup. From Annie and her sister and David … they own the land here. And the house is a gift from the entire family."

"You're kidding."

"No kidding."

I sat on the sandy ground, unconcerned about my good suit. Nate took a seat beside me. I couldn't fathom it. I went from scamming these people to being a member of the family. Too many thoughts and questions flew around in my head. "I didn't think Dominguez Construction did residential buildings."

Nate laughed. "They do whatever Raphael tells them to do. His name is on the business."

I started to giggle. "So how did the family find out about our marriage plans?"

"That kiss on the beach the other morning was their clue."

I shook my head. "I knew it, Nate. Those catcalls. They knew something was up."

Nate's marriage proposal was serious now. We were talking houses. Giggles turned to tears of joy. "It's really going to happen? I'll be Gracie Goodwin Cavelieri Rhodes."

He drew me close in a sideways hug. "Gracie Goodwin Cavelieri Rhodes … hmm … It has a certain ring to it."

We cuddled there awhile, silently with our own thoughts. The sound of the waves lulled me into contentment.

"One thing, Gracie." Nate's baritone refocused my attention on his serious face.

"What?"

"We can't do this unless we promise to be honest with each other. I know it's hard, but we have to. No matter what."

My head rested against his arm, and my gaze returned to the horizon. I wondered if we were capable of that.

"Gracie?"

A warm wind rustled my hair and swirled around us. *Holy Spirit?*

"I understand we're both working for Lambrecht now, and in different capacities. I know it can make things difficult … awkward," he said.

I lifted my free hand into the air and the wind twirled in the palm of my hand. *He has showed you, O man, what is good. And what does the Lord require of you? To act justly and to love mercy and to walk humbly with your God. Micah 6:8* It was Holy Spirit. I knew it deep down inside.

"Gracie?"

Gratitude bubbled up. "We can do it, Nate. Like Cat said, we'll have God with us this time around. We'll put each other first. Not that we won't do a good job for our employers, but our marriage has to come first."

"Right."

Later on that evening we joined the crowd of family on the beach for a cookout. After hamburgers and conversation, Nate deemed it the right time to formally announce our engagement. There were cheers all around, and then we accepted their offer of a new home on the northern end of Annie's property. We thanked each of them for their thoughtful generosity.

I was so emotional by then, I hugged them all. Debbie was crying harder than I was. When I looked up at her husband, I blurted, "On my wedding day, I'm going to be Gracie Goodwin Cavelieri Rhodes."

He didn't know what to make of me. Nate stepped in to explain how I became Grace.

TWENTY-ONE

~ Gracie ~

It was almost impossible to catch David alone, so when I heard it was girls' day out again, I thought I'd have a shot. I found David and Eduardo on the beach with their male children. I bent over the rail on the bottom step of the stone staircase that led to the sand, hesitant to walk out to them in my good suit. And it'd be hard enough to talk to David about my request, never mind the two of them.

David noticed me and headed over. Despite the T-shirt and baggy old khaki shorts, he had a presence about him that took my breath away. I think he had that impact on most people—a strange mix of stark fear and adoration.

I spoke over the sound of the surf before he could say a word or I could lose my nerve. "David, I need to see Joey B. Can you arrange it?"

He removed his sunglasses. "I don't suppose Cat has anything to do with that."

"Uh … well, yeah. I need to forgive the guy, so I can start to get him off my resentments list and out of my head and move on. I'm not sure how I can do that, but I at least need to give him a good talking to. I need to face him."

"Like you faced Pearson?"

"Yeah. But I promise not to knock him out."

He wiped the grin off his face. "Good."

"I can't promise what my new angel is gonna do, though."

He smirked. "I suppose not."

"So you'll arrange it?"

"All right." He glanced back at the kids rollicking in the water with Eduardo, then lifted a brow in my direction. "Just how long is your resentments list?"

An audible groan percolated from the depths of my stomach, and I gripped the railing tight. "Uh … kind of long." The persistent breeze flopped my hair into my face, and I held it back. "Uh … so Joey B is at the top right now, but you're on there." I couldn't believe I said that, but there it was. I looked down at the sand. "Like, right below him."

"Lena." There was empathy in his voice.

I looked up at him. His eyes were empathetic too, and I almost twisted off the stone into the sand. But I remained standing.

He hesitated, and I knew he wanted to correct himself. "Grace … Gracie … I do owe you an apology. It was a long time ago, but it still needs to be said. I was very wrong. I caused you more pain than I ever realized or intended. I thought only of myself. Now I understand the consequences of my actions, and I regret causing you such pain. I should have had the courage to speak to you about it last summer, but I didn't. So please accept my deepest apology now." That smirk was nowhere in sight. He was serious.

I managed to look him straight in the eye. "I accept your apology." Hair flew in my face again. "And I'm sorry for my part in it, too."

Something in me couldn't leave well enough alone. I blurted it out. "So if I'm working for you now, why not tell me about Joey B sending his goons to Annie's gate?"

His smirk was back. "I didn't want to add to your worries. Pearson was responsible for that attack. He was working with Joey B."

My response was an unladylike barrage of coarse language that only seemed to amuse him.

When I paused to take a breath, he said, "I didn't think Pearson wanted you dead so bad."

"Well, you insisted Keith go to New York with me. I didn't think I'd need a bodyguard."

"Can't be too careful."

"Yeah. Thanks." I fought the wind, stroking more hair out of my face. It started to sink in. *I'm part of the family here.* Aside from the shock about Pearson, it was a good feeling. "So I hope you know you can trust me. You can keep me in the loop. I'm grateful for everything you've done for me and my family. You didn't owe me anything. You could've turned me over to the feds a long time ago."

"That wouldn't have done either one of us any good. I'm grateful for your help with The Golden Bowl, keeping an eye on things." He nodded. "When do you want to go to New York?"

~ *Nathan* ~

As I returned from a meeting at the food prep facility, I took a turn onto the dirt road that would become our new driveway. Blue sky and water ahead drew me into the property. I walked the perimeter that had been staked out by the surveyors just this morning. Things were moving quickly.

Dominguez Construction was efficient and precise. Gracie and I would own a full acre of prime real estate atop a rugged granite cliff with magnificent views of the Atlantic.

It was almost surreal how this had all unfolded. I could understand why Gracie was hesitant to move too quickly. We both probably needed to take more time "to work on ourselves," as she put it. The sense of joy that built as I paced began to diminish with an old fear that began to gnaw.

The sound of an engine caught my attention, and I looked over to see an SUV pulling alongside mine. Cat and her bodyguards exited the vehicle. I had to wonder how she managed such perfect timing. She was almost like a genie in a bottle.

She dropped her backpack in the grass and approached me. "This is a gorgeous view, isn't it?" Her enthusiasm made me smile.

"The best," I said.

"Let's walk the land and bless it. Raphael said they'd be starting work this week."

"Uh … yeah." I wondered what was involved in blessing the land, but I supposed it couldn't hurt.

Cat uttered a soft prayer to start, but was mostly silent as we walked the periphery of the lot. Then she led me onto a rocky ledge where we took a seat. She smiled up at me. "You'll make a beautiful home here."

I exhaled a sigh of relief. "Thanks, Cat. That makes me feel better."

"Why are you anxious?"

Since I couldn't put my finger on that, I came out with a flip reply. "Uh … well, I was kind of wondering if an angel might show up. Not sure what I'd do if that happened."

She made a funny little face, like she goofed.

"What?"

"Oh, you have an army of angels here … all around the boundaries of your property. I'd say they mean business."

I almost slid off the rock. "What?"

She let out a little giggle.

"Like … like the angels on the stage with you?" I didn't intend to let that slip, but she obviously knew I'd seen Debbie's artwork.

"Angels are everywhere, Nathan, doing God's bidding. You and Gracie are precious children of God. The Precious Blood protects you. The enemy has no place on your property." She pushed back windswept hair. "Or in your marriage."

She was a mind-reader all right. I looked her straight in the eye. "Are you saying Gracie and I are fit to be married? To each other?"

"I can't think of a finer couple. Like your home, which will be built on solid rock, so shall your marriage be."

I liked the sound of that, but felt the need to push. "You think we can really get beyond the mess of our past?"

I swear her eyes sparkled, and then a gust of wind struck the side of my head. The shock knocked the wind out of me. I gripped the edge of the stone. "Okay, I get it. Holy Spirit promises to lead us into all truth."

"See? You did learn something last summer."

~ *Gracie* ~

It was kind of nice being included in this huge extended family. I was beginning to feel like a rock star myself. Since Nate's proposal, I was walking on air. Here we were discussing details of our new home, and I could see that could easily become overwhelming.

I'd told Nate I needed a little more time to work on myself. He respected that, and said he'd been doing the same. He'd already sat down for coffee with Carter Lewis and forgiven the guy. Carter congratulated him on our marriage plans, and they talked about the process of making amends. Then Nate wrote a letter to his dead mother, and another to his estranged father, and showed them to me before burning the first and mailing the second. I told him Cat would be proud.

I think we both freaked a little over the whole honesty thing he'd brought up. Neither one of us had a good track record with that. Especially me. I guess I was a little worried he'd think it'd be too easy for me to revert to my old self.

I was helping Annie by setting the table for another huge dinner, unconsciously precisely arranging each place setting. If I could only get myself to take care of my unfinished business with Joey B, maybe I'd feel better about setting a wedding date. I really didn't want to dredge it all up with Nate. I wanted my past in the past. But he was going to be my husband, so he really should know. But did he have to know now?

The clinking of silverware roused me from my daze. Debbie took a fistful and began laying it out.

David came around the table to me. "Cisco is going to New York tomorrow. I can arrange your appointment if you'd like to do it then."

My insides twinged in protest. "Uh … sure. Tomorrow. What time?"

"We leave here at seven."

"Okay." My voice was croaking again.

David gave his wife a quick kiss and left. Her pink blush told me she was as crazy about him as he was about her. She really was a sweet girl. It was hard to believe she had six kids. It was impossible to not like her. She was just as nice as Annie, quiet and always polite. We were done with the table in no time.

She took me by the hand. "I have something for you to take with you. I left it in the studio."

We went upstairs to her art studio, and I gasped at the room full of paintings. "Wow! Angels." They were everywhere around the stages of all the band's concert venues.

She had a soft little giggle, much like Cat's. "David says when I start a new theme I go crazy." She took a postcard from a drawer and handed it to me. "I want you to know you're never alone. I'm sure Cat told you. God is always with you. And I think that's your guardian angel."

My jaw was frozen open.

"I wanted you to have that as a reminder for tomorrow so you won't be scared."

"Thank you." I sat in the window seat and stared at the tiny painting. Flames blazed at the back of the fearsome angel. In spite of that, it gave me a strangely comforting feeling. "Now … I know what my angel looks like. I won't be afraid. Cat says that fear isn't from God anyway. I'll always remember that now."

"Yes." She smiled a shy smile.

For some reason, I flipped the small canvas over, and my eyes popped in surprise. *God help me.* The prayer I'd first put in the golden bowl, and the date, was printed in ink on the back. "How did you know?"

She shrugged. "I just knew it was important."

All I could do was shake my head.

"I have one for Carter, too. David said he decided to stay in Maine for a while. He's falling in love with a woman in his Step group."

"Why am I not surprised?" I burst into laughter, and Debbie did, too.

That kind of broke the ice between the two of us. Not that there was any coldness—we just didn't really know each other. And with my history with her husband, I didn't think I should try and befriend her.

Debbie took a seat in a comfy chair in front of me. Her face went pink, a lot like Annie did when she was emotional. "Sometimes I have strange dreams. Lately, you've been in my dreams. I'm glad you're calling yourself Gracie now. You're Gracie in my dreams."

A lump started in my throat. "Oh."

"Did you lose your brother in a fire?"

She had to have been talking to Cat—or David—about me. "Uh ... yeah. Long time ago."

Her hands were shaking in her lap. I couldn't help but stare. "Are you okay?"

"Yes ... I'm sorry. The dreams wouldn't stop, and I didn't want to ask Cat or Annie and put them in an awkward position. I wouldn't want to gossip." She stared at her lap. "I'm so sorry for you. I hope this angel helps you." She started to cry. "I think it must have been Joey the mobster—he started the fire."

I knelt in front of her. "That's right ... But don't cry. It was a long time ago."

"David lost his brother, too. In a plane crash. There was a fire, too. Lately, I keep having these dreams. I realized that you need to know. God can heal the pain. You're not alone in your pain, Gracie. That's when I painted the angel for you."

Cat wasn't the only prophet in this family. I fell back on my rear end. "Oh." *My grace is enough; it's all you need. My strength comes into its own in your weakness.*

Debbie's tears wouldn't stop and mine started. My voice cracked and croaked. "I'm not alone anymore, Debbie. I know that now. I'm God's Gracie ... and I have you and Cat alongside me now ... and my angel, too. Thank you for ... for reaching out to me. I'm so grateful."

The next morning I drove to The Golden Bowl to drop a prayer in the bowl before leaving for New York. I'd scribbled it on one of Mom's construction paper tickets after writing it in my journal over and over again, like a kid with a penmanship assignment. *Thank you, God! Your Grace is sufficient.* It was burned in my mind along with my image of the angel. I knew I wouldn't be alone to face Joey B.

In fact, I wasn't alone. David arranged for us to meet in an interrogation room, and he remained by the door along with two other guards as I took a seat across the table from Joey B, who was in shackles. His hair was unkempt and his expression defiant.

We were both silent, and fury built behind my eyes as I stared him in the face. My thoughts were all over the place. Everything from how dare he look such a mess when I took pains to be impeccably groomed and dressed for the occasion, to visions of cousin Lena in her yellow sun suit peddling into the flames ... and David had lost a brother as a child, too. No wonder he was as messed up as I was. Panic rose as I wondered where I'd put that love pendant. *Safe at home.*

I broke out in a sweat. Rehearsing my speech had done me no good. I couldn't remember a word of it. I wasn't sure I could even speak at this point. I focused on his eyes, and I knew there was pure evil there.

After a few minutes of turmoil, I remembered Debbie's angel painting. I took it from my suit jacket pocket and laid it on the table in front of me. As I gazed at it, my mind quieted. I began to identify my emotions—a whirl of pain, anguish, confusion, and fear. I didn't want to look the devil in the face.

God help me. I remembered I was God's Gracie. I wasn't alone.

I lifted my eyes far enough to focus on his orange jumpsuit and the bright white cotton undershirt that filled in the V-neck. "You're the one that's responsible for torturing me and my family ... destroying lives. Murdering my dad, my brother, my sisters, my aunt, and my cousin ... and my dog, Peppy. They suffered unspeakable horror and died in an inferno. My mother never recovered from the trauma of it. She's suffered from dementia for years since. My aunt and uncle and their boys went through their own hell because of you. And I lost my life that day, too, even though I'm still breathing."

I inhaled the tears that had started, and pulled a fistful of tissues from my purse. My eyes returned to the angel painting as I blew my nose and collected myself.

Then I looked up straight into the abyss of his eyes. "I'm here to forgive you, even though I don't know how I can do that. But I know I'm supposed to. I know it'll help me recover. Help me move on and have a life. It doesn't even matter what you think of all that. As long as I forgive you, I'm forgiven. I can heal. I don't have to be bitter and hard."

Don't blame us for the sins of our parents. Hurry up and help us; we're at the end of our rope. You're famous for helping; God, give us a break. The words from Cat's prayer note came to mind, and I realized Joey B was born into violence, abuse, and dysfunction, like my family. And it occurred to me that he'd never be getting out of here.

I kept my eyes on his. "I'm not suffering from the sins of my father anymore. I'm not staying in bondage and bitterness. And you don't have to either. If you're smart, you'll figure that out. Even though you'll have lots of time to think here and no one to help. God help you."

I slid Debbie's painting across the table to him. I couldn't believe I was parting with it. My guardian angel in the hands of Joey B. I think it was Holy Spirit that reminded me it was the other way around. Joey B was in his hands.

"I forgive you, Joey, for myself, and hopefully for you, too. Maybe this angel will help you. He helped me, and he knocked some sense into one of your crooked friends."

He looked down at it then up at me without a word. But I saw him flinch a little. I saw his eyes water. Maybe it was a start.

I took my purse and stood. "Goodbye."

David opened the door for me, and I rushed to the restroom. I didn't want him to see me shaking.

Cisco's jet was somewhere over southern Maine before I took my face out of the window, resigning myself to the fact that my angel wouldn't reveal himself to me. I don't know why I thought I was any more likely to see him in an airplane. I guess I thought he'd be out there flying around and protecting the plane. Maybe he was, but he was incognito.

Cisco was passed out in his seat. He must have been exhausted after a sleep-deprived night with his baby boy followed by a string of television interviews for the financial stations and capped off with a business lunch in the city.

David was flipping through papers, soaking up the information quickly. I'd witnessed his many abilities in the course of my employment with Pearson.

He and Debbie made an interesting couple, to put it lightly. From my talk with her, it seemed like he kept her mostly in the dark about his business dealings. I got that impression from his colleagues and family, too. Debbie had a history of anorexia that left her with a weak heart. He did whatever he could to avoid stressing her. And what could be more stressful than being married to the likes of David who worked for the most powerful of the powerful?

But somehow Debbie knew the score. It sounded like God was speaking to her through her dreams and artwork. How else could she have painted so many angels no one else was seeing? And I knew in my heart they were there, even though I couldn't see them either.

David returned his papers to their folder and caught my eye as he reached across the table for a water bottle. I leaned into the aisle between us. "Thanks for making that appointment happen. I appreciate it."

He nodded. "I hope it helped you."

"It was tough, but I feel better now. I think I can move on."

"Good."

I pressed on. "I hope Debbie can paint another angel for me. It really helped me focus. But I got this urge to give it to him. Maybe it'll do some good."

He took a swig of water. "I'm sure Debbie will be happy to paint you another angel. I wouldn't be surprised if it was a duplicate."

"She's an amazing talent."

"She is."

"And you're telling me she knows what my guardian angel looks like? She's seen him in person?"

He smirked. "I wouldn't be surprised."

Then I realized that "duplicate" remark meant that Debbie probably knew I'd hand that angel over to Joey B. I could only imagine what her dreams revealed from the supernatural world. At this point I was too afraid to push David on that topic. What if that angel showed up in front of me right now?

"I'm so sorry about your brother." I bit my lip as soon as I said it. My eyes filled. "I'm sorry … I know how it feels … to lose your family like that."

His face was solemn. "I know … thank you. I'm sorry for your loss … I should have said that a long time ago."

"Thanks."

How long ago was a long time ago? David was a mystery. For that matter, so were his cousin and his wife.

I put my head back on the headrest and closed my eyes, vaguely muddled and upset that I'd brought up David's deceased brother. Newspaper headlines and television reports ran through my mind. It wasn't long after David's exploits made international news that his entire family history had been splashed over the media—including the loss of his brother and Cat's parents and brother in a terrible plane crash when they were kids.

If I'd been with it lately, I'd have remembered that. I supposed David was well used to people dredging up the past. It'd been fodder for the press for years.

But I'd wasted years hating him, dreaming of revenge, any little thing that would hurt him. *What a waste of time*. It never occurred to me that his actions were a reaction to his sad past. Just like mine were.

I think it was in that moment I truly forgave him. I could only feel concern for him and his wellbeing. Then I realized that was love. And love is what is important.

TWENTY-TWO

~ *Nathan* ~

Helena and Teddy were making progress, becoming friends again. Cat had managed to spend some quality time with them, and that did a world of good. My visits with them were interesting and enjoyable for the most part. I think we all got some insight on the important things in life.

When Gracie came through the door, Julia's face lit up. She stifled a shocked, "Oh!" when she saw me, dropped her bag, and went to her mother for a hug.

When Gracie straightened up from the recliner, she looked at me. "Hi, Nate." She smoothed her hair. "Uh … Let's take a little walk. The sky's such a pretty shade of dark blue. Lots of stars out tonight."

She didn't wait for my answer before disappearing into her bedroom to change her clothes. I remained in my seat and watched Julia amble into her room. Helena had barely struggled out of her chair to follow her when Julia reappeared with a beat-up three ring binder.

She dropped it into my lap. "Gracie and Nate!"

My eyes watered as I flipped through the pages of our makeshift wedding album. It consisted of four or five pages of snapshots taken with a disposable camera, placed in a dime store binder. Julia gurgled incoherent comments and giggles, touching each photo with her finger. As her balance began to fail, I got up to help her back to her recliner. I resettled the album in her lap. "Thank you, Julia. It's beautiful."

I looked up to see Gracie in the doorway. She held out her hand to me. As I approached her, I could see her eyes were red. I'm sure mine were, too.

"You need a jacket," I said.

"Okay."

Silently, she led me down the path to the rocky cliff overlooking the black sea. Moon, stars, and my flashlight provided the only illumination. She settled on a large smooth slab of granite, and I took a seat beside her.

"Where were you today, Gracie?"

She sounded tired. "David told me he notified you that we were going to New York."

"Yes." I'd wait for the explanation.

She rubbed her face. "I found out last night that Cisco was going to the city on business. I'd asked David if he'd arrange a meeting for me with Joey B. I wanted to face him and get some kind of closure. I had to do it. And I know I could've told you about it last night, but I purposely didn't. I didn't want to take the chance you'd tell me no. It was something I had to do for me. And I know you're thinking I'm dishonest."

I heard her sob. "I guess I was dishonest. I'm sorry, Nate. Maybe you want to rethink this … marriage. But I hope you don't. I hope you see that I'm just trying to get myself straightened out, so I'll be a good wife to you. An honest and true wife. That's all I want to be."

My eyes stung. "So if I said you need to quit your job with The Golden Bowl and David's organization, you'd do that?"

"If that's what you want, Nate. If you'll truly be happy with me if I do that, I will." She found a tissue and wiped her face. "But you'll have to ask David if he'd allow me to do nothing and stay on their payroll. Otherwise, I could end up in prison."

Soundless laughter started deep in my gut where the pain and doubt had been. "So you wouldn't mind conjugal visits in prison?"

She let out a sarcastic sound. "Um … no."

"Okay then."

She sniffed tears. "Okay then."

A surprisingly warm gust of wind blasted me in the face. Apparently Holy Spirit thought I'd taken this far enough.

Gracie raised her hands as if to catch the whirlwind. "This is where I met Holy Spirit with Cat not so long ago. I'm not alone. We're not alone, Nate."

"So … since we have a personal counselor built in here, why not just get married? That house is gonna be ready before we know it."

"Yeah?"

"Yeah."

She threw herself at me, and we busted out laughing.

~ *Gracie* ~

By the time Nate was done, our impromptu wedding on the beach would become quite the affair. With all our new "family" in attendance, it'd rival the scale of Billy and Lisa's. Nate made a point of hiring a celebrity photographer. I guess our crude album I'd assembled the first time around didn't impress him.

I sat in my office pondering all this, nerves getting the better of me, when Nate came through the door. He twirled my chair to face him and gave me a quick kiss. "The photographer is confirmed. Joe Harris was kind enough to seal that deal."

He wheeled a chair over. "So everything is pretty much set. I think we've got it all down in record time."

I let out a nervous giggle. "Okay then." I realized I just wanted it over. I wanted to be Gracie Goodwin Cavelieri Rhodes. Living life with my husband. I collided my chair with his and leaned into him. "Do you have some fortune I don't know about? Cuz that photographer is probably gonna take it."

His eyes revealed something I'd call pain, something I'd never seen from him. His usual authoritative voice wavered. "You looked so beautiful … on our first wedding day. And no one was there to see you … to care." He cleared his throat. "This time I want you to have what you deserve. We'll get one of those big white padded albums with the gold lettering … whatever they're supposed to be … this guy'll know."

I bit back laughter, thinking of my parents' old wedding album. Mom had seen to it they did everything right. "Okay, Nate." I kissed him. "I guess I better get a dress for the pictures."

As it turned out, the album was perfect, and the party was fun. Annie's adoptive father, Pastor Auclair, officiated at our ceremony on the beach, right on the spot where Nate proposed. Cat was my matron of honor, and David was Nate's best man. Mom, Auntie Helena, and Uncle Teddy stood with Roger at the top of the stone stairway overlooking us. The rest of our guests surrounded us on the sand. Shoes were optional.

After the ceremony, we had a celebratory barbeque, and the

weather was so spectacular we didn't even need a tent. It turned out to be the low-key celebration I wanted.

After Auntie Helena and Uncle Teddy left with Mom and Roger, we ended the evening on the beach toasting marshmallows supplied by pop icon, Aubrey Rose.

I nestled into Nate's side. "Uh … Nate?"

"Are you cold?"

"Um, no. Did you make any arrangements for tonight?"

Laughter boomed out of him. "You don't want to stay here on the beach?"

I made a face. "Uh—"

"Yes, I made arrangements."

"Oh, good. Mom's not too with it, but it'd be weird to spend our first night in the apartment." As relief washed through me, curiosity rose. "So where are we going?"

I could see his mischievous smirk in the dim light. "Let's go."

After more fanfare, we took off in the SUV. "I forgot to pack a bag, Nate."

"No problem." We careened into our new driveway. "We're here. We're home."

The frame of our new house stood in front of me, aglow with the same tiny white lights that illuminated the front porch of The Golden Bowl. Tears welled up. "It's gorgeous!"

"I can't think of a better place to spend our first night."

"It's like we have our own moonroof."

Nate chuckled. "Yeah, I think the roof goes on soon."

He came around the vehicle and took me in his arms. "Now let's see if we can find the door frame."

I couldn't stop laughing. But Nate found the threshold and carried me safely through. We spent the first night of the rest of our lives under the stars snuggled in a big brass bed brought in for the occasion. I believe it stood in the middle of our future living room. We'd never have a more unobstructed view of the ocean. Or all those twinkling stars in a midnight blue sky.

Neither one of us wanted to leave that spot the next day, but we had a week off to enjoy together, and the construction crew was scheduled to continue the following day. So Nate lured me from the comfort of that brass bed to a stately old mansion on the Maine coast that catered to honeymooners.

It was the following Friday, now early in October, when Paulo and his band would wrap up The Golden Bowl Tour in Portland, Maine.

I was excited that Nate was taking me to dinner and the concert. We stopped in to Mom's room to visit before leaving.

"Gracie and Nate." She smiled up at us and picked up on my excitement. She handed me a fake ticket I'd made for Paulo's concert. "Going with Ricky."

"Okay, Mom. See you soon." I kissed her goodbye. We waved to Roger, who was working on her dinner in the kitchen, as we left.

Nate joked about taking me to The Golden Bowl, but we zoomed through Marberry and south to Portland where we had reservations at Annie's friend's restaurant. It was a nice, secluded spot, and we had a great view of the water. Private and perfect for a romantic dinner.

At the concert venue, Nate ushered me to a prime box seat with excellent acoustics. I remembered my experience in Philadelphia as the auditorium lit up in golden light. *What a difference a year makes.* Life had turned around.

Aubrey Rose rocked the place, and then Paulo and his band played on. I was swept away in the music. I think we all were. Having Nate beside me, I was on top of the world.

When they sang Cat's new song, *Grace and Mercy Rain*, people inside and outside the venue went crazy, singing and shouting that they'd been healed. The atmosphere was electric, and I recognized the power of Holy Spirit.

For their last song, Cat took center stage. "Thank you for joining us on The Golden Bowl Tour. If you've participated in taking and leaving prayers in golden bowls all around the world, you will have discovered what you knew in your heart all along. Love is what is important. This song is called *Tickets*, and it's all about love. I wrote this for Julia and Ricky."

My jaw dropped in shock and the room went silent as Cat sang her song. The lyrics brought me back through my childhood, remembering two ticket stubs Mom had always kept tucked in the frame of the mirror atop her antique cherry dresser—mementos of their first bus trip to the Catskills for their honeymoon.

How Cat knew these things astonished me. I'd long since forgotten those ragged, yellowed stubs that were tickets to a new life for Mom and Dad. They must have been lost in our move to Maine. I wiped my tears and thanked God for a ticket to a new life with Nate.

He must have read my mind. He took out our ticket stubs and handed them to me. I promised myself I'd never lose these.

For so long through Mom's dementia I thought the tickets she'd been talking about had to do with entertainment. Cat's song made it clear to me she was thinking of her final trip to heaven where she'd be reunited with her husband and family. *Going with Ricky.*

In that moment, I knew Mom was gone. Glowing gold light told me she was free and happy. *Amen and halleluiah.* Then there was thunderous applause.

Nate took me right home. We found Mom in her comfy chair holding the ornate white wedding album she'd kept hidden from my aunt and uncle all these years. The bus ticket stubs were tucked into a page of honeymoon photos. Julia and Ricky in the Catskills.

The Cast of Characters in The Golden Bowl:
TICKETS

The Golden Bowl:
Anne Auclair Brewster Wynn (Annie), owner
Buckminster (Buck) Wynn, Annie's husband

Staff
Lena Goodwin, Information Technology
Ashleigh (Ash), Manager, First shift
Brianna (Bree), Manager, Second shift
Karen, Confections Manager, The Bakery & Sweet Shop
Gerald, Manager, Food Prep Facility
Tracey, Customer Service Manager
Lisa Quinn, Dishwasher

Annie's Family and Extended Family:
Dr. Craig Westcott (Doc), birth father
Pastor Mike Auclair, adoptive father
Millie Auclair, adoptive mother
Debbie Lambrecht, sister, fashion designer, artist
David Lambrecht, Debbie's husband and Annie's brother-in-law
Cat Clemente, David's cousin, rock star lyricist, philanthropist, prophet
Cisco Clemente, Cat's husband, billionaire businessman and philanthropist
Paulo Clemente, Cisco's youngest brother, rock star, composer
Ellen Clemente, Paulo's wife
Eduardo Clemente, Cisco's younger brother, security expert
Grammy, deceased maternal grandmother

The Consultants
Buckminster Wynn (Almighty Buck), Brooke, Lewis & Wynn
William Brooke, Brooke, Lewis & Wynn
Carter Lewis, Brooke, Lewis & Wynn
Joe Harris, Agent, entertainment industry
Amanda James, Journalist

The Security Team
David Lambrecht
Nathan Rhodes, Director of Security
Billy Foster
Keith
Roger
David's Team
Cole Michelson, IT specialist
Eduardo Clemente
Tony "Cookie" Cooke

Lena's Family
Kay/Julia, Mother
Edward (Uncle Teddy) Nardone
Auntie Helena

Lena's Past Associates
General John Pearson, retired employer
Joey B, mobster

The Townspeople
Peg, Lisa's babysitter/friend

About Maeve Christopher

 Ordinary people in extraordinary situations fuel Maeve Christopher's imagination. Keep asking "what if" and "why," and the plot thickens. What could be more fun?

Her bestselling Redemption Series is part family saga, part suspense, and part love story—with the touch of the Supernatural. Tongue firmly in cheek, it deals with the age-old question: What happens when an assassin falls for a woman who is trying to kill herself?

Maeve's new series, The Golden Bowl, is set on the scenic coast of Maine. This unusual restaurant caters to the body, soul, and spirit. A large gold bowl on the front porch gives the establishment its name and invites patrons to leave a prayer and take a prayer. When they do: lives change.

Maeve lives in Massachusetts with too many characters and a number of messy subplots. She loves to hear from readers. Subscribe to Maeve's Email Updates for exclusive content, contests, special offers, and more on her website.

You can also find her on Facebook @maevechristopher

Maeve enjoys hearing from her readers. She can be contacted through her website:

MaeveChristopher.com

Other Books by
Maeve Christopher

The Golden Bowl Series:
A Ring and a Prayer (Book One)
The Supernatural Diet Club (Book Two)
Tickets (Book Three)

The Redemption Series: read in order 1--5
Killer Cupid
Fame, Fortune & Secrets
In the Name of Glori
Last Tangle in Paris
Mercy's Pen

Find links to retailers at
MaeveChristopher.com

A Note from the Author

If you enjoyed *Tickets*, I'd be honored if you would tell others by leaving a review on the site where you purchased this book.

Thank you!
Maeve

www.ingramcontent.com/pod-product-compliance
Lightning Source LLC
Chambersburg PA
CBHW061232170626
46809CB00007B/2631